The Crucible
The Ember War Saga Book 8

Richard Fox

Copyright © 2016 Richard Fox

All rights reserved.

ISBN: 1539329267
ISBN-13:9781539329268

CHAPTER 1

Captain Hale stood over the shattered body of a Ruhaald. The upper half of the body was smeared across the desert in a congealed black mass that stank of rust, the still-intact leg and hip armor twitching every few seconds. A wrecked Ruhaald fighter pinged as it bled heat into the already sweltering air. Hale turned his head to a line of doughboy corpses laid out next to a distant bunker.

A pair of Marines behind him had rifles in hand, held low but ready to fight. Cortaro scanned the horizon as Orozco shifted his boots against the packed earth.

"Egan, Standish and Bailey were alive when the Ruhaald took them?" Hale asked.

"Roger, sir," Orozco nodded emphatically, "I saw them get frog-marched into the transport. Didn't seem hurt."

"None of them opened fire on the Ruhaald, just the doughboys?"

"They were trying to help whatever was flying that thing." Orozco motioned to the downed fighter with the muzzle of his rifle. "It all happened too fast. Doughboys saw the aliens and went berserk. I tried to keep them back but…"

"Why would they take our Marines and leave their dead behind?" Cortaro asked. "Orozco said this dead one looked important when the shuttle set down."

"Hard to understand a new species you've just met," Hale said. "Killing one of their leaders—or any of them—probably isn't the best way to say 'hello.' No word from the Ruhaald since the stand-down order?"

"Nothing new, sir," Cortaro said. "Couple Eagles got in a scrape with their fighters over St. George a few hours ago. Ruhaald repeated their 'no airborne craft, no hostile acts' warning again."

A wall of shadow swept across the desert floor. Hale looked up as a Ruhaald battle cruiser blocked the sun. Lines of arrowhead-shaped fighters flew tight circles around the angular ship. Light smeared across its underside, a telltale sign of energy shielding.

"You ever been in a fight without air superiority, First Sergeant?" Hale asked.

Cortaro ran a palm over his side, where Hale knew the Marine had a long patch of scar tissue.

"Sumatra, back when I was a buck sergeant. Bad couple of days."

An IR channel in Hale's helmet hissed to life.

"Roughneck-6, this is Phoenix actual. Return to base immediately. Code Gamma," said the commander of the defenders in and around Earth's capital.

"Moving," Hale replied, then cut the transmission. "First Sergeant, Phoenix reports enemy contact. We need to get back." Hale looked up at the alien ship again.

What the hell do they want? he thought.

****

The Crucible's heart no longer belonged to humanity. Most of the workstations, chairs and computers installed over the years-long occupancy had been ripped out and tossed into a mound against the control center's outer wall.

The tiers of dull basalt rings were as bare as the Xaros builders intended, all but the glowing probe in the bottom tier. Bastion's probe floated within a thin force field, its normally smooth texture fraying around the edges.

Square panels cluttered the space around the probe, each projecting thin holographic lines of alien text.

All the panels connected to one of three evenly sized boxes rimmed with frost.

Prefect Ordona floated between the holo-fields, his metal encounter suit boasting several mechanical arms connected to wide shoulders. His head was an overturned bucket with a thin red vision slit. Arms reached into the holo-fields, tweaking code. Ordona's head swiveled around, watching the effect of his changes on the Bastion probe.

One of the panels flickered and died with an electric snap. Claw-tipped hands snapped in annoyance. That was the fourth failure in the last several hours, likely due to yet another power surge from the Crucible's faulty systems.

Doors on the uppermost level opened and a Ruhaald stomped down the steps too wide and too tall for a normal-sized human. This Ruhaald bore a diagram of his species' home system across his armored chest. The flesh within his clear helmet was milky-white—a sign of advanced age according to Ordona's records.

"I render appropriate greetings," Septon Jarilla said.

"Indeed you do," Ordona said, continuing his

work.

"The occupation of Earth is complete. All surviving cities have at least one battle cruiser monitor. The humans were disciplined for breaching the no-fly order several times, all within the first hour of our restrictions."

Ordona twisted his head around to regard the Septon.

"This is irrelevant to our purposes," Ordona said. "What of the omnium reactor? The procedural technology?"

"The reactor is well defended. Human warriors and their slaves repelled our initial assault. They've used the reactor to bolster their defenses."

"I sense hesitation. Provide your excuse for our delayed success."

Jarilla stepped carefully around the panels and peered into the force field holding the probe.

"Her highness considers the lives of each of her children as jewels beyond price. Ruhaald lives are my responsibility. I could overwhelm those defending the omnium reactor, but it would be a massacre. My troops are not air breathers. Fighting in such conditions is difficult for us. We've much to learn."

"Sacrifices must be made," Ordona said. "The fate

of the least of your species is irrelevant to our mission."

"It is relevant to her. It is relevant to me. Perhaps you can explain why you do not have full control over this station?" Jarilla raised a thin tentacle and tapped the tip against the force field. Electricity snapped and singed the armored digit.

"The humans modified their probe following the Toth intrusion into their system. The source-code modifications the Naroosha purchased from Dr. Mentiq were perfectly adequate to co-opt the probe in our home world and all the probes utilized by the other races that joined our grand endeavor. The Toth program will work…in time."

"We had control long enough to send your ship to Bastion with the ancient. Yet now the Crucible is a dead satellite?"

"The probe had an independent memory partition. Most unusual. It tried and failed to regain control. I put up firewalls to isolate the program. The same firewalls block my control of several key systems. My efforts are focused on deleting the partition and rebooting the probe to a more compliant configuration. Both courses of action will result in the same end state. The Crucible will be ours."

"How much time? The humans will not sit still for

this."

"At most, two days."

Jarilla bent at the waist and turned one of his wide black eyes to look into Ordona's vision slit.

"Then you can vent the atmosphere in the omnium reactor chamber. I will not lose a life if there is a better alternative."

"Keep up the pressure on the defenders. Their use of the reactor is rudimentary. Do not give them time and space to learn more."

"This will be done. There is the matter of the Toth. The method of payment is most…unusual." Bubbles escaped from Jarilla's feeder tentacles. Ordona noted the Ruhaald nonverbal cue for disgust.

"The Toth want what the Toth want. If our species are to survive the impending Xaros maniples closing on our worlds, we will need larger fleets. The humans barely managed to defeat this last attack with a few years to prepare. The Ruhaald and Naroosha have many more years to bolster our defenses. The Toth will provide us legions of human troops and crews, but only if we give them the procedural technology."

"Why must we consort with those traitors?"

"The alternative is to assault a fortified human city and seize a fully functioning procedural farm. The casualties will be significant, which bothers that queen of yours. Sad that ideals impede progress."

Jarilla whipped a pistol off his waist and leveled it at Ordona's vision slit.

"You will not insult her!"

Ordona's helmet swiveled from side to side. "The comment is withdrawn."

Jarilla lowered the weapon, but kept it in hand.

"The procedural technology is the final prize in our mission here," Ordona said. "Once the gate is fully under my control, the Toth will send an invasion force to secure the human cities. Supreme Leader Rannik is most anxious to revisit this planet after the death of Dr. Mentiq."

"There is a procedural facility on this station. Why do we need more?" Jarilla asked.

"The memory partition ruined the storage banks and scrambled much of the system's coding. The units already in production will reach full maturity, but I cannot make more. Another of my kind is attempting to reverse engineer the process. I put his chance of success at eleven percent. The Toth do not want a possibility; they want a fully functional system. I do not wish to anger them upon their arrival."

"They will devour every last human in revenge for

Mentiq's death. The Toth are not known for their restraint. You know what the Toth did to the Karigole."

"This is not our concern." Ordona pivoted in place and floated over to another holo-field.

"She would see a better outcome for the humans. If they hand over the procedural technology and the reactor, we can leave with our mission accomplished. Scuttle this Crucible once we depart, take their jump engines. We have Malal and can create our own Crucibles, in time. Leave the humans to fend for themselves until the next Xaros attack. Let our enemies spend their strength on each other." Jarilla holstered his pistol.

"Possible. The final outcome will be the same. Ravaging Earth was not the agreement we made with the Toth, just the shared use of the procedural technology. You may pursue that course of action, but do not threaten my efforts here."

Jarilla took to the stairs, then stopped.

"She feels that the Naroosha have not sacrificed as the Ruhaald have on this mission. If you could commit resources to the siege on the omnium reactor, it would be appreciated."

A staccato hiss came from Ordona's encounter suit. "This environment is incompatible with Naroosha physiology. Our ships will control the void. For something so pedestrian as ground combat, we have you and your kind. This conversation is a distraction. Any further discussion and it may take longer than two days to assume complete control of the probe. Leave."

"I render appropriate farewells," Jarilla said and marched up the stairs.

****

The abyss pressed against Private First Class Standish, smothering his eyes with total darkness. The deck of the Ruhaald shuttle lurched beneath his feet and the grip of unseen guards tightened against his arms, which were bound behind his back at the wrists and elbows. Sweat dribbled down his face and ran over his lips as the hot, humid air clung to his skin.

His battle armor weighed heavy against his body, the pseudo-muscle layer and support lattice rendered useless once the Ruhaald ripped the suit's power pack away. Standish shifted his weight from one foot to another, trying to relieve the mounting stress on his legs.

A snarl of wet pops sounded in his ear as a guard jerked him off balance.

"Fine, fine…I'll stand still," Standish said.

A cold tentacle touched his neck and slithered

across his skin.

Standish seized up. "No talking, I remember!"

"Get stuffed, you bunch of fisho lookin' cocks! Hurt him and I'll kick you until I find a place to stick my—mmph" Bailey's invective ended with a rustle in the darkness.

The tentacle around Standish's neck withdrew, but not before the tip poked at Standish's face.

Standish cursed silently and tried to figure out just how he'd landed in this situation. He, Bailey and Egan had been shot down fighting the Xaros near Phoenix, then taken refuge in a bunker manned by bio-construct doughboy soldiers. A fleet of Ruhaald fighters turned the tide against the invading drones, and one crash-landed near their bunker. The Marines rendered what aid they could to the aquatic alien. Things seemed under control…until a Ruhaald shuttle landed nearby and a high-ranking Ruhaald set foot on Earth. Standish's memory went a bit hazy as he tried to piece together the chaos of weapons fire from doughboys and Ruhaald that left the Ruhaald leader, and a slew of doughboys, dead.

The surviving Ruhaald took Standish and his two squad-mates prisoner after the firing had stopped and hustled them into their shuttle. Then the darkness.

This can get worse. A lot worse, he thought. *Pretty sure killing an ally commander is* not *how you make friends with these...whatever they are. I'll get blamed. I know it. I was the lowest-ranked Marine out there.*

The shuttle rattled. The smell of salt water grew stronger. The grip on his arms tightened.

Here we go.

A bar of white cut across the darkness. Standish blinked hard as the shuttle's ramp lowered and light assaulted his eyes. The guards pushed him forward and the Marine stumbled. He trudged forward, his unpowered armor dragging his steps like he was walking through mud.

Cold, bone-dry air filled his mouth and nose. His boots hit the ramp with a metal-on-metal clang, then set down on what felt like loose sand.

Standish shook his head and looked up. He was inside a flattened dome. Obsidian-black walls dotted with bolted-on lighting and blinking display panels stretched around the perimeter of the small stadium. He got a glance at blocky Ruhaald shuttles arrayed next to each other as perfectly as soldiers formed up for close-order drill to one side...and piles of bodies on the other.

The dead were large and well-muscled, with mottled skin. Smoldering wounds created a fugue of burnt meat and vaporized blood that sent Standish's stomach into knots. Standish looked over the many dead and didn't see a single normal human in the pile. They were all doughboys.

A guard grabbed him by the back of his head and shoved his chin down. Standish counted his steps as the Ruhaald frog-marched him into a corridor. Ruhaald soldiers trotted up and down the corridor, all carrying rifles made of irregular-shaped blocks and pulsing wires. Clicks and squeaks sounded through the corridor. The sound of distant gauss fire echoed off the walls.

Two alien soldiers supported a Ruhaald, its armor pitted with craters and leaking brackish fluid that stank of low tide. The wounded Ruhaald lashed out at Standish, but his guards jerked him out of reach. Flecks of oily water sprayed over Standish's bare face and neck.

Not going well. At all, Standish thought.

He twisted his head aside when an anti-grav cargo pallet went by, dead doughboys stacked atop each other, all marked with burnt circles against their torsos.

The guard steered Standish down another, narrower hallway. The air was stale, cold. There was no hustle of fighters around them.

They stopped at a wide doorway and waited as the doors crumbled to the side, like a wall of sand failing against the tide. Inside, a Ruhaald held open a cell. The guards slammed the three Marines against the back wall of the cage and exited before Standish could even get to his feet.

"Hey, you want to do something about this?" Standish struggled against the bindings around his arms and wrists.

The cell door slammed shut and an energy field crackled to life around the bars. A single Ruhaald remained behind; it looked over the human captives and cocked its head to the side. The bulbous lower half of its helmet was clear and feeder tentacles writhed within as the guard leaned toward Standish.

Standish backpedaled, stopped by the obsidian wall.

The guard let off a series of clicks, then Standish's bindings fell to the floor. The green-black cords curled together and burned away in a cloud of gray vapor. Standish got a sore arm up and waved his hand against his nose to combat the sudden stench.

The Ruhaald backed away, not turning his back on the Marines, and left the room.

"Where the hell are we?" Egan asked. "One of their ships?"

"This is the Crucible." Standish rubbed his shoulders and looked over their cell. "I got a good look at the place when we were running around, trying to get

Stacey Ibarra to the control center back when we took it from the Xaros."

"Blimey, this is a cock-up, isn't it?" Bailey sat on a metal bench and tapped on her forearm screen. She rolled her eyes when it didn't respond, then removed the gauntlet with a click and set it next to her.

"Either of you two diggers catch what happened?" The Australian Marine ran her naked hand through her short brown hair. "We were out there, trying to do one of them a solid, then some alien bigwig shows up and…Christ."

"The doughboys attacked." Egan went to a small sink next to the only toilet and took a drink from the fountain. "Oro was trying to stop them, trying to warn us. Why would they do that?"

"Bailey," Standish rapped his fingers against the bars, "you remember when Steuben and Hale came back from Earth, right before we went to Europa to try and play nice with the Toth?"

"Steuben had a shiner. Didn't want to talk about it," she said. Her head perked up. "Orozco said they'd got in a fight with a doughboy some of those true-born twats had captured. Some big misunderstanding."

"Wait, the doughboys will just attack any alien they see?" Egan asked. "What about the Dotok? Steuben was walking around doughboys in Phoenix before we got assigned to that Osprey."

"Not a problem we need to solve right now." Standish removed a small armor plate from his shoulder and tossed it through the bars. It hit the energy field and quivered against the invisible wall as tiny filaments of electricity crackled. The plate spat back toward Standish. He caught the now-blackened lump of armor and frowned.

"We're in this cell because of that 'problem,' Standish," Egan said.

"You've an idea to get us out?" Bailey leaned against the wall and rubbed her temples.

"I've been in brigs, confinement, juvenile detention centers on three continents and Tijuana's seedier jail cells," Standish said. He paced from one side of the cell to the other, looking over everything.

"And in my expert opinion…we ain't going nowhere." Standish put his hands on his hips. "Bars are reinforced with graphene. Couldn't break them even if our armor was powered up. The energy going through the force field is tuned higher than penal-code standard. Dissuasion barriers are meant to sting, not fricassee. I don't know what was in this cell before us, but Ibarra must have been scared of it."

Standish clicked his tongue and looked up. His gaze stopped on a small light diode on the ceiling.

"You both saw those dead doughboys and heard the gauss fire, right?" Egan asked. "There's got to be an organized resistance to the Ruhaald. We'll wait for our chance to get free and find—Standish, what are you looking at?"

"That one light. It's fluttering," Standish pointed over his head, "but the rest aren't."

"So?" Bailey tucked herself into a corner and laid her head against the wall. "We're in the brig and I don't even know what damn day it is anymore. Get some sleep."

Egan went to Standish's side and peered up at the light, its luminosity flickering.

"R-R-A-B-I-A…Ibarra?" Egan asked. "It's in Morse, repeats and is backwards. Odd."

"Hold on, where is Ibarra? Last I remember he was inside the probe they've got running this place," Standish said.

"You tell us." Bailey sat up. "You were the one carrying one of those probes in your head on Nibiru."

"We don't speak of that. Ever." Standish pointed a finger at the sniper.

"It's changing." Egan squinted. "'Time. Short. Help.' Those words over and over again."

"We're open to suggestions," Standish said with a shrug.

"'Wait,'" Egan said. The light held steady. "I guess that's it."

"Right, I'm going back to sleep. You boys tell me when the voices start talking again," Bailey said.

"You've met Ibarra before, right, Standish?" Egan asked. "You trust him?"

"I'm acquainted with what might be his ghost. It's not like I ran in his social circles back before the war. I stole money from the Triads and he was the richest man in human history. Not a lot of overlap," Standish said. "If he's planning something, I think we've got a chance. Or we'll be killed trying to escape and end up on a Ruhaald smorgasbord. I give us fifty-fifty."

CHAPTER 2

Hale walked through a corridor, the metal grate of the walkway vibrating slightly with each step. The nerve center for all of Phoenix's defenses buzzed like an angry hive through the metal slats. The smell of unwashed bodies and stale coffee rose from the dozens of officers and enlisted soldiers clustered into little pockets of activity. The walls of the command center were bare stone, carved out of Camelback Mountain on the city's east side.

A giant map on one wall with the fixed defenses around the city—rail gun batteries and landing pads hidden within mountainsides—was awash in colored icons. Few of the big guns were still fully operational. A wide swath of red icons filled the northeast portion of the map, the same area where his Marines had been taken captive.

Hale stopped at a metal door and knocked. It slid

aside, revealing a plain metal desk and a tired-looking General Robbins sitting behind it. Another Marine stood by the desk, the back of his head scaly and gray.

"Steuben?" Hale asked as he stepped into the room.

The Karigole warrior turned around. The upper left side of his face was a scuffed metal plate ringed with scar tissue, a glowing red oval where his eye should have been. The alien raised his right hand and squeezed the cybernetic fingers into a fist. Steuben had nearly been killed fighting the Xaros general. The last time Hale saw his alien mentor was when he'd delivered him to a medical station.

"Lafayette programmed the auto-surgeons to treat Karigole physiology," Steuben said. "My new parts are from his workshop."

"You were on death's door when I handed you over to the medics." Hale looked Steuben over and found little changed in the warrior's bearing.

"We recover quickly," Steuben looked down at his metal hand as the fingers twitched, "but we do not regenerate."

The general cleared his throat.

"Sir." Hale snapped to attention and rendered a salute.

The general returned the courtesy and looked up at Hale. The older man had bags beneath his eyes and a pallor to his skin that looked anything but healthy.

"Captain, well done dispatching that…entity. That kind of bravery speaks well of your ship and the Strike Marine Corps." Robbins took a small jar of pills out of his desk and popped a pair into his mouth.

"Thank you, sir, but the armor made all the difference," Hale said.

"We'll figure out which backs get the most pats later. One of your Marines witnessed the incident with the Ruhaald. You have anything to add to his initial report?"

"The doughboys attacked the Ruhaald without provocation," Hale said. "The Ruhaald left their dead behind and captured three of my Marines. Wasn't much more to learn from the scene."

"Your Marine have any idea why the Ruhaald would attack doughboys after that incident?"

"Sir?"

Robbins reached over the desk and tapped a data slate near Hale's edge. A topographic map of the area northwest of Phoenix came up. Blue icons representing bunkers popped up across the map. Several grayed out, forming an arrow shape pointing toward a firebase inside a line of mountain peaks near the Tonto Basin.

23

"Our guests took the high ground over every single mountain fortress around the planet without firing a shot. Well, almost," Robbins said. "There was plenty of battlefield friction going on right as the Xaros pulled back and formed that construct. One minute, the Ruhaald were on our side, fighting the Xaros. Then that construct, and every other drone in the solar system, went up in smoke. Soon as that happened the Ruhaald gave every air and void craft fifteen minutes to land or be shot down. Couple ground-based rail batteries took potshots that didn't get through their shields and were promptly destroyed. Then they threatened to nuke the next city that fired on them."

"And it's been quiet since then?" Hale asked.

"Everywhere but the defenses around Firebase X-Ray," Robbins said, "which isn't far from where your Marines were captured. This is the last message we got through the fiber lines."

A small screen came up on the data slate. A Marine in full armor, his face obscured by light across his visor, adjusted the camera.

"This is First Lieutenant Bolin." Hale's ears perked up at the sound of the man's voice, which sounded oddly familiar. "My outer defensive lines have been breached by Ruhaald troops. My soldiers report that the Ruhaald are targeting and killing doughboys, but they'll take humans captive. My information's fragmentary, at best. The inner strongpoints are holding but our ammo reserves will only last another—" The camera feed shook violently and Bolin ducked as sand and small rocks rained down on him. He looked up at the ceiling, then ran from the control room. The feed corrupted and blacked out moments later.

"Why are the Ruhaald attacking that area and nowhere else?" Hale asked.

"I was hoping you knew," Robbins shrugged. A chime sounded on his desk. "Let me take this." He swung his seat around and began a low conversation with whomever had called through his earbud.

Steuben whacked Hale's shoulder with his metal knuckles. The Karigole held his forearm screen up for Hale to see. The personnel file for one First Lieutenant Mark Bolin was on the screen. Hale's face went white as he looked at the man's photo. Bolin looked almost exactly like his brother Jared, who'd left Earth years ago on a colony mission. The man in the picture looked harried, worn from years of stress, but Hale was positive that man was his twin brother.

"There is a resemblance?" Steuben asked quietly. "Distinguishing humans by your faces is difficult for me now." He tapped the metal plate embedded into his skull.

"It's there," Hale whispered. "But he's been gone for—"

"Forty-five soldiers and nearly a thousand doughboy augmentees," Robbins said, snapping Hale and Steuben out of their conference. "That's what's assigned to Firebase X-Ray. Ruhaald destroyed every IR retransmission site between Phoenix and X-Ray and they're jamming every commo freq into and out of the area. Whatever they're doing, they don't want us to know about it. I hoped there was more to learn from the site of the incident. You're both dismissed."

"What about the firebase, sir? We can't just leave them out there."

"Captain Hale, my mission is to defend Phoenix and the civilians behind our walls. We took one hell of a beating from the Xaros, and right now I have a chance to re-arm and repair and to do so without being shot at by the Ruhaald cruiser floating over our heads," the general said. "We can't poke the bear just yet. Not until we figure a way around their shields."

"There is a tunnel linking Phoenix to one of the outlying bunkers," Steuben said. "There are several cloaking devices in Lafayette's lab. We could reach X-Ray without detection."

The general sat back in his chair and folded his

hands across his chest.

"Reconnaissance," he said, raising a finger. "Gather information and report back. We're in intermittent contact with the *Breitenfeld* and the surviving ships orbiting the moon. Captain Valdar doesn't know much more than we do. Anything you can find to help us understand—and fight—these new enemies will be vital."

"We're on it," Hale said. "My Marines have snuck through worse places than Arizona countryside."

"What is it Valdar's crew is always saying to people?" One of the general's eyebrows shot up.

"*Gott mit uns*, sir."

****

Beyond the edge of the Milky Way, a multifaceted orb hurtled through the void. The great crystalline faces of the exterior shell stretched for billions of miles, connected together in an object with a circumference wider than the orbit of Saturn. This, the Apex, carried every surviving member of the true Xaros race, but not their drone servants, within.

Deep within the crystalline mountain ranges of the interior walls, a single intelligence waited. The Keeper's consciousness tapped into the vast network of jump gates seeded through the galaxy that would soon be the Xaros' new home. It reached out to the conduit that should have been on Earth, the home of an annoying resilient parasite race…and felt nothing.

The arsenal world that the General sent from a nearby star was gone. The secondary conduit that Keeper had used to converse with his peer was also absent. Keeper knew the size of the General's force, his worth as a tactician and the known disposition of the surprisingly well-equipped human resistance. Keeper's records of previous conquests lent to near-perfect models when estimating the force required to erase another irrelevant species. In all scenarios, the General should have finished off the humans some time ago.

To willingly sever his connection from the network, the General risked the ultimate fear of any Xaros: true death. The humans had destroyed the General's photonic husk before; to leave himself open to that same risk was unfathomable.

And yet…

If the General had succeeded, he would have sent word of his victory. Keeper had told his peer many times that failure to eradicate the humans would not be tolerated by the other Xaros masters. The General's silence could only mean failure.

The General had strode across the stars, the drone vanguard an overwhelming force against every intelligent race ever encountered. Never before had a Xaros perished at the hands of another species, even during their billion-year supremacy in their lost home galaxy.

And yet…

Keeper did not deny the only logical conclusion as to the General's absence. If the humans and their allies had found a way to kill a Xaros, then the rest of the species under his care was at risk. It had known of the General's failings and allowed the other Xaros to operate freely. The others had some trust in the General's abilities, but they made sure Keeper knew their safe arrival in the new galaxy—a galaxy cleansed of all other intelligent life—was Keeper's responsibility.

Keeper's prominent position in the new galactic order was in jeopardy, but the situation could be salvaged.

It snapped its point of consciousness to the tip of a massive spike stretching from the inner shell to just shy of a captured star. In the spike tip dwelt another, the Engineer.

+Awaken.+ Keeper undid the bindings that kept the Engineer asleep during the eons-long journey between galaxies. The Engineer materialized: a giant clockwork wheel, cogs within cogs all working perfectly together in perpetual motion.

+Too soon…+

+Indeed, your great work is flawed. I have called you to account.+ Keeper fed his peer status reports from the last few thousand years. The Apex was failing, albeit very slowly. The titanic forces keeping the central star corralled had developed certain idiosyncrasies, which would inevitably lead to failure and the quick and total destruction of the entire structure.

+I told the others this star was not the ideal candidate. If given enough time, I would have created the perfect solar foundry for our journey, but the annihilation wave was too close,+ the Engineer said.

+You promised the star would never fail. We could traverse the universe without fear. Now we will arrive at the nearest galaxy from our home with mere millennia to spare.+

+We're nearly there. You're welcome,+ the Engineer said. The master builder sent a pulse through Apex and took less than a second to process the enormous volume of data. +Millennia, yes. I can tell you down to the nanosecond, but that is irrelevant. Our new home should be nearly ready long before then.+

+We have a complication.+ Keeper fed the Engineer the details of the General's conflict with the humans and his deafening silence.

+The General is lost…intriguing.+

+Was your mind damaged during hibernation? One of our own is gone forever. There is a credible threat to the rest of us. I came to you for a solution, not a philosophical discussion.+

The Engineer's form morphed into an hourglass. Diamonds poured through, but the mass of sparkling jewels in the upper and lower halves remained the same size.

+The natives use wormhole technology, unfettered from the gates. Dangerous,+ the Engineer said. +They run the risk of triggering another annihilation wave. There will be no hope for our kind if that happens.+

+Give me a solution or I will have no choice but to take the issue to the others. Then they will cast us both into the intergalactic void for failure,+ Keeper said.

+One of your shades had a prisoner. A Torni.+

+How do you know this? I destroyed the data.+

+All information is sacred. I designed the system. I built data shunts to make sure heathens like you didn't destroy anything…this Minder…good that you killed it,+ the Engineer said.

Space around the two Xaros shifted to the upper atmosphere of a gas giant. A pair of stars hung beyond the hazy sky. The two Xaros loomed like disinterested gods, watching four humans and a Qa'Resh play their part in the recording as the crystalline entity extracted Malal from the human on a gurney.

+An ascended species, most interesting,+ the Engineer said.

+Why are we here?+

+This is the lynchpin to the resistance. This 'Bastion' of theirs. I can find where it is. It will just take some time to identify the binary star system with just such a planet. I'm within the data now…our new home is quite fascinating,+ the Engineer said.

+You're engaged in a hollow pursuit. The world is likely well beyond our immediate reach. The drones will overrun the rest of the galaxy in the next few thousand years, with or without the General. The damage this Bastion could do between then and now is difficult even for me to predict.+

+If we hold to our current model, then there is a risk.+

Keeper felt a chill run through its being. +What are you suggesting?+

+We must not limit ourselves to a failing paradigm. I can find data you thought hidden, but if *I* decide to destroy a record, it will be gone forever. We can solve the human problem. How we do so will remain secret from the others.+

****

Standish slid a boot off and set it next to the rest of his armor in a neat pile. The Marine, wearing nothing but a black body glove, massaged his swollen foot.

"It's like walking around in snow boots when the power systems are off-line," he said. "I swear my stress fractures will come back from Strike Marine selection. That's all I need, tottering around on broken feet."

"That's the worst you got from selection?" Bailey asked. She'd stripped off her armor and now stood at the sink, scrubbing Ruhaald blood from a thigh plate. "I got bit by a damn cottonmouth. Corpsman hit me with antivenom before I passed out. Still made it through swamp phase in one go."

"Hypothermia," said Egan, taking his turn on the sleeping bench. "Freak cold front. Woke up covered in frost and my hands iced to my weapon. Florida. The 'sunshine state' my ass. Don't know why so many guys retire there…or used to."

"So that's what you remember?" Standish worked a knuckle against a knotted muscle in his calf. "Because you're a proccie. It didn't…you know…happen."

"Huh," Egan frowned. The Marine was a procedurally generated human, his body flash gown in a tube and implanted with memories, skills and abilities from a supercomputer. "Guess you're right. But damned if I don't feel the ache in my fingers and my ears when I think of that morning."

"So what if he's a proccie?" Bailey asked. "Yarrow's a proc. Rohen, God rest his soul, was a proc. Bet most every swinging Richard on Earth and the fleet came out of a tube."

"It doesn't matter to me," Standish said. "Just hard to process. Egan's memories are his memories. They're just as real to him as mine are to me. Egan came to us purpose-built to fly Toth shuttles for the mission to Nibiru. If Ibarra can make someone that specific, why can't he recreate any of us? That probe's got a copy of his mind. Why isn't he walking around in flesh and blood? Why didn't he bring back Admiral Makarov and all of Eighth Fleet? Sure could have used them against the Xaros."

"Rohen…" Bailey's lips quivered for a moment. "He's a good lad. Died for us all. Why couldn't Ibarra bring him back?"

"They told me what I was," Egan said. "I woke up

in Hawaii, did a check flight in a Mule around the Big Island then went to debrief. Couple guys in suits said that I'd been 'decanted' that morning, and I was meant for a secret and dangerous mission. I took the news about as bad as finding out the mess hall was out of bacon…I was born that morning and went right to work. Never occurred to me that sort of thing was unusual. You think Ibarra made me so I wouldn't care?"

"Well, you weren't a big weepy mess like Yarrow when he found out," Standish said.

"You remember his face when you told him he was a virgin?" Bailey snickered. "Thought the poor kid would—"

The door to the brig opened. The Marines scrambled to their feet as a single Ruhaald strode into the room. It was almost a foot taller than the guards they'd seen before, a constellation of black stars and alien writing stenciled across his enviro-armor.

The Ruhaald carried a metal box by a handle and came to a stop a few feet from the cell. Standish saw wide black eyes like a squid's darting from side to side within the semi-opaque helmet.

"I render appropriate greeting," came from a voice box mounted on the alien's shoulder.

"Are you the slimy bastard they've sent to kiss our

bums and apologize for kidnapping us?" Bailey asked.

"I am Septon Jarilla of the Ruhaald expedition. You will answer my questions."

"How about you let us out of here and give me back my damned rifle, my Bloke, you calamari-looking mother—" Bailey stopped mid-breath when Egan raised a hand...then pointed to a light in the ceiling that faded and brightened ever so slightly.

"Your hostility is noted," Jarilla said. "Your subspecies is cooperating in some locations, yet actively resists our efforts on the Crucible. Are you beyond command of your leadership caste? My soldiers are dying against your warrior breed. If there is a way to end the bloodshed, you will tell me. Continued conflict puts this station in danger. My subordinates and allies urge my brood mother to destroy one of your population centers to force compliance. She is merciful, but her patience has limits."

"Most of what you just said doesn't make any sense to us," Standish said. "Didn't you come here to fight the Xaros? They're gone. Why are we fighting each other?"

Jarilla snarled and stepped toward the cell. A balled fist made up of a dozen armored tentacles slammed against the energy field.

"Your warrior spawn murdered a brood father.

Treachery! Your commanders agreed to a cease-fire once we seized the void around this station. The battle was over yet you took him from us. Why?"

"Whoa there, buddy." Standish held his hands up. "We don't know why the doughboys attacked your brood daddy…guy. We were out there trying to help that pilot of yours. Your shuttle lands and then everything just got crazy. You guys are here to help, right? Why would we…wait—why would you attack the Crucible?"

The tentacles within Jarilla's helmet twisted into knots.

"Our reasons are not your concern," the Ruhaald said. "We have observed your subspecies commanding the warrior spawn. They follow your orders. This is correct."

"No!" Standish shook his head from side to side. "Just because we're regular humans doesn't mean the doughboys will do whatever we tell them. I don't know who told you that but we sure didn't get that memo."

Jarilla set the box at his feet and opened it, slipping long tentacles into the box. The alien leader lifted up a doughboy's severed head and held it toward the Marines. The dead bio-construct's face was slack, one cheek burned away. Blood dripped through the alien's digits and pooled on the floor.

"False. We have sequenced the warrior spawn's

cortex with the aid of the Naroosha. They obey you. You ordered the death of the brood father. You will suffer for it." Jarilla dropped the head into the box.

"I don't know what a Naroosha is," Standish said, "but they sound like a bunch of lying assholes. We were trying to help that crashed pilot. That's what friends do. They don't attack your Xaros jump gate and throw you into a dark shuttle that smells like the bottom of a fish tank. OK?"

"You will order the warrior spawn to lay down their weapons," Jarilla said. "I offer this clemency only because pilot Third-Vorinth confirms some of your story. You will do this or you will receive justice for the brood father's death."

"No," Egan said. "We demand arbitration. The blood debt is not ours to pay."

"How do you know of this?" Jarilla asked.

"That's a good question," Standish muttered.

"I know your laws. Our ambassador on Bastion told us you were coming to help. We prepared as best we could." Egan glanced at the ceiling. "This is a normal human custom before joint operations."

"It is?" Standish asked. Egan jabbed an elbow into the Marine's side, and Standish added, "It is! Yes, I was just about to mention…that."

"The ship loci will convene for arbitration," Jarilla said. "It will take one and three-eighths rotations before a judgement is obtained."

"Do we get a lawyer? What about our testimony?" Bailey asked.

"You've already given it," Jarilla said and then picked up the box and left the room.

Standish looked over the small pool of blood beyond the cell and grimaced.

"So, Egan, what the hell?" he asked.

"Ibarra started talking soon as that thing came in here," the Marine said. "Told me to stall, then gave me that line about arbitration. I don't exactly understand what I was saying either. Figured you would, jailbird," he said to Standish.

"You think I'm an expert on alien squid-monster jurisprudence? For all I know, that thing's going to come back in here and tell us we have to swim to the bottom of some giant tank filled with tentacle-sharks and recover a gold coin tossed in by the Princess Froo-Froo or they'll chop us into sushi." Standish looked up at the now-still light. "Thanks, Ibarra!"

Bailey sat on the bench and crossed her ankles.

"Normally I'd tell him to shut up by now, but I'm about as nervous as a gypsy with a mortgage," she said.

"Without better options I don't know why we shouldn't trust the…blinking light on the ceiling." Egan's arms flopped to his side. "Oh balls, what have I done?"

"If it is a giant sharktopus tank," Standish said, "*you* are going in first!"

Egan's hands balled into fists. He took in a deep breath, then froze, his gaze fell on something behind Standish.

Air shimmered near the doorway. An apparition in the loose shape of a human came toward the Marines with halting steps.

"Anyone else see that?" Egan asked.

"Egan, the light," Bailey said, pointing to the ceiling.

"Clear," Egan said, "it's blinking the word 'clear.'"

The shimmering air around the apparition ripped aside, and a woman in an armored vac suit stumbled to the ground. She ripped her helmet off and tossed it aside as she fell to the ground, her lungs heaving.

Standish crept toward the bars, his eyes on the woman with neck-length black hair who was gasping for air. Even under such duress, Standish couldn't help but notice her exotic features and dark eyes.

"You OK out there?" he asked.

"Air…I love air," she said. She struggled to her

hands and knees then took a deep breath. "Had to use the suit's air supply around the Ruhaald or their enviro sensors would pick up my DNA. Tanks went empty while you all were gabbing with that big one. Thanks for that."

"Sheila," Bailey said, "let's get down to brass tacks. You here to get us out?"

"You," the woman said as she got to her feet, "you're the sniper. Boss doesn't need you. Which of you is the commo expert, Egan?"

"That's me," Egan said. "Who're you?"

"Shannon. I work for Ibarra."

"Hold on, you're getting us all out, right?" Standish asked. "Admiral Squid-Face is coming back and it's not like we can explain how one of us is missing."

"You're all getting out." Shannon took a small canister off her belt and shook it. "Just need to know which one of you I have to keep alive."

"Nothing like an adventure where I'm expendable. Sure sounds fun, doesn't it?" Standish asked. "Lady, you want to get us up to speed?"

"The Naroosha and Ruhaald came through the Crucible. The Ruhaald fleet made for Earth and helped turn the tide against the Xaros. Soon as the Xaros burned away—boss thinks Torni managed to hack their self-destruct commands after the General was killed—the

Naroosha opened fire on the ships we had guarding the Crucible. Forced our fleet to stand down. The Ruhaald sent boarders and I got squeezed out of the control room. Managed to grab a Karigole stealth emitter and lay low until the boss got ahold of me." She held up the canister and sprayed a golden mist onto the force field. Tiny particles seeped into the force field and hung like smoke in a dark room.

She traced the spray over the cell door and stepped back. The force field over the doorway flickered and vanished with a loud pop. Shannon pressed a small cube against the cell lock and pulled it open.

"Out. Hurry," she said. "Leave your armor. It's useless without power and enviro packs."

"Nothing like running around a space station full of hostile aliens in our underwear, right?" Standish asked as he and the other Marines hustled through the open doorway.

"Neat toys you've got there," Egan said to Shannon. "Maybe you've got a gauss rifle somewhere?"

"Boss and I have had contingency plans in place since he took over years ago," Shannon said. "Naturally, all our plans didn't survive contact with reality. At least one of you is useful." She took a spindle of orange twine off her belt and handed it to Standish. "Burn cord. Lay out a breach hole big enough for one of us in the floor."

Shannon jabbed a finger into Egan's chest.

"Ibarra needs to get secure contact with Captain Valdar and the *Breitenfeld* in orbit around Luna. How can you make that happen?"

"Does the Crucible still have its IR network set up?"

"No, the Naroosha tore out everything. I can link you to Ibarra through the lighting system. That's the boss' only way of communicating," Shannon said.

Egan chewed on his bottom lip for a moment, then said, "I need a KR-12 system with auto-connect base, and I need my gauntlet powered up. Do you have a KR-12?"

"No, but I know where we can build one," Shannon said. "Trick is getting there."

"Build one?" Egan asked. "The KR-12 is a precision piece of equipment. It took Tirium Engineering weeks to put them together. Back when there was such a company."

"We have the omnium reactor in node four that can make anything from a pound of freshly ground coffee to a fusion bomb in minutes." Shannon frowned. "Again, trick is getting there."

"Got the burn cord set," Standish said. "I would

like to point out that us being in this room when the charge goes off will definitely kill us."

"Different kind of cord," Shannon said. "Step back and watch."

Standish jumped back from the circle he'd made like it was a live wire. Tiny laser beams lit up within the circle, bouncing off the inner edge until a deep yellow field filled the interior. Heat emanated from the circle and it sank into the floor slowly.

"Wait until it cuts through," Shannon said. "Won't have much time before the floor repairs itself."

"You want to fill us in on the rest of your plan?" Bailey asked.

"The Crucible's nodes are linked through the attenuation thorns, which change position to create the wormholes used in jump travel. Thing is, this Crucible isn't one hundred percent complete. Wasn't when we took it away from the Xaros and finishing it hasn't been our number-one priority. We're in node one. Node four has the reactor. Because of how the thorns are arrayed and that there's a giant gap between thorns, we can't get to node four by foot."

"No," Standish said, wagging a finger at Shannon. "Not no, but hell no."

"So we need to do a little space walk," Shannon

said.

"We're in our skivvies," Bailey said, "and your suit's out of air. How're we going to get through hard vacuum?"

"We need to make a pit stop." Shannon looked into the hole, then grabbed Egan by the arm.

"Few more seconds. Should be good, but don't touch the screen." Shannon jerked Egan off balance and sent him down the hole. Shannon stepped on the edge of the hole as she peered down. She tried to step back, but her foot caught on the edge. She twisted her foot loose and went pale.

"Shit, self-repair just started. Go. Go!" Shannon jumped into the hole.

"I hate me job," Bailey said and jumped in after Shannon.

"Should we get—" Standish looked at the armor in the cell. He turned his gaze back to the hole and found a rapidly shrinking opening.

Standish dove headfirst into the pit. He bounced off the smooth side, scraping his scalp. There was a light at the end of the tunnel, but it was getting smaller by the second. Air whistled past Standish's face as he fell, the thought of being buried within the alien construct filling him with a newfound sense of claustrophobia.

He reached out, grasping for the light as he bounced off the now gravelly walls, ripping the outer layer of his body glove.

Standish jerked to a halt as his leg caught against a spur growing out of the wall…several feet short of safety. A hissing sound squeezed around Standish as the hole tightened.

"Son of a—" Standish kicked his legs and tore loose from the wall. He fell and his body passed through the opening a little wider than an escape hatch. A floor rushed up at him and he barely had time to throw his arms in front of his face. His body glove tightened across his body with a jerk.

Standish looked through his fingers. The floor was several feet away. He bent at the waist and found the right heel of his body glove held fast in the ceiling. The fabric stretched away from his foot, distending like pulled elastic.

He went slack and found the other three staring at him.

"Ideas? Anyone?" Standish asked. "Great timing on the cord. Real fun on the way down."

"He always talk this much?" Shannon asked.

"You have no idea," Bailey said.

The ceiling released its hold on Standish and he fell to the floor with a yelp. He popped to his feet and brushed dust off his suit.

"No points for that landing," he said. He turned around and froze.

A dead doughboy sat against a wall, legs as thick as tree trunks sticking out straight, his head lolling against his chest, his hands at his side—palms up. A smear of blood ran down the ceiling to the soldier's back.

"Franklin," Standish said. "Neither of you knew him. He died here, on the Crucible, saving Stacey Ibarra from a drone. He was just like that when we found him." He backed away from the body. "He was…he—" Standish took a quick breath and started gulping for air.

Bailey grabbed Standish by the arms and shook him hard enough to snap his head back.

"Hey! Come back here right now, Marine," Bailey said.

Egan touched Standish's shoulder.

"We've had a long…shitty day," Bailey said. "It's not over yet, Standy. We need you to keep it together a bit longer, all right?"

"Yeah." Standish wiped his sleeve across his eyes. "Sorry. It's just…" He looked around. "I hate this place."

"Try living here," Shannon said. "The body's a good sign. Means the Ruhaald came through. Haven't seen them spend much time or effort covering cleared ground.

We aren't too far from the crèche. Let's go."

****

The situation within the holo table hadn't changed in hours, but Captain Isaac Valdar kept staring at it, looking for a missing detail, a hidden bit of data that would change his objective assessment.

Valdar tapped a screen and called up the damage reports for each of the ships circling the moon alongside the *Breitenfeld*. None were unscathed. Many teetered on the brink of being abandoned to the void, their crews transferred to other ships in the hopes of adding one more ship capable of manning a battle line.

A battle line that had no hope of saving Earth.

The *Breitenfeld* had survived the conflict over Pluto, the skies of Mars and the assault on the extinction arch over Japan with minor damage. Also exiled to lunar orbit were twelve *Manticore*-class frigates armed with Toth energy cannons, sixteen cruisers, a dozen frigates and destroyers and a hodgepodge of Eagles and Condor bombers from hundreds of different aviation wings that found refuge on the ships like wet navy sailors clinging to lifeboats.

The fleet that survived the battle against the Xaros. The sneak attack from the Ruhaald and Naroosha when they seized the Crucible was a confused mess until Valdar took the reins, but he wasn't sure he should be the one in charge. During the chaos of battle, the navy had a simple tradition of linking authority in the chain of command to the largest surviving ship, and her captain. The many carriers and battleships larger than Valdar's ship had been lost early against the Xaros, and the *Breitenfeld*'s arrival through the Crucible with the *Manticore* frigates had shifted the mantle of leadership to him.

Even the greenest ensign knew the mantra of "when in charge, take charge," and Valdar had stepped up to the challenge. Fighting the Xaros had been simpler: destroy them and the construct ripping Japan apart. Trying to stop the world killer made up of all the remaining drones had been nearly impossible, but the planet had been saved when every Xaros drone in the system suddenly self-destructed.

Valdar didn't understand exactly why that happened, although he had his suspicions.

But once the Xaros threat was gone, and their allies betrayed them, the leadership equation changed. Valdar now faced a problem he didn't have an answer for: how to save Earth before the Ruhaald and Naroosha could destroy it.

Valdar swiped his fingers through the holo and brought Earth to him. Every human city built into the mountains had at least one Ruhaald ship hanging over it like a guillotine. The alien ships had thick Toth shields that could withstand the few surviving rail guns the cities had for defense. The ships were vulnerable from above…but the no-fly zone the Ruhaald had imposed on the Earth meant any fighter/bomber attack from the ground would be spotted quickly.

He'd seen the Ruhaald fighters in action and knew the aliens were a match for human pilots in ship-to-ship combat…and each Ruhaald ship carried hundreds of fighters.

No…an attack from the ground had little chance of success.

He double-tapped the enemy ship over Bern. Basic information collected by the defenders below came up, and a nuclear-radiation report blinked at Valdar. The ship had lowered a portion of their shields an hour ago and let Bern see the bank of nuclear-tipped missiles aimed right at them. The Ruhaald had missiles that could burrow into the mountains and set off a seismic event that would wreck the subterranean city. Neutron bombs that would poison the soil for hundreds of miles. Fusion weapons that could flatten mountains. It wouldn't take many warheads to send the planet into a nuclear winter that would make the weather effects from the final Indo-Pak conflict look like a chilly afternoon.

Every alien ship looming over Earth's cities could rain down destruction within minutes of receiving their orders to do just that.

The Ruhaald fleet over Earth was double the size in hulls than Valdar's assemblage around the moon, but it was spread thin over the planet. If Valdar brought his fleet to bear, he could defeat the Ruhaald in detail…but they'd wreck the entire planet before he could even get his guns within range. If the Naroosha ships came out of hiding from around the Crucible, then his chances of beating the Ruhaald were almost zero.

If he left the moon, he'd lose the Earth to nuclear fire and the battle to a numerically superior foe. If he stayed in place…the Earth remained under alien domination. The Mars fleet could tip the scales, but they were days away and if they left orbit, the nukes came down.

He hadn't heard from Fleet Admiral Garret since Valdar and the *Breitenfeld* returned to Earth with the *Manticores* in tow. Part of Valdar worried that the admiral would resolve this situation immediately, no matter the cost.

Valdar did some calculations in his head. He didn't want to risk the chance his bridge crew would see his thoughts played out in the holo tank and let them know he'd even considered the possibility. The Mars fleet weighed anchor, making best speed to Earth as Valdar launched a desperate attack on the ships over the cities. Some Ruhaald ships would be destroyed, but *Breitenfeld* and her fleet would be lost. The aliens would complete their nuclear destruction and undoubtedly poison the atmosphere with enough fallout to render the surface inhospitable to any form of life.

By the time the Mars fleet reached the Earth, the enemy would have left through the Crucible and scuttled the jump gate with left-behind explosives set on a timer. Humanity would be nothing but the surviving Mars fleet and whatever else was scattered through the solar system.

No one celebrates Pyrrhic victories, he thought.

He wanted to return to his ready room, scream in frustration and break something out of frustration, but his mask of command had to remain. His ship, his fleet and his home needed him focused on a solution, not admitting defeat.

A text message appeared on his screen. His guest was about to arrive.

Valdar hoped a second set of eyes—very different eyes—might uncover some detail he'd missed.

The door to the elevator opened, and Captain Gor'al of the Dotok battleship *Vorpral* entered the bridge. The alien's head jerked from side to side, his blunted beak snapping at the air. Gor'al was tall for his kind, a hair under six feet, with white age splotches on his gray-toned skin. The roots of his head quills tended toward the color of old snow near his scalp. His escort, Commander Utrecht, gestured to Valdar with an open hand.

Gor'al tapped the knuckles of his long fingers together and went over to Valdar, ignoring the human's offered hand. Gor'al pressed the side of his shoulder against Valdar's. Valdar took a half step aside, only to be joined by Gor'al again.

Valdar remembered Durand complaining about the Dotok concept of "personal space" and decided to endure the discomfort.

"Thank you for coming, Gor'al," Valdar said.

"The *Vorpral* has seven decks still open to the void and two of my three generators are off-line. Thank you for waiting. If I'd come sooner, my ship might have joined the *Naga* and plowed into your moon. A poor end to the Dotok's last warship," Gor'al said. "Some of the human ships asked me for instructions after the *Europa* was lost and before your arrival. This confused me. Guests do not instruct their hosts."

"That's fleet standard operating procedure, but joint operations with allied species…isn't standard operating procedure. We can work the details out later, but let's go over the situation together." Valdar zoomed the holo tank away from the Earth and laid out how he saw their situation, and how little they could do about it.

Gor'al listened, asking a few minor questions as Valdar went along. When Valdar finished, the Dotok clicked his tongue several times.

"There's a crack in the hull and our rank is low," Gor'al said.

"I'm sorry, what?"

"The situation is poor. Very poor. Tell me, do you have nuclear weapons?" Gor'al asked.

"No. The Xaros generate some sort of energy field that stops them from functioning. The only reason that one device worked on Takeni was because it exploded deep within a mountainside where the Xaros field was blocked. All my nuclear munitions and the mines were taken off the ship. One less thing that could go catastrophically wrong if the *Breitenfeld* was damaged. None of my other ships have nukes."

Valdar reached into the tank and called up a

logistics report listing everything his fleet carried down to the number of food paste tubes by ship.

Gor'al scrolled down the list with flicks of his fingers, too fast for any human to read.

"No word from Ibarra? Garret?" Gor'al asked.

"Nothing from the Crucible. I'm expecting a message from Mars any minute now."

"Do you know our enemies? Their culture? How they fight?"

"I'd never even heard of them before they showed up and started shooting at the Xaros. There's video somewhere of the ship-to-ship combat around the Crucible between the Naroosha and what I left to protect the facility. I have my gunnery team looking it over."

"We don't know what they want. We don't fully know how they fight. Poor. Very poor for us." Gor'al ran a flight plot from lunar orbit to the Crucible orbiting Ceres. "We have the *Breitenfeld*'s jump engines, but I think the enemy will consider your sudden departure a hostile act."

"The time between jumps depends on how far we go and how much other mass we take with us. I looked at—"

"Priority communication from Mars, sir," the comms officer said through Valdar's earbud.

"Put it on the holo tank…no, on the tank's

control screen," the captain said. If the message was dire, and it probably was, putting it in the holo where the crew could see would only invite panic. If only he and Gor'al saw the unvarnished message, the fear would spread no farther than them.

A grainy video square appeared on the screen. It resolved to show an exhausted naval officer with the rank of rear admiral on her vac suit.

"That is not Garret?" Gor'al asked.

"It is not." Valdar felt the icy touch of fear blossom in his chest. Where was Garret?

"This is Admiral Michaud with Mars Command. There's a twenty-light-minute delay on communications, but we monitored the Ruhaald demands…and we have no real choice but to comply, for now.

"Admiral Garret is…indisposed. He suffered a psychological break after receiving news of the Ruhaald betrayal. The chief medical officer informed me that the admiral had a critical level of stimulants in his system, a level Garret apparently maintained for the last several weeks." Michaud shook her head. "We expect him back on his feet soon, but that doesn't mean he'll be ready to take the helm again.

"As of now, the macro-cannon batteries on Mars—and across the system—will stand down. We cannot risk the collateral damage to Earth or the Crucible from the cannons." She ran a hand through her short hair, exhaustion writ across her face. "Valdar? I assume you're still alive. I'm sorry to say this, but you're on your own for now. The intelligence officers have high confidence the Ruhaald and Naroosha *don't* have the combat power to take the cities and fully occupy Earth. They're most likely waiting for reinforcements to come through before they launch an all-out assault. You've run the same simulations. Mars can't get in this fight without losing Earth in the process, same with the rest of our forces through the rest of the solar system. So consider yourself on your own until we can get some actionable information. Make re-contact with Ibarra and the Crucible your top priority. Michaud out."

"That could have been worse," Gor'al said.

"Not by much," Valdar said as he closed the video and leaned against the holo tank.

Gor'al pulled out a field from the *Breitenfeld*'s readiness reports and pointed to a single line of text.

"What is this here?" the Dotok asked.

"That's our Mule equipped with a Karigole cloak. I had it mothballed since the Xaros could…the *Xaros* could see right through the cloak." Valdar ran his fingers through his beard as new ideas came to mind.

"Seems we've found a new option," Gor'al said.

Valdar pointed a finger at Ericcson, the XO. "Get Durand up here."

CHAPTER 3

The Phoenix cemetery held ten coffins for armor. A pair of flatbed trucks, each holding one wrecked suit, were parked next to repair cages in the center of the warehouse-sized room. Only two suits stood upright in the coffins, one with an unblemished new helm, the other boasting heat-warped armor plating and an exposed hip joint.

A human and a Dotok in loose coveralls stood on a catwalk that ran waist-high across the mostly empty coffins, both huddled over a diagnostic station attached to a beam that ran parallel to the catwalk.

"Elias." Bodel lifted his head from the station and looked to the armor with the exposed hip. "There's a cascading servo fault down your right leg. Check your plugs."

Elias said nothing. His armor remained stone still.

"Elias?" Caas, one of the new Dotok armor soldiers, cocked her head to the side and clicked her beak.

The armor raised a hand and banged it against his leg. Icons on the diagnostic screen went from red to green.

"Is something wrong—" Bodel stopped Caas' question with a press of his nerve-damaged arm against her side. The stroke he'd suffered after being cut from his armor on Takeni left him reliant on a cane to move about and half his face slack. In his armor, he was nigh unstoppable, but a cripple without it.

Bodel tapped a mute button on the screen.

"He's...having trouble," Bodel said. "It's Kallen." The third Iron Heart had died on Mars, her armor left in the red sand.

"I don't understand human grieving rituals," Caas said. "Is there something I can do?"

"And how do the Dotok handle the loss of one they...held dear?" Bodel twisted a knob and shook his head as the synch reading between Elias and his armor remained below normal.

"We hold a *shran*. Those who were part of the deceased's life witness the body being returned to nature. The spirit fills the world, remains with us. After we left Takeni, we carved the names of those we lost onto *ganii* nuts and planted them in Maui. They grow well in your soil, a good omen."

"I like it," Bodel said, "simple, peaceful. Elias and I, we are soldiers. We are armor. Death in battle is expected. We bury our dead in their wombs, then hold a remembrance, a wake. After that…individuals grieve on their own. Some move on…others can't."

"What about you? Elias?"

"Kallen was a good Christian woman. I believe she will be judged worthy of heaven and find peace. As for Elias, he believes as she did, but…she was his anchor. He was badly wounded, red-lined, after we took back the Earth. It was her plan that brought him back. She called him out from the darkness, and now I don't know if we can hold him back."

"What're you talking about?" Elias' voice boomed out of his armor.

"Your organ function is below nominal," Bodel said. "You need another round of dialysis and muscle rehabilitation."

"Get me green across the board. Then worry about getting your own armor back in the fight," Elias said.

Bodel looked at the wrecked suit in the back of the truck.

"We can do rudimentary part replacements. We need our maintenance crew off the *Breitenfeld* to put my armor—and Ar'ri's armor—back together," Bodel said.

"Is Ar'ri in any condition to wear his armor?" Elias asked.

"Physically, he's fine," Caas said. "But fighting that...thing...rattled him. He's resting right now."

"Colonel Carius sent another platoon, with their maintenance teams, from St. George." Elias tapped an antenna on the side of his helm. "They'll have you fully mission capable in no time."

"Until then we've got two suits to defend the city," Bodel said.

The door to the Cemetery slid open. Hale and Steuben walked in, both in their power armor. Caas ran her fingers through her head quills and cleaned a bit of dirt off her beak.

"Elias, you all right in there?" Hale asked, looking up to the three armor soldiers.

"Never better. You need us?"

Hale and Steuben traded a glance.

"There's a firebase under attack by the Ruhaald. I'm taking—"

"I'll go!" Caas said. "I can be suited up in ten minutes. Whatever you need." Caas' hands clenched and her head lowered like a scolded child. She gave Elias a bashful look, her beak clicking rapidly.

"I mean, if Elias says we can," she said.

"She and I are with you." Elias hit his fist against his chest plate.

"We step off in thirty minutes," Hale said. "Subterranean tunnel nine."

"We'll be there," Elias said.

Caas watched as the Marines turned away and looked at Elias with pleading eyes. Elias flicked his fingers at her. Caas vaulted over the catwalk and landed in a roll. She ran up to Hale and gave him a little pat on the shoulder.

"Yes?" Hale half turned around.

"Lieutenant—no, Captain—I'm Caas. Do you…do you remember me?"

Hale's lips pressed together. "You're familiar…"

"You and your Marines saved me and my brother from the *noorla*, the banshees. When I came of age, I joined our militia to repay what you did. Now I…is Mr. Standy OK? I'd like to see him again. He was so kind to me."

"I'm sorry, but the Ruhaald have Standish. Last we saw him, he was alive. We'll get him back. Marines don't leave anyone behind." Hale's eyes darted to the patches on her shoulder. "You have your plugs?"

"Yes, sir."

"I didn't make it through selection. You must be tough." Hale gave her a nod. "Glad to have you with us."

****

The subterranean terminal was a wide cylinder with heavy doors over each of the mag-lev tracks leading to and from Phoenix. On Takeni, the Dotok survived within the deep canyons scarring the planet. The atmosphere over Takeni's tall plateaus was thin and swept by massive storms. The Dotok opted to dig tunnels through the planet's crust to connect the scattered settlements, rather than continuously risk flying over the hostile and deadly terrain.

As the Dotok integrated into Earth and took an active interest in defending the planet from the next Xaros attack, Ibarra and Admiral Garret saw the tactical and strategic usefulness of using Dotok techniques and technology to link defenses beyond the reach and detection of the enemy. The tunnels, some running hundreds of miles below ground, were coated in quadrium, which thwarted Xaros sensors.

If the Xaros ever did find their way into the tunnels, they were rigged with enough high explosives to collapse with the press of a button.

Hale picked up a belt of gauss magazines from a supply cart and fixed them onto his armor. The plasma weapons he'd used on Pluto were experimental…and the power cores were manufactured by the omnium reactor on the Crucible. None of his Marines had complained about returning to the familiar gauss rifles and carbines.

"Sir," said Cortaro, already in his full kit, as he held a hand out to what was left of their company. Fifteen Marines stood in uneven lines. All squads had taken casualties on Pluto and defending Phoenix from the Xaros.

Elias and Caas waited in their travel configuration behind the Marines, the tracks within their leg armor exposed and set against the heavy steel of the terminal floor.

"Marines," Hale said, swinging his rifle off his shoulder and slapping in a fresh magazine, "we're tired. We're beat up. There's an enemy hanging over our head like the Sword of Damocles. We don't know what they want or why they turned on us, but we know they're on the offensive. They've got Firebase X-Ray in their sights and we need to find out why. The more we learn, the better chance we have of ending this standoff with anything but another battle."

He pointed to the number-nine gate.

"In a few seconds this door will open and—"

A buzzer sounded and warning lights flashed…over the number-three gate on the other side of the terminal.

Hale glanced down at the map on his forearm screen and double-checked that the ninth track did lead to X-Ray and he hadn't just made a fool of himself.

The metal doors on gate two slid aside on massive rollers, and three armor soldiers entered the terminal bearing red and white flags painted on their shoulders. Their helms had a metal plate shaped like a double-headed eagle over the lower half of the face. The side and back of the helmets were linked plates, like a lobster's tail.

Hale's head tilted slightly at the weapon mounted on the new arrivals' backs; next to their rail cannons and rotary cannons was a spear.

"Which one is Hale?" the lead armor asked.

"That's me." The captain raised a hand.

The armor rolled over to him and saluted, two fingers to the right temple.

"Vladislav, Armor Corps. I've got Ferenz and Adamczyk with me. Sorry I couldn't bring more. Casualties. You are *the* Hale?"

Hale tapped the name stenciled onto his armor.

"Last one…far as I know."

"I thought you'd be taller," Vladislav said. "We need fresh power packs. It was a long road march from St. George."

Hale pointed to pallets loaded down with batteries against a far wall. Vladislav nodded and rolled away. Hale got another look at the spear on the armor soldier's back. The weapon was nearly as long as his rail cannon.

A truck loaded with soldiers in light armor and tool chests came through the open gate.

Warning lights flashed over the ninth gate and it opened into an abyss of darkness.

"Caas and I will take point," Elias said through the IR net. *"The new arrivals will follow you and your crunchies."*

"Fair enough…Elias, why are Vladislav and the rest of his men carrying spears? They know it's the twenty-second century, right?"

"Because they're Hussars," Elias said the words as if they made perfect sense and rolled into the tunnel.

****

Standish's hands opened and closed over and over again. He brushed fingertips over his thigh, reaching for an absent weapon. Moving through the dead-silent corridors of the Crucible brought back more combat memories than

Franklin's end. Being without his gauss rifle, the familiar weight of his armor and the near constant chatter through his abandoned helmet made him feel almost naked.

They'd come across more dead doughboys, but not the enormous gauss weapons the bio-constructs carried into battle.

Shannon, in front of the Marines, held up a hand as she came to a stop. She watched as a door light blinked rapidly.

"Got something coming our way," she whispered.

Standish looked over his shoulder for any kind of cover, something to hide behind, but the corridor was bare.

"Come here," Ibarra's employee said, waving them over. "Don't say anything. Try not to breathe hard. Or at all."

Shannon grabbed Standish as he got close and pulled him so close his face mashed against her hair. The other Marines tucked in close and Shannon activated her Karigole cloaking field.

A shell of air shimmered around them; colors from beyond the field came in gray-scale. Standish turned his face to the side, still pressed against Shannon's head. The field buckled, distorting like he was looking at a cracked mirror.

He'd seen this effect before. The field was losing power.

A deep buzz filled the air. Long shadows crept out of a nearby intersection and grew longer as something approached.

Standish heard a little whimper escape from Shannon.

A metallic gray robot floated into view. Spindly arms ending in hooks and tools dangled from broad shoulders. Its head looked like an overturned bucket and a red visor slit ran across the front. Its torso was a series of interconnected plates with small bright lights embedded between the seams. The robot stopped in the intersection, turned to face the corridor where Standish and his fellows were cowering, and continued on. Standish felt a vibration go up his legs as the machine moved past, held up by an anti-grav field.

The humans stayed still until the robot had turned down another hallway and the corridor was dead silent.

Shannon snapped off the cloak and pushed Standish away.

"Ugh, when was the last time any of you showered?" she asked.

"Good question, princess," Bailey said. "Between running around Pluto, fixing a shot-up ship, getting chased through Phoenix by drones and being kidnapped by Ruhaald, no worries, mate. We'll find time for a pop over to the spa."

"We also got shot down in the Osprey. Don't forget," Standish said.

"What the hell was that?" Egan pointed down the hall to where the robot had disappeared.

"A Naroosha, I think," Shannon said. "Saw some of those heading for the control room when I was on the run. Sure don't look or act like the Ruhaald."

"It was a robot. Why would they send robots to fight the Xaros? I thought the drones could hack computers," Standish said.

"I bet they'd look at our armor and think the same thing," Shannon said. "I'd bet real money there's something inside that robot. Probably something we don't want to see. We're almost there. Come on."

They found a broken barricade around the corner. Plates of aegis armor as thick as castle doors had been twisted open and pushed against the walls. Slain doughboys lay packed against the walls, leaving a path to a doorway marked AUTHORIZED ACCESS ONLY.

"Boss will open the door for us in a second," Shannon said.

Egan went to a doughboy weapon half-buried

beneath a body. He pulled it free with a grunt and tried to lift it. Standish got his arms under the barrel and together they lifted it into the air.

"Not…happening," Egan said. He guided it back to the ground and tilted it onto a corpse.

"Magazine's empty." Standish tapped a metal box on the underside of the weapon. "Bet the recoil would kill us."

"We could manage in power armor, yeah?" Bailey said.

"Orozco could do it. Don't think we can," Egan said. "Why the hell do the doughboys have weapons that are so crude?"

"So they don't break them," Shannon said. "They're not the smartest things on the battlefield. It took more engineering to make doughboy-proof weapons than it did to design those brutes."

Standish looked closely at one of the bodies. The skin was the color of wheat, desiccated. A straight, blackened line of seared flesh traced from the body's ear down the neck and into the armor.

"What happened to them?" Standish asked.

"Not our problem," Shannon snapped over her shoulder, "and it'll stay that way if the boss would just…there we go."

The door crumbled aside and they rushed into a darkened room.

Standish's shin bashed against something hard and unfriendly.

"Not my day," he moaned through gritted teeth as he fell to his side, clutching his injury.

Lights snapped on and grew brighter.

Upright tanks filled the room, all tethered to a frost-covered computer bank in the ceiling. Bubbles the size of coins floated up the sides of the tanks. Floating in the lime-green fluid was a naked human being.

"Is this a…" Standish tapped on a tank. "Well, it must be."

"Procedural generation crèche number twelve," Shannon said. "Boss doesn't let anyone in here. Says it would be bad for morale if pics ever got loose on the net." She stepped onto a control platform and tapped at a keyboard.

Egan stared slack-jawed at a tank holding an emaciated body, limbs pulled into a fetal position.

"You remember any of this, Egan?" Standish asked.

Egan shook his head.

"I don't like this," Bailey said, touching her stomach. "I carried my baby girl. Felt her moving. Sang to her. What's even happening to them?"

"Bodies grow to maturity within a day," Shannon said. She pointed to the computer in the ceiling. "Consciousness gets etched into the neural pathways over the next eight days. The system makes sure the desired traits are trained, plenty of wiggle room for personality development and idiosyncrasies. Boss says we could have a trillion tubes going for a billion years before a duplicate mind came through the system."

"When I was twelve," Egan said, "I fell into the Mississippi. I stayed afloat for…God knows how long. People on the riverbanks tried to throw ropes to me." His hands reached out and grasped at the phantom memory. "I went under. I remember the taste of river water in my mouth, my lungs. A highway patrolman tossed a rescue bot into the river. It got me out and did CPR until I came to. None of it…happened?"

"Memories are as real as you want them to be," Shannon said. "You all see why the boss wants to keep this part of the sausage making off-line? Expect to sign a very serious nondisclosure agreement when this is all over."

"How long have you worked for Ibarra?" Standish asked. "Was this his plan from the very beginning? Flood the solar system with super soldiers."

Shannon huffed as her fingers danced across the

keyboard. "I was one of his off-the books employees, and even I didn't know about the probe Ibarra kept squirrelled away under Euskal Tower. *Nobody* knew. Man can keep a secret. But…the boss tells me he couldn't have made any of these proccies before the probe sent Stacey to Bastion. The big brains out there made the gene-tech. She brought it back through the probe."

A strobe light flashed against a back wall.

"There," Shannon said, "that's our gear. The tube techs will outfit the newbies before their higher functions kick in, let them become fully awake in a natural environment. Bring it over while I cover our tracks in the system."

Standish nudged Egan, snapping him out of his reverie.

"I would've made a couple dozen of that one guy," Standish said. "What's his name? My grandpa was always talking about him. Got bit by a rattlesnake and three days later the snake died."

"Chuck Norris," Bailey said. "You know he was Australian?"

"What? He was Canadian. Grandpa said so," Standish said.

"Both of you are on drugs." Egan shook his head. "He was so American it's not even up for discussion."

Shannon slapped a palm against the control station several times.

"Children!" She pointed to the flashing light on the other side of the room. "I just got a text update from the boss. We either get in touch with the *Breitenfeld* and figure out some way to save the probe or Earth will be nothing but a breeding ground for slave soldiers. Now focus!"

Standish lowered his head and hurried over to the blinking light on the fabricator. He heard the whirr of gears within the machine, but nothing came out from the small door beneath the light.

The Marine turned around, looked over the tubes, and did a double take at one a row away. His brow furrowed as he stepped over a frosted cable running between the tanks. Inside the tank was a woman with long black hair, her face pressed against her knuckles. Standish touched a screen on the tank and frowned as an information panel came to life.

"What're you doing, you pervert?" Bailey slapped Standish on the back of the head.

"Look at this one," Standish whispered.

"You think I need to see some stretchy Sheila to remind me I'm tottering around on short sticks? We—" Bailey's mouth snapped shut with a click of teeth. She leaned close to the tank and cupped her hands around her eyes to take a better look at the woman in the tank.

"Hey, Shannon?" Standish asked. "I thought Ibarra didn't make doubles."

"He doesn't," Shannon called out. "Why?"

Standish and Bailey looked at each other. The sniper shrugged.

"Is your last name Martel?" Standish said, reading from the information panel.

Standish heard Shannon jump off the control station and make her way toward them.

"How is it you three can be so famous but not able to focus for more than three minutes on an important task?" Shannon asked. She raised a finger at Standish, then looked into the tank.

Inside, her perfect duplicate floated in the faux-amniotic fluid.

Shannon's face went white. Her mouth moved, but there were no words.

"The panel says 'Shannon Martel Mark V,'" Standish read.

"No…" Shannon said. "That's not me."

"The one in the tank has a crescent-shaped scar on her neck," Bailey said. "So do you."

"That's not me!" Shannon shoved Bailey aside and

hammered a fist against the tank. Shannon let out a primal scream and struck again.

Standish wrapped an arm around Shannon and wrestled her to the floor, pinning her beneath his body as she screamed and flailed against the Marine. Standish got a hand over her mouth and stifled her screaming.

"This is weird for everybody," Standish grunted, "but all this noise will get us noticed. Ah! No biting! No biting!"

Shannon stopped struggling. Bailey and Egan gathered close, confusion writ across their faces. She lifted her head up from Standish's grasp and took a ragged breath.

"I'm fine," she said. "I'll be fine. Let's get this done. Then I'll have answers from the boss."

Standish let her go and helped her up. She kept her gaze away from the doppelganger in the tank.

A bell dinged from the fabricator and shrink-wrapped sets of power armor rolled off a conveyor belt.

"There's our armor, full life-support systems," Shannon said. "Let's get it on and get the hell out of here."

****

A thorn as wide as a football field and several

miles long scraped against smaller segments of the Crucible, balancing the quantum field spreading through the center of the great edifice. A tiny pinprick of yellow light appeared on the thorn's hull, growing larger as a burn cord cut a hole.

The charge fell into the void, flopping around like a sail lost to the wind.

Standish, wearing full void battle armor, emerged from the hole moments later.

"Nope!" he shouted. "Nope nope nope…" He repeated the word as the gravity linings in his boots pulled him against the thorn.

Egan followed close behind.

"Seriously, Standish," he said as he landed next to the other Marine, "you can't let one bad experience taint you forever."

"Oh, do you want to go play kissy-face with the next Toth tentacle monster you see?" Standish asked.

"There are none of those krait things out here." Egan looked across the void. "I mean, why would there be?"

"That's what I thought, hypocrite." Standish grabbed Shannon as she came through the hole and set her down next to him. Bailey emerged a moment later, forming a loose circle with the others.

"OK, let me find the reactor node," Shannon said, looking over the Crucible.

"It's so…weird," Bailey said. "The whole thing's moving like a ball of snakes."

"Are those our ships?" Standish pointed to a derelict hull floating just beyond the outer edge of the jump gate. He zoomed in with his helm optics and sent the feed to the others. A *Manticore*-class frigate that used salvaged Toth energy cannons drifted on their visor screens. Tendrils of atmosphere and broken hull fragments drifted behind the ship like blood seeping into water.

"Scorch marks on the hull," Bailey said. "Xaros didn't do that."

"The Naroosha," Shannon said. "Took out everything we had guarding the Crucible in minutes. Their ships are lurking near the outer edges. There—the silver-looking corkscrews. See them?"

"They look 'bout the same size as the *Breit*," Egan said. "Why're they so close to the Crucible? Where are the Ruhaald ships?"

"They're afraid of the macro cannons on Mars and the Jovian moons," Shannon said. "So long as the Naroosha ships are tucked in close, Admiral Garret can't hit them without destroying the Crucible. Ruhaald are in Earth's atmosphere floating over the mountain forts.

Macro cannons can't attack their ships without destroying the cities. Hit or miss."

Shannon pointed to a dome across from the gap in the Crucible's ring.

"There's the reactor. We need to hurry," she said.

The Marines stretched metal tethers off their suits and mag-locked the lines to each other. The lines tightened, pulling them into a circle.

"I ever mention how much I hated Dutchman training?" Standish said.

Egan took a propellant gun and shook it.

"No grav linings," the commo specialist said. "We do our best to act like another hunk of broken space junk and no one'll notice us." He led a brief countdown and the four jumped off the thorn and into the void.

Standish kept his gaze on their destination, the dome housing the omnium reactor. He felt a slight tug at his waist as Egan used the propellant gun to adjust their course.

"You want to hurry this up?" Shannon asked. "The Naroosha ship with their jump drive left a day ago. I'd rather not be floating in the middle of the wormhole when it comes back. Ibarra ran a few experiments years ago. Any matter caught in a forming wormhole—and not protected by a jump engine—gets smeared into subatomic particles."

"You're telling us this now? *After* our little space walk got going?" Standish asked.

"Oops," Shannon said bluntly.

"I've got enough propellant to maneuver a bit and slow us down," Egan said. "We go any faster and we'll skip right off the hull."

"Bloody Crucible," Bailey said. "Hate this arsed-up alien hunk of…whatever it is. Should have blown it all to hell the moment we had the chance."

"If we'd done that," Shannon said, "no proccies, no aegis armor, no allies. We wouldn't have stood a chance when the Xaros returned."

"Now we've got our 'allies' ready to nuke our cities if we don't fall in line. Great plan, but," Standish said, "not like we could complain if we're all dead. We've got that going for us."

"Standish, I know you were in the Crucible when Stacey Ibarra and the probe took it over," Egan said. "Where were you, Bailey?"

"That one." She nodded to a dome farther along the ring of thorns from their destination. "Was with 2nd Raider battalion. Our landing was a complete goat screw. The colonel and most of his senior staff died right as we disembarked from the *America*. Lost half my team to drones in the first couple minutes. Then the lieutenant saw her husband's ship explode and she dropped out of the fight. It was a long day."

"I remember sitting in a search-and-rescue shuttle on the *Constantine*," Egan said. "Up here," he said, tapping his helmet, "I saw the whole battle play out. Never got to be a part of it."

"Everyone remembers that battle," Shannon said. "Boss incorporated it into the first batch of proccies, helped them integrate into the fleet after all the personnel shake-ups."

"Wait…that's why I was reassigned from the Raiders?" Bailey asked. "So Ibarra could do some social experiment with his tube babies? Sorry, Egan. No offense."

"None taken," Egan said.

"You wouldn't believe what the boss has done to get Earth to this moment—well, not the Ruhaald and Naroosha betraying us. The moment before that when our skies were free from the Xaros," Shannon said.

"Like?" Standish asked. "Was he the one that made NuMeat popular? That fake stuff really hurt my rancher family."

"Yeah, kid, Mark Ibarra and the probe from an alien alliance went to the effort to make sure fast-food joints sold vat meat instead of dead cows." Shannon rolled her eyes.

"He stopped the campaign for Darwin back in '68, didn't he?" Bailey asked. "The Chinese 9th Army was broken. Atlantic Union armor was outside Daly Waters when the stand-down order came through. The official explanation about 'overextended supply lines' never made sense. Have you seen armor in the field? They run off bloodshed and pure hate."

"Beijing was a day away from using nukes. The boss didn't want World War IV to start right when the Saturn colonization fleet was being built. He made a few calls, ensured the right politicians had 'accidents' and made sure the armistice kept military tensions high enough that the AU was happy to lend war ships to the colony mission," Shannon said.

"He didn't see the refugees coming out of Daly Waters. I was knee-high to a joey when me pa took me to the evac center outside Alice Springs. Those poor bastards were skin and bones. All women, children and oldies. Pa wouldn't tell me where all the men were. At least the armor got video of the mass graves, got my answer years later. Did Ibarra know about the war crimes?"

"He knew. There was only so much he could do. The only reason any civilians got out of Daly Waters was because he altered Chinese military transmissions to make that happen," Shannon said. "Ibarra was a wreck for weeks after the armistice, kept watching the vids of armor digging up the graves. You may think he's some kind of heartless monster. He's not. He knew there were consequences behind every decision and when the innocent suffered, he suffered."

"And the not-so-innocent?" Standish asked.

"He had me, and one other person, to deal with those," Shannon said with a chuckle. "I always liked that part of my job."

"Almost there." Egan let off a few quick bursts from his propellant gun and angled them toward a gap through the inner ring of thorns.

"Mind the sharp, pointy bits," Standish said.

They floated between two thorns as they slid against each other, closing the entrance seconds after the Marines made it through.

Standish used his helmet's optics to zoom in on the dome, still several hundred yards away. Angular plates of aegis armor covered the surface, gleaming like obsidian beneath the sun's light. Several wrecked bunkers dotted the surface.

"I don't remember any of that," Standish said. "Are those point defense turrets? Bet we could find weapons in there. We get in a fight and my cutting wit won't do more than hurt feelings."

"We reinforced a couple key facilities before the Xaros arrived," Shannon said. "Defenders didn't last long. Aegis armor works against Xaros disintegration beams. Naroosha lasers? Not so much. Get us to the nearest bunker. That's our way inside."

A ripple of light appeared beyond the dome as a squadron of Ruhaald fighters came around the far side.

"Think we've got a problem," Standish said.

"Loosen up. Play dead." Shannon hit the release on her lifeline and pushed away from Standish. The lights within her helmet switched off.

"Open your air valves and cut power." Egan put a boot against Bailey's side and shoved her away.

Standish's ears popped as his helmet flooded with air pressure. Strike Marines' evasion techniques did everything possible to limit their electromagnetic signature if an enemy was close. Active air-tank regulators and the power armor's heating systems would generate a great deal of attention if the Ruhaald looked too closely. Unpowered, floating loose, they might be mistaken for Marines blown from warships during the battle…who died waiting for recovery.

A chill pressed against Standish's body as the void

leached heat away. His teeth chattered as his exhalations frosted the inside of his visor. According to the suit's specs, he could survive for nineteen minutes in an unpowered suit. As numbness crept up his fingertips, he had serious doubts about the manufacturer's promises.

The Ruhaald fighters flew a lazy orbit around the dome, then veered toward a dome on the opposite side of the Crucible. A single blocky transport ship trailed behind the fighters.

Standish's teeth chattered. He felt a nip of frost against his earlobes and cheeks, a familiar pain from enduring Canadian winters.

There was a tug against his lifeline. He looked over and saw Bailey slapping at her forearm computer.

Standish poked his control screen with dull fingers and felt a wave of relief as his suit came back online and the heaters kicked in.

"—way too fast. Hold on!" Egan shouted.

Standish looked up. The dome was close enough that he could make out the individual plates of aegis armor and noted just how quickly the unforgiving surface was coming right at him.

"Get your hooks out." Standish unspooled his secondary lifeline from his belt and spun the weighted magnetic tip like a bolo.

The line attached to Bailey jerked as Egan used the propellant gun to slow his momentum. Standish felt his speed slow as the complexities of a four-body vector dynamics equation played out.

"Really should have paid more attention to high school physics," Standish said as they crossed over the edge of the dome.

"I'm out." Egan flung the gun away and removed the lifeline attached to Shannon from his belt. "I'll drop her line and—damn it!"

Egan clawed at Shannon's lifeline as it slipped out of his grasp.

"Drop hooks! Now!" Bailey yelled.

Standish released his secondary line and bit his lip as it darted toward the dome. The magnetic anchor skided over the surface…but didn't find purchase against the armor plating. His line went slack as the anchor bounced away. Standish's panicked breathing thundered in his ears as he slapped the lifeline housing on his hip and waited for the winch to reel his line back in. He might get a second chance, if his connection to Bailey held.

Egan jerked to a halt as his anchors gripped tight. Bailey slammed to a stop as her line to Egan went taut.

Standish gripped the line to Bailey in his hands and held on with all the strength his suit could muster. The graphene-reinforced cable lengthened until it was nearly straight. The force of his momentum hit like a truck as the line ran out. His head rattled like a pea in a can as his body jerked against the lifeline.

He flailed around, grabbed the line and looked down at his belt…it was stretched, nearly torn open by the shearing force that brought him to a stop.

"Oh no…" Standish gripped the line to Bailey in one hand and grabbed the line to Shannon in the other. He had only seconds to save Ibarra's spy.

"Shannon, listen to me. My belt is compromised. You need to use your anti-grav linings in your boots to—"

The line to Shannon went tight, then snapped loose as Standish's belt ripped apart.

Standish reached for the belt, the last connection he could make to Shannon, and missed it by inches.

Shannon's arms flailed as she tumbled end over end, away from Standish and into the black. She faded into the void within seconds.

"—suit! Nothing's working!" Shannon's transmission was full of static.

"Shannon? Shannon, answer me!" Standish called out. He caught a few bursts of static…then nothing.

The line in his hand tugged at him. He looked down and saw Bailey and Egan reeling him in. He stumbled onto the dome and struggled to get a firm grasp with the magnetic soles of his boots.

"Did she say anything to you? Can she get back here?" Bailey asked.

"Her IR was weak." Standish looked into the abyss, searching for Shannon. "Her suit might have malfunctioned when she brought it back online. Did she even know how to do that right? You try and bring up life support before the temperature regulators and the batteries might dump their charge."

"I thought she knew," Egan said.

"I didn't ask her," Bailey said, touching her fingertips to her visor.

"Damn it, why the hell didn't any of us make sure she knew how to use her armor right when we put it on her?" Egan asked.

"She was in a hell of a rush to get away from the other…her. Remember? Excuse me for thinking Ibarra's ninja-woman knew how to cold-start mark-nine armor," Bailey said.

"I'm going to get blamed for this." Standish put his hands on his hips and shook his head.

Egan slapped his forearm screen and his icon dropped off the IR net. The Marine balled his fists and screamed a single word into the void.

He reopened his comms and let out a deep breath.

"All right…we need to get out of the open." Egan pointed to a ruined bunker a dozen yards away. "Shannon wanted us to go to one of those, must be a way inside."

"Wait…what about her?" Standish waved a hand over his head. "She's gone Dutchman. We don't know how long her suit will last or…even how to find her."

"Our suits have exactly jack and shit left for battery power and life support. We go looking for her and we'll end up dead in the void…or back in that cell," Egan said. "We still have a mission. Get Ibarra and Captain Valdar connected. Let the brass figure out the rest of this mess. Come on."

Egan kept his feet locked to the surface, skating across the metal on a loose magnetic grip like he was gliding over ice. The other Marines followed.

The bunker's roof was torn open like flesh assaulted by a jagged blade. Standish came to a stop next to a firing slit and took a quick glance inside. Blackened bodies fused to gauss cannons manned the firing positions.

"God bless 'em," Bailey said. "Hope it was quick."

"The rest will be just like this," Egan said.

"I'm not going to say 'I told you so,'" Standish said as he climbed up the side of the bunker and dropped into the wrecked interior. "Mostly because I didn't.

Shannon frightened me. But I was *thinking* this was a bad idea."

He scraped his boot over the charred floor, sending black flakes floating into the void. His toe caught on a depression.

"Hello, what's this?" Standish ran his fingers over the dip, then grasped a handle. He pulled, using much of the augmented strength his armor provided before a hatch popped open.

"Good job." Bailey looked over Standish's shoulder. "You've found a very small box."

Standish looked into the hole. There was a solid base of metal two feet down.

"No doors on the outside. This is wide enough for us. How'd they get in here?" Standish asked.

The metal base slid aside, revealing an inky darkness below.

"You found it. You first." Egan nudged Standish's shoulder.

"In all fairness, I think its Bailey's turn to go face-first into the dark scary place." Standish looked up at the other two and found no sympathy. "Fine. Where's that damned new guy when I need him. Whole company of new guys and I'm still the one that—don't push me!"

Standish shrugged off Bailey's hand and slid into

the opening. He landed a moment later and switched on his IR filters. A narrow passageway barely taller than him extended away from the opening.

"Clear." Standish took a few tentative steps away from the hatch. He lifted a hand and let it fall naturally to his side as Egan and Bailey joined him. "We've got gravity…but no atmo."

"Are we inside the dome?" Bailey asked.

Standish rapped his knuckles on the wall.

"That's armor plating," he said. "We're in the aegis shell over the dome."

"Move," Egan said, "our air tanks aren't getting any fuller."

Standish swallowed hard, then started running.

CHAPTER 4

The *Forever Tide* was not a perfect vessel for the many Ruhaald subspecies. Septon Jarilla was reminded of this each time he walked through the passageways with his helmet removed. The high methane-nitrogen mix of atmosphere suited some of the crew that walked upon the many islands of their home world, but not a locus like Jarilla. His body demanded frequent returns to the many pools of seawater where the truest strains of Ruhaald lived and worked.

His queen demanded his company and counsel, and that could not be given while he tottered around on two legs and his lungs demanded gas to function. Undergoing the metamorphosis back to his oceanic form took time and was quite painful when rushed.

The larger Ruhaald vessels catered to the seaborne

castes, fully aquatic and compartmentalized to survive void combat. Assault vessels had nothing but the land walkers and a few pools to rejuvenate the crews. Most of Ruhaald civilization existed beneath the waves of their home world, and even those specially bred to expand beyond the surface still needed the embrace of the sea.

Jarilla's long-toed feet sloshed through the passageway; the feel of sea grass beneath his bare feet was comforting, at least. The *Forever Tide* had to carry the loci, the leadership caste like him that transcended the stratified Ruhaald society to guide the species, and that meant air and sea segments within the ship.

He turned around a clear tank, one set directly on his path to the bridge, forcing a detour that would take him several minutes to circumvent. He swore a water dweller designed the ship just to confound the land walkers. The aquatic crew often complained to him that a land walker had designed the layout, and either failed to consult the swimmers or made sure the ship was as inconvenient as possible for them.

Jarilla thought there was truth to both opinions.

He entered the walker's bridge where the crew handled the external concerns of the ship: navigation, combat, communication. The swimmers controlled internal duties: life support, the hatchery, propulsion and power systems. The swimmer command center formed the back wall, a clear wall where the two aspects of the Ruhaald coordinated with each other.

Jarilla flicked his tentacles at the swimmer officer in charge across the glass and went to a communication screen. He scooped water from the floor into his helmet and placed it on his head. The moisture against his skin was therapeutic, and he would need some comfort to steel himself against this next conversation.

Jarilla opened a channel to Ordona on the Crucible.

The Naroosha's bucket helm appeared on the screen.

"Report," Ordona said curtly.

"I am your ally, not your servant," Jarilla said.

"The Bastion translation software conveys our meaning to each other. That is sufficient for our needs. Expending mental energy to appease your cultural expectation is wasted mental energy. Report."

Jarilla wondered if the Bastion technology could fully convey the Ruhaald's opinion that Ordona was a ruptured cloaca. He decided not to test that question in the interest of diplomacy.

"I wish to open negotiations with the human authorities."

"Irrelevant to our timetable. If you have nothing to add, I will close the channel."

"Wait," Jarilla's toes writhed in annoyance, splashing in the shallow water. "My queen requests that we reconsider the terms of success."

Jarilla looked to the side where a pool of black water sat separate from the swimmers' bridge. She dwelled within her own tank, perfectly suited to her physiology and linked to the hatchery where her offspring were cared for. He longed to join her in the tank, feel the meld of her consciousness with his, but his duty kept him away.

"Your queen, all proper obsequious notions rendered, agreed to this with the Vishrakath representative. As did my leadership committee. I am not authorized to deviate from our objectives unless there are unforeseen and very extenuating circumstances. Explain yourself."

Jarilla gave thanks that he was not on the Crucible at this moment; otherwise he would have ripped Ordona's suit open and found out if he had a neck to strangle.

"My queen believes the humans are not as Ambassador Wexil and the Vishrakath made them out to be. They could be more valuable in the war against the Xaros as willing allies, not the slave caste the Toth will provide."

"I have studied some human documents stored in

the Crucible's data banks. They are as craven and untrustworthy as Wexil describes, but their actions in regards to the Karigole and the Dotok do not fit this classification. Regardless, I reject your queen's suggestion, with all appropriate respect."

"Why?"

"Your ground forces are engaged in a limited offensive outside the settlement designated as Phoenix. Is this some manner of gross error? Was a memo as to our tactical and strategic objectives not distributed? Explain."

Jarilla felt his feeder tentacles twist together.

"It is unavoidable. Human slaves killed the scion of an assault brood. They must generate a replacement to…it is a biological imperative. Their aggression must have an outlet," Jarilla said.

"Promising reconciliation while engaged in a purge is incompatible with human diplomatic concepts. Additionally, the survivors of the first Xaros attack were from a culture known as 'the West.' Our actions mirror prominent historical events known as Pearl Harbor, 9/11 and the *HMAS Mendelson* incident."

"I don't know human history. How did those events play out?"

"Very poorly for those that acted against what the West considered 'honorable.' Our initial attack and

Ruhaald continued actions make the chance of reaching our goals ahead of schedule unlikely. I will have complete control over the Crucible soon, then I will summon the Toth. Continue your negotiations, the distraction seems to be all that the Ruhaald are good for."

The channel shut off.

Jarilla slammed a fist against the screen, cracking a spider's web across its face.

Our survival is more important than the humans, he thought. *We will not have a fleet strong enough to defeat the Xaros when they arrive. That is why we are doing this.*

He looked to the dark water where his beloved queen dwelled. Her every wish was his command; his failure to save the humans would be accepted. Especially when so much was at stake.

****

Stacey Ibarra paced back and forth across her living quarters. She glanced at a panel recessed into the wall showing the time, Congress meetings and her schedule for the next few days. The last few meetings were highlighted in red: not attended.

Pa'lon sat on a couch, bent forward with his hands interlaced between his knees. Bastion projected a perfect disguise over his Dotok body, making him appear as a well-dressed man in his late forties with a close-cropped beard and swept-back hair.

"This activity of yours does nothing for our situation," Pa'lon said.

"What else am I supposed to do?" she asked, tossing her hands in the air. "The Naroosha and Ruhaald fleets should have arrived through the Crucible hours ago. For all we know the Xaros are defeated, or the battle's still going, or the defenses have broken and our people—including the Karigole—are dying. Why are you so calm?"

"We've spent many years preparing for the Xaros assault. The outcome is beyond our control. There is no point in fretting."

"You returned to Takeni when the Xaros came for the planet. Why the hell didn't one of us go back to Earth?"

"Because we needed you here on Bastion to negotiate for reinforcements. I'm an old, sickly Dotok and the great-great-etcetera ancestor to much of my people. If I go back, everyone will be concerned over my health and not fighting the Xaros. Dotok do not take the ill health of relatives well. I can barely pick up a rifle. No good in a fight."

Stacey went to a fabrication unit and ordered two

cups of coffee. A small shutter opened up and she reached in to remove the drinks. Both were in clear glass cups with no handles.

"Chuck, how many times do I have to tell you the correct way to prepare coffee?" she said to her AI concierge. The heat built in her hands slowly, which meant the coffee was lukewarm and not brewed correctly.

"The most technologically advanced place in the galaxy and we're drinking coffee like refugees." She handed a cup to Pa'lon. He reached for it but was stopped when a force field materialized around his hand and drew it back.

"Ambassador-to-ambassador contact is forbidden as per section three thousand twelve of the Bastion protocols," Chuck said from a ceiling speaker.

"Why can't I even hand him...forget it." She set the Dotok's drink onto a coffee table and went back for sugar and cream.

"It's a holdover from the Toth betrayal." Pa'lon took a sniff from the cup and set it back down. "Several lives were lost when the Toth landed a strike team on Metrica, the forerunner to Bastion, and attempted to kidnap a Qa'Resh. After that our hosts moved us to this undisclosed location and abolished the old missions. Only one representative from each race. No touching. Rapport projections over everyone. Most everyone's managed to get along quite well since then."

"Pain in the ass is what it is," Stacey said, adding copious amounts of sugar to the coffee and a dash of cream. Her hand shook as she tried to lift it to her mouth and ended up slamming it back to the table.

"This is worse than with the Toth!" She wrapped her arms around her chest and crossed her legs. "At least then we had a decent chance of winning without Bastion's help. Did you see the projections on the size of the Xaros fleet?"

"I did. Your grandfather has been preparing for this for a long time. The macro cannons across the solar system can make more of a difference than you think. Let's not forget the *Vorpral* and the new Dotok armor units."

"Yes, your people's contribution to the defense of Earth is greatly appreciated."

"Don't get all diplomatic with me, young one. It is our home too. There aren't procedural crèches across the solar system producing us by the millions, but we'll do our part," Pa'lon said.

"If Bastion had created the technology to…create Dotok-like the proccies, would you have agreed to it?"

"That is a hard question to answer. The thought of eggs maturing beneath hot lights and under the care of a machine and not a doting mother…it goes against the Dotok concept of family. It would be debated by the council of Firsts, then likely put to a vote." Pa'lon stroked his beard.

"So the decision wouldn't have been made decades in advance, sperm and ovum collected and hidden in a colony fleet, and proccies fed into the general populace without anyone's knowledge or consent until some alien race showed up demanding to eat all of them?" Stacey asked, giving humanity's truncated history with the program.

"It would have been handled differently."

"Now who's being diplomatic? You know…we don't *have* to wait here. Any ambassador can return home whenever the conduits are free. If the Xaros do conquer Earth again, I don't want to stay here with those poor souls down in the legacy barracks."

Of the many races that had been part of the Alliance, some had succumbed to the Xaros advance, others were lost to celestial events, and more than one species had collapsed from the pressure of knowing a fleet of xenocidal drones was heading right for them. Surviving ambassadors from the lost lived in a segregated part of Bastion.

Stacey had been to visit the barracks once. The

thought of ever going back and seeing her possible future was more than she wanted to deal with.

"Chuck, show us the conduit schedule," Stacey said.

A holo tank appeared over the coffee table and a list of ambassadors with their departure times came up. Stacey set her coffee down and stood up. She leaned closer to the list and frowned.

"Pa'lon, why hasn't anyone left since the Naroosha and Ruhaald ambassadors went to rally their fleets to Earth? Every departure schedule since they left has been missed…and no one else is in the queue to go home," she said.

"That is most irregular. Perhaps they're waiting for word of the battle? Bring some good news to their people?"

The lights went red, accompanied by a *ting-ting-ting* alert sound. The holo scrambled, replaced by a silver corkscrew-shaped vessel floating in the void.

"Chuck, what race is that and why aren't they in a pocket dimension like the *Breitenfeld*? I thought we had security protocols in place…Chuck?" Stacey looked up, waiting for the AI to answer. "Still irregular, Pa'lon?"

"Most." Pa'lon stood up, spoke something in the chattering Dotok language, then said, "My AI isn't answering me either."

"Let's get to the conduit," Stacey said. "We need to get out of here."

The only door to her quarters slid aside. A half-dozen ambassadors stood on the other side, a mix of men and women, all glowering at Stacey.

"What is this?" Stacey asked.

"The end of an error," the Tinnial ambassador said, appearing as a short woman with a wide Slavic face. Stacey recognized the others, all well-known allies of Vishrakath Ambassador Wexil.

The Tinnial reached out and grabbed Stacey by the arm. The touch was ice cold. Stacey froze in shock at the once-forbidden contact.

More freezing hands grabbed her and hauled her out of her room. Stacey managed a weak protest before a dark cloth bag went over her head. She heard Pa'lon shouting as she was carried away.

****

The moon beneath Valdar's feet was the same as he remembered from years of visits to Earth's first natural satellite. The feel of loose dust beneath his feet (which was destined to cover his vac suit in a fine coat of grit before long), the gentle pull of weak gravity, all the same. The sky, however, had changed. A haze of high clouds of dust blown up by whatever glassed the dark side of the moon cut his visibility of the surrounding stars to the point it was almost like he was looking through the polluted skies over the Richmond of his youth.

He looked over a Mule's wing and watched as his ship and his small fleet vanished over the horizon.

"We're alone now," Gor'al said from the open ramp. The Dotok captain hadn't set foot on the moon yet.

"Now we wait." Valdar picked up a rock and chucked it farther than he could have ever thrown it on Earth. "There's an old story about one of the first men on the moon. He brought a golf ball and club with him and hit a couple drives. When he got back to Earth, he asked people how many golf balls were on the moon. The answer was three or four, I don't remember. Then he'd ask how many golf balls were on Earth. The answer was 'all the rest.'" Valdar chuckled.

Gor'al cocked his head to the side. "Are your oxygen levels sufficient?"

"Earth humor," Valdar said as he looked to the void and the Crucible orbiting distant Ceres.

"Got something," Petty Officer Perez said through

the IR from the Mule's top turret. The sailor had the sharpest eyes on the *Breitenfeld*, and Valdar needed a spotter more than a gunner for this mission. *"Shuttle that originated off the ship over Knoxville is heading right for us. Had it on scope for the last hour. Damn fast too, no escort."*

"Good work." Valdar made a mental note to increase surveillance on that ship. They hadn't identified the Ruhaald flag ship yet, if they even had such a concept.

"To be clear," Gor'al said, leaning over the edge of the ramp, the flesh over his beak twitching, "we will agree to nothing. Yes? Then why are we out here on this ugly rock?"

"They asked to talk to us. The way I see it, we can learn a hell of a lot about them and what they want, and we don't have to give up anything—assuming they do want to talk and this isn't just another sucker punch," Valdar said.

"That we trust them enough to parley is difficult for me," Gor'al said.

"I looked through the logs right after the Xaros superweapon was destroyed. The Ruhaald ships never fired on us. The others, the Naroosha silver ships, those attacked the picket ships I left around the Crucible," Valdar said.

"So you trust them?"

"No, I distrust them a fraction less than the Naroosha. Do you have a guess as to why the Ruhaald demanded that we come without any doughboys?" Valdar asked. "I've never had those...constructs on my ship."

"Perhaps he saw one up close. They are quite repulsive, even by human standards."

"Bogey coming in low." Perez turned the gauss cannon turret away from the approaching Ruhaald ship as it skimmed over the surface with ease.

"They're good pilots," Gor'al said.

The Ruhaald craft slowed and a maneuver thruster twisted its tail toward the waiting captains. The shuttle's ramp lowered, revealing a tall alien in a bulky environmental suit. The Ruhaald stepped off the ramp and landed on both feet, sliding over the rocky surface and kicking up a plume of dust.

Valdar's hand twitched, eager to grab the sidearm absent from his thigh. The alien stood a head taller than him and walked forward with a grace that shouldn't have been possible on the moon.

"I am Septon Jarilla. I render appropriate greetings," it said.

"Captain Valdar of the *Breitenfeld*," he said, gesturing to his Dotok companion and adding, "Gor'al, First of the *Vorpral*."

"I witnessed your skill and bravery against the Xaros," Jarilla said. "These circumstances are not…ideal. This was not our intention when we arrived."

"Your intentions are irrelevant. Only your actions matter," Gor'al said. "Do not waste our time with posturing. Tell us what you want."

"Our conflict is not with the Dotok. If you would—"

"It is with us!" Gor'al smacked a fist against the ramp's hydraulic brace. "The blade you've leveled against the humans' throats crosses ours. What you speak to Valdar you speak to me."

"Why don't you tell us why there's a conflict at all, Scepton," Valdar said.

"The Alliance will not tolerate further human independence. The Crucible is ours. For now, it remains our greatest weapon in the war against the Xaros. There is another issue that may be negotiated," Jarilla said.

"What do you mean 'for—'" Gor'al stopped as Valdar raised a hand.

"The other issue?" Valdar asked.

"Know that this offer is a courtesy, not one I choose to give. Surrender the procedural-generation technology to us. Every crèche tube, human spawn material bank, and procedural-intelligence generation computer. Intact and functioning. We know the crèches are beneath your mountain cities. Do this, and further bloodshed will be avoided."

"Why don't I put out a radio call to every city and tell them to smash the tubes?" Valdar asked.

"Do not think that the Alliance cares for your continued existence. One greater than I believes you must be saved from the depths. If you willingly give in to our demands, we will protect you. Lives can be saved, Valdar. Your civilization will continue. Demilitarized, of course."

Valdar clasped his hands behind his back. He looked toward the Crucible.

"You came riding in like the cavalry," Valdar said. "You and the Naroosha. You didn't see the swarms of drones over Mars. The thousands and thousands of drones pouring out of the gate over Anthalas or Malal's secret world."

Jarilla's feeder tentacles clenched together at the mention of the ancient entity. Valdar didn't know Ruhaald body language, but that sudden change was telling.

"The Xaros are legion, do you understand that?" Valdar asked. "We killed one of their leaders, but I'm betting they'll come back. We had a fleet, led by a brilliant woman, that sacrificed itself to buy Earth a little more time to prepare. We survived this time, but barely. The Xaros will return, and in greater numbers, in a few years. If we can't rebuild with the help of the proccies, what chance do we have? Will you escape through the Crucible the instant the Xaros arrive, or will the Ruhaald put themselves between Earth and annihilation?"

Jarilla's eyes twitched back and forth.

"That will not be my decision," he said.

"And giving up the proccies isn't mine, but I can take your offer to those who can say yes or no," Valdar said.

"Know this," Jarilla said as several of the tentacles on his hand straightened toward Valdar, "the procedurals are the only thing that stops us from destroying your planet. Do not sabotage the crèches. There will be no mercy if you do."

Jarilla turned toward his shuttle and began to walk away. Then he stopped and looked back to say, "I am sorry we are enemies, Valdar and Gor'al. No matter the outcome, my actions are without malice."

"Soldiers can act with honor, even if their cause is unjust," Valdar said.

"I give you three days." Jarilla walked away.

Valdar climbed back into the Mule and ordered the pilot to take them back to the *Breitenfeld*. He strapped himself into a seat across from Gor'al as the craft powered up.

"Well?" Valdar asked his Dotok companion.

"Give up the only hope of defending against the Xaros or wait until the enemy takes that hope away from us." Gor'al tapped a finger against his faceplate. "Either way, we are doomed."

"They don't need the Crucible anymore," Valdar said. "They have Malal. That was why the single Naroosha ship went through the wormhole right after they attacked. They were taking that monster somewhere else. Malal has the blueprints for more Crucible gates...and the Alliance already has the omnium reactor tech."

"If they get the procedural technology...Earth will have no value. The Alliance can make their own humans." Gor'al clicked his beak together.

"If we fight them on the ground or wreck the tubes, they'll nuke us," Valdar said. "The only bargaining chip we have is whoever sent Jarilla to speak to us." Valdar felt anger well up inside him. He looked around, making sure that the crew chief wasn't watching, then slammed a fist against the bulkhead in frustration.

"That last time the Dotok faced such an impossible situation," Gor'al said, "*you* arrived in the skies over Takeni. Something tells me you did not have the perfect solution to beating the Xaros at the moment, but you figured it out."

"That was catch-as-catch-can for a while," Valdar said.

"We return to the *Breitenfeld* with more—more insight, more information—than when we left. Every step forward is a step in the right direction…unless you're walking toward a cliff."

"Are Dotok always this cheerful and despondent at the same time?"

"You sound like several of my ex-wives. Let's get back to your ship. I have some ideas."

CHAPTER 5

The thump of armored boots echoed through the tunnel. Hale's pace was a bit faster than a jog, his power armor assisting his stride and reducing some of his effort, but after several miles of running, his breathing was labored and sweat ran down his face.

If this war ever lets up, I'm going back to the gym, he thought.

The tunnel ran beneath old Highway 87, wide enough for a cargo truck and almost twenty feet high. Unmanned supply shipments had run along the tracks recessed into the ground. Mile markers and arrows in luminescent paint told the distance to the next stop. Even with the ambient lighting, Hale felt a nagging sense of panic in the back of his mind.

It had been days—possibly, keeping track of time

while jumping from one crisis to the next was problematic—since he'd led his company of Strike Marines into the Xaros mines beneath Pluto and destroyed the factory providing raw omnium for a Crucible gate. Every few minutes he thought he heard the distant scream of a Wight, the thrum of a Xaros drone coming for him. His IR radio hissed in his ears, which did nothing to calm him down.

He ran past a cutout along one side of the tunnel, a divot big enough to accommodate a freight car and with a ramp leading to quadrium-clad locked shutters.

The Marine ahead of him slowed to a stop near a bend in the tunnel and raised a fist. He went down to a knee and waved Hale over.

"Armor up front needs you, sir. Said something about a blockage. The IR's shot to hell down here," said Weiss, a new addition to his company and a Marine that had distinguished himself during the battle on Pluto.

Hale muttered thanks and slowed to a walk. He tried and failed to open a channel to the Hussars at the leading edge of his force in the tunnel. He found Steuben waiting for him around the bend.

"The tunnel's quadrium plating and a significant amount of humidity are interfering with our communications," Steuben said.

"It's monsoon season, shouldn't be surprised." Hale's face pulled into a grimace. He should have anticipated the interference. As the company commander, everything that his Marines did, or failed to do, was his responsibility. Leading them underground and relying on shouting or the crack of gauss weapons to communicate a problem was not a winning strategy.

Hale and Steuben walked together, passing more Marines kneeling along the tunnel walls every few tens of yards.

"You believe your brother is at Firebase X-Ray?" Steuben asked.

"It…can't be him," Hale said. "Jared left on the Terra Nova mission years ago but I never had the chance to say good-bye because we got stuck in the void for years after we pulled Malal's codex out of his lab. But that Bolin guy, he has my brother's voice…his face. Jared and I are twins. I don't know how it is with Karigole, but human twins share a strong bond that begins in the womb."

"Those of my Centurion are my brothers. Karigole families are not bound to lineage like humans. Tell me, if this Bolin did not resemble your brother, would you have volunteered for this mission?" Steuben held up his new metal hand and tried to squeeze the fingers into a fist. The artificial joints twitched, then closed slowly.

"Strike Marines don't do well sitting behind fortifications. We're meant to be beyond the front lines gathering intelligence, carrying out sabotage missions or targeted killings. Figuring out what's going on with the Ruhaald and the firebase is what we were made for."

"You did not answer my question."

"Yes, XO, we'd still be on this mission. Bolin being the spitting image of my brother just made the decision easier for me." Hale rolled his shoulders back and adjusted the grip on his rifle.

"Have you heard from Lafayette?" Hale asked.

"Nothing. Last time we spoke was on the *Scipio* after we returned from Pluto."

"I'm sure he's fine," Hale said. They came around a bend and found the three Hussars, all pressed against one side of the tunnel. Ahead of them, the tunnel's walls had partially caved in. Cortaro, halfway up the pile of shattered rock, peered through a gap at the top of the tunnel. Hale smelled a thick aroma of ammonia and copper in the air.

A Hussar pointed a finger to a severed cord along the wall.

"Someone tried to blow the tunnels. Looks like a bit of shrapnel cut the wire to the explosives down the line," Vladislav said.

Hale climbed up the rubble and stopped next to Cortaro.

"The door to the bunker is blown open," Cortaro said. "We can squeeze through one at a time. Armor can't."

A breeze blew through the uneven tunnel to a mangled door a few dozen yards away. Hale rapped his knuckles against the ceiling.

"You think the rest of the mountain will come down on us?" Hale asked.

"I grew up crawling around abandoned mines. No dust coming off the roof, no sound. The mountain sleeps again, sir," Cortaro said.

Hale twisted around and said, "Vladislav, you and the rest of the armor head back to that last emergency exit. We'll scout ahead and get a look at the next tunnel."

"Fair enough." The armor's treads turned the soldier around and the Hussar rolled away.

"Wait for me to get through, then send the rest." Hale drew his pistol and crawled into the void between the rocks and pulled himself forward one handhold at a time. The bunker remained quiet as Hale approached, but he stopped every few feet to listen and watch. If the Ruhaald were in the bunker, they'd find him an easy target.

The rocks quivered. Hale felt the vibration

through his armor and his heart skipped a beat as dust filled the air like a thin fog. Abandoning the stealth approach, Hale scrambled forward. The tremor eased seconds later, but Hale kept moving fast.

The rifle slung against his back bumped against a rock just as he reached the end of the tunnel. He pushed himself back and tried to cross the last few feet again, but his rifle thwarted his progress with a loud crack as it butted up against a low-hanging rock.

Hale winced at the sound. He flattened his belly against the broken floor and tried to inch his way forward. He reached over the edge of the tunnel and grabbed a rock bigger than his chest, then scooted forward another half-arm's length.

The rock broke loose from the pile and carried Hale down the steep slope. He tried to roll forward, bouncing against every sharp edge in a small avalanche. His feet hit the ground and he lurched into the bunker, his pistol up and ready.

The bunker was empty. Dark sunbursts of energy weapon strikes scarred the walls and the firing slits along the walls. Bright sunlight cut into the circular room, reflecting off pools of drying blood. A ramp on the other side of the bunker led to the shut doors of the next tunnel segment.

"Clear," Hale said through the IR. When there was no response, he went back to the cave-in and flashed a thumbs-up to Cortaro. The first sergeant returned the gesture.

Hale took the gauss rifle off his back and returned to the bunker. He ran a finger through a smear of blood on the wall. The reddish-black bloodstain spread with his touch, and he flicked his thumb against it.

"Still wet...where are the bodies?" Hale mumbled.

The sound of a wet thump came with a gust of wind.

Hale activated his cloak and crept up to the destroyed bunker doors. Across the packed desert earth and scorched shrubs, a Ruhaald shuttle sat on skids extended from its belly. A half-dozen alien soldiers clustered near the blunt nose of the aircraft. Hale watched, half-hidden behind the bunker. The Karigole cloaking technology wasn't foolproof, and he didn't want to learn the hard way how good the aliens' scanners were if they could detect him easily.

One of the Ruhaald pulled away from the group, dragging something behind it. Hale zoomed in with his visor optics. The alien had a doughboy by the scruff of the neck. Silver wire ran from bonds around the doughboy's hands and feet to his neck, his face contorted in agony.

The Ruhaald threw the doughboy into the dirt and then raised its arms up as a wet trill filled the air. It hauled the doughboy onto his knees. The Ruhaald clapped its hands twice over its head, then drew a knife from a scabbard on its chest and raised it to the sky. Sunlight glinted off the blade.

"No…" Hale looked back to the cave-in, but no other Marines had made it through.

The Ruhaald twirled the blade around and slammed it into the doughboy's skull. The knife sank down to the hilt and smacked against bone with a dull crack. The other Ruhaald trilled and beat fists against each other's armor.

The doughboy wavered for a moment, then collapsed to a side. The executioner wiped its fingers through the blood gushing from the dead soldier's head, then slathered the vitae over its helmet. It yanked the blade from the body, then proffered the pommel to the other Ruhaald.

Clicks and pops of Ruhaald language echoed from the knife-wielder.

Another alien stepped away from the pack, dragging a bound doughboy.

"Damn it." Hale ran toward the Ruhaald transport. The Karigole cloak flickered as a gust of wind peppered him with sand. The alien with the still-living doughboy accepted the blade.

Hale's thumb flicked between the gauss rifle's HIGH and LOW power settings. He didn't know how strong the Ruhaald armor was. A high-powered shot could crack the shell of a Xaros drone, but the recharge between shots would leave him vulnerable and in a slightly worse position than if a low-powered shot did nothing but tickle their armor.

One of the aliens looked at Hale, then pointed a pair of overly long fingers in his direction.

The knife-wielding alien raised the blade over the prostrate doughboy.

Hale brought his rifle up and snapped off a low-powered shot. The magnetically driven slug hit the executioner in the chest and sent it staggering back. A second shot pierced the damaged armor and shot out the back in a spray of green fluid. The wounded alien collapsed like a puppet with its strings cut.

Hale kept running and swung his weapon toward the Ruhaald that noticed him. The aliens began to spread out, speaking to each other with high-tempo clicks. Hale fired and hit the alien in the forehead. Its helmet burst like a balloon.

The cloak died with a loud pop and a whiff of

ozone.

Hale was barely twenty yards from the rest of the aliens. He put three shots into a Ruhaald struggling to pull an energy weapon slung over its back and knocked it into the dirt. Hale let out a war cry and lowered his shoulder as he rammed into the next alien, knocking it onto the companion Hale had just shot.

The Marine dodged a clumsy punch and jammed his muzzle into the thin armor covering the Ruhaald's neck. He fired and the bullet pierced the thin armor then bounced off the interior armor and ricocheted around, shaking the alien like a rat caught in a terrier's jaws before the bullet exited through a hip joint.

Thick arms grabbed Hale from behind and lifted him off the ground. Hale slammed his helmet back and felt a solid contact as the sound of glass shattering filled his ears. The alien let Hale go.

He whirled around and faced a panicked Ruhaald slapping at its broken helmet as fluid poured from the cracks and evaporated into mist almost instantly. Behind the alien, the last standing Ruhaald had a weapon in hand and aimed at its fellow's back.

Hale grabbed the alien with the broken helmet and pulled it close, making it impossible for the armed alien to fire without hitting them both. He stuck his gauss rifle beneath the Ruhaald's armpit and fired as fast as he could pull the trigger.

A bullet hit the Ruhaald in the knee and blew the limb away. The alien dropped its weapon and squealed as it clawed at the bleeding stump. Hale shoved his impromptu shield away and shot the other alien in the head. He swung the rifle toward the one with the broken helmet and found it lying flat on its back, the feeder tentacles making up the lower part of its face trembling in the open air, its limbs jerking feebly.

Hale's finger tightened on the trigger, then hesitated.

A high-pitched whine filled the air from the transport. A double-barreled energy cannon rose from the top and swung toward Hale. He ran toward the alien craft and leapt into the air. The cannons lowered to track his flight and stopped short as he hit the ground within the weapon's defilade, close enough that the guns couldn't fire without hitting the ship.

The guns fired anyway, twin bursts of energy hitting the ground with a thunderclap. Searing heat flashed against Hale's armor and the blast wave sent him tumbling like a log. He slammed into the shuttled landing skids, right next to the lowered cargo ramp.

The blast sent Hale's balance reeling, but he

struggled to his feet and grabbed a grenade off his belt. He clicked the activation switch twice, tossed it into the shuttle as the transport doors began to close. He lurched away and fell to the ground, covering his head with his arms. In the split second before the grenade went off, Hale wondered if the aliens carried any high explosives in their shuttles.

The grenade blew out the front windows. The Ruhaald spat out and smacked against a boulder with a sickening crunch.

Hale rolled over and got to his feet. Smoke poured from the shuttle, now canted on its side from a broken landing skid. The cannons on the roof burned treetops in a blaze. He swept his weapon over the aliens lying in the dirt and found one, the first he'd shot, reaching to the sky with one arm.

Hale kept his rifle on the alien as he walked over. The Ruhaald lay in a growing puddle of lime-colored fluid as more burbled out of a bullet hole in its chest. Black eyes the size of Hale's palms darted from side to side until fixing on the Marine.

"I render appropriate greetings," came from a voice box mounted on its shoulder. The feeder tentacle writhed as tiny bubbles poured from the mouth area. "You have killed me. Why? Why is your caste in conflict with us?"

"You were about to murder a prisoner. We don't stand for that. Why are you attacking the firebase and nowhere else? Why did you kill that soldier?"

The fluid leaking from the Ruhaald's chest slowed to a trickle.

"I die beneath a yellow star. My prophecy lies," it said.

"Hey," Hale said, nudging the alien with his foot, "answer me. At least tell me how I can stop you from bleeding out."

The Ruhaald lifted its other hand, the blood-encrusted, thin-bladed knife still in its grasp. It tossed the blade at Hale's feet.

"Vendetta. Blood between us and your slaves. Our scion will have justice." The alien reached to the sun…and its arm fell to the side. Hale removed the voice box and slipped it into a pouch on his belt.

"Sir!" Cortaro called out from behind Hale.

The Marine and Yarrow knelt next to the doughboy. The bio-construct bled from a dozen tiny cuts up and down his body, his face twitching in pain.

Hale jogged over.

"Nice of you two to show up," Hale said.

"I had rifles trained on each and every hostile,"

Cortaro said, "then *someone* dropped his cloak and got into a knife fight, ruining our shots."

"Sir," Yarrow said, pressing his fingertips against the doughboy and giving him a gentle push, "he's got strong vitals. I think the wiring is doing something to his nervous system."

Hale looked to the sky, which had gone beige with wind-blown dust. "The longer we're out here the more likely we'll be spotted. Figure something out."

"Right." Yarrow put his hands on his hips, thought for a moment, then reached down to grab the silver cord running from the doughboy's neck to his wrists. When the medic grabbed the cord, electricity arced from the cord and jabbed Yarrow's fingertips.

Yarrow jumped up, shaking his hands furiously.

"Cotton picking son of a—" Yarrow groaned and squeezed his hands into fists.

"Yarrow, if you're going to curse you need to do it like a Marine." Cortaro unsnapped his Ka-Bar blade from the forearm housing and touched it to the silver cord. Tendrils of electricity danced along the blade as the gunnery sergeant sawed through it.

"I'll be sure to tell everyone those things are electrified," Yarrow said, "and remind them that our Ka-Bars have rubber stoppers between the blade and our armor."

"Knowing is half the battle," Cortaro said as he tapped the back of his hand against the severed cord, then unwound it from the doughboy's neck and hands.

The doughboy let out a grunt and ripped the rest of the cord away. He threw it on the ground and stomped it into the dirt.

"Hurt me. Bad." The doughboy ground a heel against the wire.

"You got a name, big guy?" Cortaro asked.

The doughboy's head snapped toward the Marine, then to Hale. The construct snapped to attention with his heels together, chest puffed out and hands balled against the sides of his thighs.

"Sir! Nickel Three-Seven. Enemies took my sir, killed other Nickels."

"Sir, you met this one before?" Cortaro asked Hale.

"No, last doughboy I spoke to was on Hawaii during the Toth attack," Hale said. "Maybe he saw that damn movie everyone's talking about."

"Nickel lost weapon. Nickel sorry. Sir Bolin punish Nickel?"

"What did you call me?" Hale asked.

"Sir is gone." The doughboy pointed a meaty

finger at Hale. "Bolin bigger sir. More sir."

"Isn't there a Lieutenant Bolin at Firebase X-Ray?" Yarrow asked.

"There is, but I'm not him," Hale said. He felt a vibration through the ground and looked over to see a pair of armor rolling toward him on their treads.

"We took a look in the other segment," Cortaro said, "blown. If we want to get to X-Ray, it'll be overland. Next bunker is three kilometers away. That one connects directly to the firebase. Could still be our way in."

Elias came to a stop in a cloud of dust.

"I take it there's a good reason why we're all standing in the open," the armor soldier said.

"Hold on." Hale looked at a map on his forearm screen, then pointed to a ridgeline a few miles away. "There's an emergency access point to an auxiliary tunnel at the base of the mountains. Looks like it was supposed to run to a bunker that never got built, but it's on the defense grid. Should take us straight to the firebase."

The sound of muted thunderclaps came over the mountains. Heavy weapons fire.

"Let's get moving before it's too late," Elias said. His treads pivoted him in place, then he and Caas rumbled away.

"First Sergeant," Hale said, "get the rest of the

company out here. We'll go by foot." Hale touched his cloak-activation controls, then put his hand down as windblown sand hissed across the ground. "Sand will screw up the cloaks, won't it?"

"Karigole tech ain't perfect," Cortaro shrugged. "Don't tell Steuben I said that. He's sensitive."

"Nickel," Hale said, pointing to the bunker, "you're big but you can squeeze through that opening. Go back and don't stop until you've made it to Phoenix. Understand?"

Nickel shook his head emphatically.

"Dark in there," he said. "No leave sir."

"Soldier, you don't have armor or a weapon and I can't—"

"No leave sir!"

"He's just like a puppy, isn't he, Captain?" Yarrow asked. "A giant, Cro-Magnon puppy that could crush my skull with two fingers."

Hale's gaze wandered to the dead doughboy lying amongst the slain Ruhaald. He sighed and said, "I thought everything would be easier once I pinned on captain. Come on, Nickel. You have to keep up."

****

Hale stepped on a half-buried boulder and then up to the edge of the ridgeline. Windblown sand scoured across his cloak, and error messages popped on his visor. Hale looked up and saw nothing but a tan pallor across the sky. The smell of smoke came with the breeze, artifacts from the battle that wrecked Phoenix.

He cut the cloak and climbed the last few feet to the top of the ridge. Steuben, already poised against the summit with a set of optics in hand, appeared as his cloak faded away.

"Jacobs is in the tunnel. Path's clear as far as she can tell. She hasn't made it to the firebase yet," Hale said.

"It may not matter." Steuben passed the optics to Hale. The Marine peeked over the edge, and dread gripped his heart.

Firebase X-Ray's mountain façade was pitted with broken impact craters. Two of the rail gun emplacements smoldered, the heavy guns blasted into pieces and strewn around the mountain. The landing pad cut into the center had collapsed.

Between the firebase and Hale's ridge, an energy field several stories high and miles long blocked the line of sight from the human fortifications and a sprawling base full of Ruhaald soldiers and equipment.

"That's...not what we were expecting," Hale said.

"You engage in understatement to cover for a poor tactical situation," Steuben said. "I've observed this leadership trait in other officers."

"Combat leaders can't show fear, or doubt. Troops get a whiff that things are wrong and all of a sudden it's *sauve qui peut* and the battle's lost. Christ, how many are down there?"

"I counted roughly three thousand nine hundred individuals, fourteen artillery pieces, three equally sized large pieces of equipment receiving attention from what appear to be technicians and dozens of temporary structures. They're armed with—"

"More than we can handle." Hale frowned. "Looks like they're preparing for another assault on the base."

"Our mission is reconnaissance, intelligence gathering," Steuben said. "We are not a relief force."

"But what if we…" Hale looked at his forearm computer, then back to the valley full of enemy soldiers.

"You have been visited by a deity? The one known as the 'good-idea fairy'?"

"You could say that. She comes to captains more than lieutenants." Hale pointed to a pair of tents next to an artillery piece, an energy cannon hooked to several battery stacks the size of cargo containers. "There's another access hatch down there. Doesn't look like the Ruhaald know it's under their noses, or whatever they have."

"You propose a raid?" Steuben asked. "Even with the element of surprise, we'll be at a distinct tactical disadvantage."

"A good old smash-and-grab. We've got more than surprise. We have Iron Hearts and Hussars. Now help me find their headquarters tent."

****

The Marines came to a stop in front of a vault door flanked by a single inactive control panel.

Standish glanced at his forearm screen.

"Eight minutes of air left." He tapped the control panel, but it stayed dark. "That's not helping."

"Move." Egan ran a wire from his gauntlet and plugged it into the panel. The panel powered up, then went completely blue. "Command prompts are scrambled, but the power shunts are still accessible. Maybe if I…"

The panel sparked and Egan jumped back.

"Seven minutes," Standish said.

"Can you get it open?" Bailey asked.

"Do you have a pneumatic vice some—" The vault door swung open. "I mean, obviously I can get it open," Egan said.

An unlit airlock lay beyond the armored door. The Marines stepped inside and the door closed behind them.

A red light twirled over their heads and air pumped into the tiny space through nozzles built into the wall. Standish waited until the sensors in his suit flashed green, then opened the visor on his helmet and took a deep breath.

"Ah, sweet, sweet, fart-smelling air." Standish wrinkled his nose as he took another breath.

"Standish, sometimes I swear you'd complain if your ice cream was too cold," Egan said as he removed his helmet.

A shadow passed over the small view port on the inner door. The door swung open violently and a giant arm shot through the opening. A hand the size of a frying pan clamped on to Standish's neck and yanked him off his feet.

Standish beat against the vice grip around his throat and found breathing impossible. The Ka-Bar knife in his gauntlet sheath snapped out. He slashed the blade against the arm and heard a grunt of pain before he found himself flying through the air.

He smashed into a bulkhead and fell to the floor, his armor absorbing the worst of the impact. Standish looked up and into the barrel of a very large gun.

"Stop! Stop!" A Marine in power armor pushed the weapon aside and put himself between Standish and his assailant.

"Marines, good! Remember?" The Marine put his hand on Standish's shoulder and looked him in the eye. "Where the hell did you come from?"

Standish pulled in a ragged breath and grabbed his neck as he began coughing. He fell onto his rear and slapped the Marine's hand away.

The passageway was full of brutish doughboys, their weapons and armor soot-stained and beat-up. Their Cro-Magnon features glowered at Standish. One doughboy lifted his arm and sniffed at the bleeding cut across the forearm. The soldier opened his mouth and licked a black tongue over the wound.

"Standish, you OK?" Egan asked as he stepped out of the airlock.

"I really don't like these guys," Standish croaked.

"Lieutenant Douglas, Crucible garrison command," the man said, shaking hands with Egan. "Who are…wait—are you Sergeant Bailey?"

"That's me," she said.

"I've seen *The Last Stand on Takeni* at least fifty times. That part with you and that village gets me every time. Does this mean the *Breitenfeld*'s here? Are we finally getting some help?" Douglas asked.

"Sir, can we talk and walk?" Egan asked. "We need to find the omnium reactor."

Douglas pointed down the passageway and led Egan and Bailey away.

The doughboy with the bleeding arm reached down and lifted Standish onto his feet like he was a child.

"Sorry. Thought enemy," the doughboy said with a gravelly voice.

Standish brushed his armor off and motioned to the cut. "Same here. Thought you were trying to murder me."

The rest of the doughboys stood impassively, heavy brows twitching.

"You have a name, big guy?"

"Onyx Twelve-Twelve."

"That's not a name I've heard before, but OK." Standish walked after Egan and the lieutenant, and the doughboys followed in lockstep.

"You know what's happening out there?" Standish asked.

"Enemies." Onyx hefted his oversized rifle.

"More than that, maybe?"

"Many enemies." Onyx nodded fervently.

Standish shrugged and caught up to the other Marines as Egan finished detailing their escape from the Ruhaald and their arrival at the dome.

"So the squids, these Ruhaald are all pissed off because *you* killed one of their leaders?" Douglas asked.

"Wasn't us," Standish said, jerking a thumb over his shoulder, "it was those boneheads."

"Something tells me the Ruhaald and Naroosha stabbing us in the back and taking a spot over our cities wasn't a flash reaction to fratricide," Douglas said. "I'm glad to give you three rifles and put you on the line, but we're hanging on by a thread in here. So there's no more help coming with you?"

"We're it, for now," Egan said.

"I'll barricade the bunker tunnels." The lieutenant pressed a knuckle against the bridge of his nose. "Can't believe I forgot that. Wouldn't have known you were here, but the airlock tamper alarms went off."

"You slept lately?" Egan asked.

"Heh heh, sleep." The passageway ended in stairs that led into the ceiling. A set of heavy doors slid open as they neared and bright light flooded around the Marines. Standish put a hand over his eyes as he took the steps. He blinked hard and came to a stop.

The hollow interior of the dome stretched around

them, a two-story barricade of aegis armor plates with integrated towers full of doughboys. The bio-constructs hauled heavy boxes of ammunition from a cube-shaped building in the center. Smaller Marines in power armor mixed with the doughboys along the wall, directing repairs and standing shoulder to shoulder on the firing steps.

"We had to abandon the outer wall after the last push," Douglas said. "Squids tried to swarm us through gate Charlie. Some of them got to the top of the wall before we pushed them back. Lost three Marines to their damn armor. They ain't as bad as the Toth, but they ain't pushovers in a fight either."

"The reactor's undamaged?" Egan asked.

Douglas snapped off terse commands and the doughboys turned away. The lieutenant motioned to the cube.

"The only reason we're alive is because they must want that thing intact," he said. "I saw them using heavier weapons during the mad scramble to get in here when the attack started. Squids aren't even using explosives. I thought about scuttling the reactor. Our back's to the wall here, but we can still fight."

"Do you know what we had to go through to get that damn thing?" Standish asked.

"Who're you?" The lieutenant gave him a once-over.

Standish groaned and tossed his hands up in despair.

Douglas grabbed a handle on a sliding door and opened it with a heave. Inside, the reactor stretched across the length of the cube. Pallets full of glowing omnium cubes filled a corner. A robot arm grasped a cube and slid it into an open slot on the far end of the reactor. On the other side, a thick plate of aegis armor slid out of a sparking field and onto a conveyor belt.

The lieutenant pointed to a computer terminal hewn from stone. Strips of paper attached to the many buttons and dials fluttered in a slight breeze. Waist-high piles of green notebooks formed a berm around the side and back of the computer.

"That looks familiar," Standish said. "We got that off Anthalas."

"Sure hope you guys know how to use it," Douglas said. "I futzed around with it and got it to keep making the last item in the production queue, aegis plating. You put something in that scanner box in the middle of the device and it'll make that. We use it for ammo, parts."

Egan walked up to the computer and frowned. He bent over and looked closely at the alien script on the buttons and dials, then compared it to the very different alien markings on the labels.

"This must be Shanishol," Egan said as he touched a button, then lifted the attached ribbon, "and this is…"

"Karigole, I guess," Douglas said. "Lafayette was the only one that worked in here."

"I need to tell this alien artifact to make me a KR-12 IR receiver-transmitter," Egan said, "and the control panel is in two languages I have no idea how to read."

A small lamp attached to the control panel flickered. Egan's gaze snapped toward the light, and he nodded.

"Ibarra says the production code is in one of these notebooks." Egan flipped through a book, glancing back at the light as the flickering intensified. "Lafayette scanned thousands of items. We just need to find it…and figure out how to use the interface."

"What? Ibarra's in the lamp?" Douglas asked.

"He's in the Crucible's power systems. He also said he's been trying to communicate with you for hours." Egan set the notebook aside and picked up another one.

"Huh, I just thought the light was on the fritz." The lieutenant frowned as the flickering continued. "What's he saying now?"

"You don't want to know." Egan tossed another

book from the pile to Standish and Bailey. "Lafayette wrote down an item description or a stock number in English for what he scanned. Last four digits are two-seven-two-two for the transmitter. Find it."

The pound of heavy gauss rifles echoed through the dome.

"Balls, not again." Douglas ran for the door.

"I thought Lafayette was some kind of Karigole mechanical genius." Standish ran a finger down a list of numbers. "You'd think he'd be more organized than this."

The lamp flickered.

"Ibarra says you've never heard of Nikola Tesla…and he's got an idea that might help us." Egan put his helmet over the lamp and ran a wire from his gauntlet to a port on the back of his headgear.

The light flickered rapidly as Egan's fingers danced over his control panel.

Marc Ibarra's head and shoulders appeared on Egan's visor and looked around.

"That's a little better," Ibarra said through the helmet's speakers. "You have no idea how cramped it is in here."

The clatter of gauss weapon fire grew louder.

"No time for chitchat." Ibarra clapped his hands twice. "Flip pages in front of the helmet's camera. I can read and process the information a hell of a lot faster than any of you, and time is not on our side here."

Bailey opened a notebook and turned the pages one by one.

"Faster, my dear. I'm not a Commodore 64," Ibarra said.

"A what?" Bailey bent the pages with her thumb and let them flip open with a rustle.

"Before your time. Not that one. Next."

Standish picked up an armful of notebooks and passed them to Bailey one by one.

"Mr. Ibarra, we've got some bad news about Shannon," Standish said.

"I noticed her absence. She will be missed." Ibarra's eyes barely twitched as he scanned through another book.

"Well, we were sad to see her go," Standish said, "but we were wondering—ow!"

Bailey stomped on the Marine's foot and snatched another book out of his hand.

"We were wondering what happened to you," Bailey said. "Shannon couldn't explain your…situation."

"My mind's been inside a secure memory partition within the probe since Bastion tried to screw us over with the Toth. Stacey and I had a few failsafe programs installed for this kind of situation…but the Naroosha are better hackers than I gave them credit for. They don't have full control over the probe—yet. But they will soon. I can play around with the maintenance systems a bit and assert control over a few key areas in a pinch. If they figure out where I'm hiding, things will go south real quick."

"What do you mean by 'south'?" Standish asked.

"The Naroosha had complete control for a few hours before I threw my sabots into the works. They sent their one and only jump-capable ship to Bastion. Now they're trying to jump from Bastion back to their home world through our Crucible," Ibarra said. "If they do that, we'll be neck-deep in Naroosha ships and troops. I'll let you speculate on how that'll play out."

"And you think Captain Valdar can pull our asses out of the fire?" Bailey asked.

"The *Breitenfeld* is our wild card, my dear. Ah…there it is. You," Ibarra said, pointing at Egan, "the tall one, enter this code."

Bailey tapped her finger against the helmet over the light, jostling it from side to side. Ibarra's arms shot out and pressed against the side of the visor.

"Soon as he makes your little toy," Bailey leaned in close and pointed a finger at Ibarra, "you're going tell him how to make me a new Barrett rail rifle to replace

Bloke."

****

Standish craned his neck up, peering across the void. His visor cycled through spectrums, searching for heat blooms of enemy ships and graviton emissions from anchored ships. A sliver of the moon showed on the far side of Earth, scorched soil creeping around the horizon like a scabbed-over wound. He pushed down from the torn roof of the bunker and landed gently.

"Clear," Standish said to Egan. "Anyone know what the hell happened to the moon? Looks like somebody took a flamethrower to it."

"Better that ball of rock than the Earth," Egan said. He opened a box and removed an IR transmitter the size of a gauss rifle. "It'll take a few minutes to get this emplaced. Cover me." He touched a button on his chest and vanished beneath a Karigole cloak. The transmitter seemed to lift up of its own volition and floated onto the roof, a fiber-optic cable trailing into the open hatch.

Standish leaned next to a firing slit, keeping his distance from the charred bodies still manning their posts.

Bailey ran a loving hand down her new rail rifle, scanning the dome through a handheld scope.

"Hey, Bailey, why didn't you let me say something to Ibarra about the tube Shannon?" Standish asked.

"The look on her face." Bailey snapped her gum and ran her scope across her firing slit. "She was terrified. If she's the first—or third—one of her running around, she never knew about the others. Ibarra kept that from her. He keeps a secret like that from someone that does his dirty work…bet he doesn't want anyone else to know about it either."

"What do you think she is? A clone? Everything in the news about the proccies says cloning is impossible…which means Ibarra's been lying to everyone. Again."

"You think that bloke's above killing people to keep things quiet? Shannon said she did just that kind of thing for him."

"Jesus." Standish tapped a finger against his gauss rifle. "He could be making clones of us right now. We'll get bumped off and replaced by compliant…pod people! Can you imagine, another me running around the galaxy?"

"I'd rather not," Bailey said. "You guys ever hear about that mess in Saigon couple months before this war started? Some Chinese People's general whose head mysteriously exploded while he was enjoying a getaway with a mistress?" She gave Standish a look out of the corner of her eye.

Standish shifted uncomfortably against the wall.

"I saw a Marine team in High Orbit Low Opening gear get into a Mule on the *Breitenfeld*. I got curious and dug around. Turns out the flight wasn't on the schedule and the personnel logs didn't show any departures. Two days later Major Acera calls me into the office and rips me a new one for unauthorized data access and tells me to forget I saw anything and never mention it again. Which I just did. Oops."

"Just keep your mouth shut about what you saw," Bailey said with a wink. "Leaks get plugged."

"Wait…how did you know about that?" Standish asked.

"I'm in!" Egan said with a little laugh. "Bounced the transmission off the Ceres relay and into the fiber network running through Phoenix and every other fortified city. Ibarra's got comms to the whole planet and to the *Breitenfeld*…so long as they're on the right side of the moon. Thank the signal corps. You can talk about us, but you can't talk without us."

"Is setting up the transmitter all you're doing up there?" Standish tapped the roof. "Can we leave? I don't want to be out here in case Standish Two comes along to dispose of the evidence."

"There's a Ruhaald ship coming in," Egan said. "It's heading for the far side of the dome...and one of the thorns over there just broke off the side."

"It's an attack," Bailey said. "Let's get back to the barricades and do something useful for once."

****

Ibarra, Gor'al, Utrecht and Ericcson stood around the *Breitenfeld*'s holo table, watching icons of Ruhaald shuttles trace between the alien ships over the Earth.

"We had ships put camera and optics to every Ruhaald ship in view during our last two orbits," Ericcson said. "The enemy keeps up regular cargo shipments between all ships at a pretty regular interval. From a frequency analysis, we can't pinpoint any ship that's more important than any other."

"Jarilla's shuttle returned to the Ruhaald craft over Lima. He didn't return to Knoxville," Gor'al said. "They're hiding their command ship quite effectively. But..."

Gor'al touched the ship menacing Anchorage and zoomed in. He shifted through footage until he stopped at a Ruhaald shuttle leaving the ship's hangar bay. The shuttle had a bulbous center, like a water tender that would service his ship at anchor.

"Notice the flare off the engines?" the Dotok asked.

"The ship's carrying a decent amount of mass," Valdar said. "What of it?"

"This particular type of cargo shuttle goes between every single ship," Ericcson said, "but the engines work that hard when—and only when—it leaves the Anchorage vessel."

"So there's some sort of liquid on that ship that all the other ships are consuming…" Valdar stroked his beard. "Curious."

"It's a single point of failure in their system," Utrecht said. "Which would make it an ideal target."

"Our stealth Mule can reach Anchorage," Valdar said, "but that's a big ship. All I can send as boarders are armsmen. Gor'al, you have a contingent of Marines on the *Vorpral?*"

"Space is limited on your Mule. This is not a time to hold back. I suggest sending soldiers with more firepower," the Dotok said.

"Armor…but they're all on the surface. How many suits could it—"

"Sir, priority communication for you," the comms officer said through his earpiece, *"from the Crucible!"*

"Put it on the tank," Valdar said.

Marc Ibarra's static image came up next to Ceres within the holo-field. Ibarra brought the transmission to the fore with a hook motion toward the new moon.

"Valdar? Sure hope it's still you over there. All I've got is audio and about ten minutes before you orbit out of my line-of-sight transmission," Ibarra's tinny voice said.

Valdar tapped Ericcson on the shoulder then tapped their status report screen. She nodded and sent the data through the open line while Valdar spoke.

"I'm here. Got Gor'al from the *Vorpral* with me. More data's coming to you. We had a conversation with the Ruhaald admiral that—"

"Yes yes yes. I'm monitoring everything within the Crucible. There just isn't much that I can do about it. It won't be long before the Naroosha have complete control over the gate, and then there's no chance of us winning this thing," Ibarra said.

"If you've got a plan to retake the Crucible, save our cities from the nukes and have us hold on to everything long enough for Mars fleet to get here and beat those bastards into dust, we're all ears," Valdar said.

"We can pull it off, but several things have to happen all at once. The hardest part will be getting rough men and women ready to commit violence into the

Crucible's control room," Ibarra said.

"I think we've got that covered." Valdar brought Ibarra up to speed on the cloaked Mule. "The nukes are the sticking point for us. Doesn't do us much good to retake the Crucible just to watch the home world go up in nuclear fire."

"Nukes are easy," Ibarra said and rapidly laid out a plan.

"It could work," Gor'al said. "If everything goes perfectly. Fail one part and every human, Dotok and Karigole on Earth is doomed."

"There is a demon named Murphy," Valdar said, "and we will not let him win this day."

CHAPTER 6

Streaks of fire ran across the sky. The broken remains of fighters, orbital emplacements and ships ranging from corvettes to *Midway*-class supercarriers made their final descent to Earth as brief red-hot comets. Those near Perth saw the re-christened *Gallipoli* fall into the atmosphere and begin shedding its hull to a conflagration that stretched all the way to Hawaii where the bus-sized remains of the carrier splashed into the sea.

The shower of burning wreckage would continue for days as dead ships and their abused remains slowly succumbed to Earth's gravity.

Over the American West, a darkened lump of metal the size of a fist passed into the lower atmosphere, slowing precipitously in the thicker air. It reached terminal velocity within seconds and began the long parabolic arc to the ground. By the time it hit the lower extent of the Rocky Mountains, it was little bigger than the palm of a child's hand.

The lump bounced off a boulder and settled into a pile of loose rock. Embers burned across the warped metal, flaring as a gust of wind swept over the surface. The metal lay dormant for nearly an hour…then its shell shifted color into a deep gray. Tiny black squares appeared on the surface, swirling into larger fractal shapes.

The metal sank into the surface, growing larger as it devoured rocks and soil into it. The metal stretched out into four spindly limbs. It grew larger, fuller, as it fed on the earth around it, morphing into a humanoid shape.

A head spilled from the body, hanging by thin stands until those merged into a neck. A too-wide mouth bit into a boulder, chewing off a fragment and swallowing it whole.

Torni's naked form collapsed to the ground. She fought to recreate open eyes from her shell and managed to look around. Mountains to the north, rising sun behind her and the remains of a city to the front. Many of the skyscrapers were splayed open, half-demolished by Xaros drones during their scouring of the planet's surface. One building's upper floors were blown apart and blackened by fire.

"I...know this." Torni stood up, remembering the training exercise with her team in the city and their failure to defeat the faux-drones Steuben used to ambush them. She'd landed near Tucson.

She looked down at her naked shell and gave off a startled yelp. She scooped up a handful of dirt and rubbed it over her arms, transforming the mass into a plain jumpsuit. She grabbed a rock and squeezed it between her hands, absorbing it into her body, which changed her color to mimic a pale, blond-haired woman in dark blue coveralls.

Fireballs streaked through the upper atmosphere.

She remembered the General's call, sending her to merge with the rest of the Xaros drones forming a planet-killer weapon over India. She remembered releasing the dormant kill command she'd carried for years. After that…

Torni tried to tap into the electromagnetic spectrum to pick up anything from the defenders, but her shell collected nothing but mangled static. She willed an antigravity field into being to take to the air. Rocks exploded away from her as the rogue gravitons emitted off her body.

"Not everything works," she said. She looked at her hands and saw waves undulating over her surface. They calmed as she concentrated on holding her form, but the control she'd once had over her Xaros body was gone.

She dropped her hands to the side, thankful there wasn't a mirror nearby to reflect her face.

The remnants of old I-10 extended from the city to the northwest…toward Phoenix.

Torni made her way down the mountain.

****

Hale, hitching a ride atop the armored skirt over Elias' treads, held onto the soldier's arm as they rolled through the low tunnel. The armor leaned forward, ducking beneath the unfinished ceiling, the treads kicking up a cloud off the dirt floor.

The unfinished tunnel felt too much like the caverns beneath Pluto to Hale, the nagging press of claustrophobia stirring in the back of his mind. Years before, Hale had volunteered for armor selection at Ft. Knox. He'd done well during the first few months, scoring top marks in neuro synthesis with the suit systems and combat ability. His dreams of wearing armor came to a screeching halt during isolation testing.

Prospective armor soldiers were required to withstand the psychological stress of being trapped within the suit's womb until rescued. Tests inside the pitch-black tanks filled with salt water could last from hours to days. During his second stint in the tanks, Hale snapped. The instructors found him weeping and hysterical when they opened the tank. There were no second chances for cadets that washed out of the isolation tests.

Claustrophobia hadn't been a problem for Hale before his time at Knox. Since then, the press of tight spaces brought an air of anxiety—not because he was truly afraid, but because of the memory of abject failure.

Elias came to a stop next to a group of Marines huddled near the ramp leading to the emergency access and Caas.

Lieutenant Mathias and Cortaro stood up when Hale jumped off the tread.

"We've got an IR relay to our Marines and the Hussars on the ridge," Mathias said. "They know the target area and will lift and shift fire soon as we open the hatch."

"Thank you, Lieutenant," Hale said, then raised his voice. "Mission is to grab a Ruhaald leader and get back to the tunnel and move with urgency to the tunnel network leading back to Phoenix. The confusion of our ambush and the casualties we'll inflict should give us enough time to withdraw. We will hit them like a thunderbolt and fade away like ghosts. These squid-looking bastards have never fought Strike Marines, and now it's time to teach them a lesson for setting foot on Earth. Any questions?"

"What're we waiting for?" Elias asked. The rotary cannon on his shoulder began to spin slowly. Metal clinked as his mechanical hands opened and closed.

"Mathias, tell your team sniper to knock on the door," Hale said.

The lieutenant nodded and touched a control pad on the back of his hand.

"Thibodaux, take 'em."

The tunnel shook as a rail-rifle shot smashed through Thibodaux's target and into the earth a few tens of yards away. The muted sound of gauss fire and the pitter-pat of bullet impacts drummed through the tunnel.

"Ambush team will shift fire after the second rail shot," Mathias said.

Elias rolled to the base of the ramp, grabbing either side of the walls and holding himself back as his treads ground against the loose sand. His helm twisted to look at Hale.

"Cry havoc."

The tunnel shook with the impact of another rail slug and Elias roared up the ramp. He lowered a shoulder and smashed through the hidden exit. Light flooded down the tunnel and the sound of Elias' gauss cannons echoed off the walls.

Caas rolled up the ramp and Hale followed. He would never let his Marines charge ahead of him, but using the armor as a shield made perfect tactical sense.

Caas' treads lifted her torso away from the ground and the actuators whined as the treads transformed into legs. She lifted her forearm cannons and opened fire, double claps of gauss shells slapping the air. Her rotary cannon twisted the opposite direction from her gauss cannons and let off a storm of bullets.

Hale ran up the ramp and veered to the right. A Ruhaald artillery emplacement burned in front of him, the barrel blown open like a used firework and smoldering in the sand. Dead aliens lay around the emplacement, lime-green fluid seeping into the dirt around their corpses.

The mountains behind the camp flashed with gauss fire from the Hussars and his Marines. Thibodaux's rail rifle split the air and a distant tent exploded into a ball of fire.

A high-pitched gurgling sound filled the air, emanating from scattered tents and Ruhaald vehicles. A few of the aliens attempted to return fire: short lightning bolts snapped up the mountain side and were answered with aimed fire from several Marines.

The Marine ran toward the gun, jumping over the

wrecked tube. Glancing over his shoulder, he saw the rest of his Marines following close behind. He cleared the emplacement and saw a circular tent with garlands of shells over the fabric and several antennae poles in a loose circle around what he and Steuben assumed was a headquarters area.

Chest-high blocks of gray stone formed a berm around the tent with a wide opening to the rear. A pair of Ruhaald ran out of the corral, both carrying the lightning guns their infantry seemed to prefer.

Hale shot one in the head. It fell in front of the other and tripped it to the ground. Hale put two rounds into the survivor as he passed and ran into the berm. He swept his rifle around the corner and found an alien soldier struggling to load a glowing pill into a rifle stock. The alien glanced up and froze when it saw the Marine.

Hale's armored heel kicked out and crushed the alien's head, splattering deep-purple ichor against the wall.

"Assault team ready!" Matthias shouted. The lieutenant and four Marines were just outside the tent flaps. The rest of the Marines that followed Hale into the camp were crouched against the blocks.

"Go!" Hale stood up and fired at a group of soldiers fleeing Elias and Caas.

Heavy gauss cannons blew the soldiers into

bloody fragments.

Elias, the cannons on his arm glowing red hot, jammed an arm into a tent and pulled a Ruhaald out by the leg. Elias leaned back and hurled the alien through the air. The enemy soldier tumbled end over end, arcing over Hale's head and slamming into the shield wall.

A twenty-foot-wide segment of the energy shield flickered as the alien burned to a crisp like meat forgotten on a hot skillet.

Elias let off an ear-splitting roar and smashed a black berm aside with the back of his hand. He hoisted another Ruhaald over his head with both hands…then ripped the alien in half. Elias dropped the bleeding hunks to the ground.

"Sir! Got one." Matthias came out of the tent, limping badly, a blackened circle marring his right thigh. A pair of Marines dragged a Ruhaald with thin arms and a lower body shaped like a tadpole's tail.

"It had bodyguards," one of the Marines said. "Guess this one's important, right?"

A horn blast hit Hale hard enough that he reflexively ducked behind the berm. Caas thundered past, her cannons blazing.

A Ruhaald vehicle built like a scorpion broke through the wall of one of the large buildings. Its oversized forelimbs, a pair of flattened stalagmites made of dark metal almost fifteen feet high, pawed at the ground like a bull readying to charge. Gauss bullets ricocheted off the dark metal in a starburst of sparks. A ball of sensors and thick cables hung just behind the shield-limbs, bobbing up and down as it scanned for threats.

Gauss shells bounced off the armored fore limbs without leaving a dent.

"Anchoring!" Caas yelled. She raised her right leg and a drill bit popped out of the heel. Her aegis shield unfolded from her forearm in segments.

The scorpion tank's tail snapped up, a wide-barreled energy cannon on the tip.

Caas slammed her anchor into the ground just as the Ruhaald tank fired. A thin, jagged line connected the alien weapon to Caas' shield, then a bolt of lightning so bright it left an afterimage against Hale's eyes, burst through the air. The Dotok armor slammed to the ground and slid back like she'd fallen on an icy lake.

The cannon swung toward Hale and their prisoner.

"Down!" Hale twisted around and covered the prisoner with his body.

Blazing heat cut through his armor as the scorpion let off another blast. A concussion shook the ground...yet everything was intact when Hale looked around. He lifted his head up over the edge of the berm.

The entrance to the tunnel was a burning crater. A straight channel of collapsed earth ran through their escape route. The scorpion had destroyed their only way out.

A flurry of bolts snapped over Hale's head and smacked into the berm with a hiss of smoke. The Ruhaald had recovered from the initial onslaught and Hale realized that he had very little time to salvage the situation.

Elias charged the scorpion, his cannons firing on the tank's tail. The scorpion pivoted toward Elias and scuttled forward. The armor jumped to the side as the thin, jagged line shot from the cannon. Elias twisted in the air and dodged the next blast.

A burning line of fire cut through the air as a rail-rifle bullet hit the scorpion's tail. The severed cannon went spinning through the air. The scorpion charged toward Elias, heedless of the loss of its weapon.

Elias' fist retreated into the forearm and a diamond-tipped spike emerged. He dashed aside as an armored forelimb snapped out so fast Hale's eye could barely follow the strike. The thick plate clipped Elias' flank and sent him spinning.

Elias' cannons fired as he hit the ground in a cloud of dust, the bullets striking the scorpion's exposed underbelly. It pulled back like an injured animal, then sprang forward, raising its forelimbs and slamming them toward Elias. The armor rolled aside, got to his feet, and backed away, peppering the scorpion with cannon shots that bored into the forelimbs and beat the scorpion back.

Hale ducked as Ruhaald fire came over the other side of the berm. He looked up the mountainside, the only avenue of escape he could think of. Charging up hundreds of yards of rough terrain would make him and his Marines slow targets to every gun the Ruhaald had.

Think. Think!

An explosion smashed through the berm and threw one of his Marines against an antenna. Hale rushed to the new gap in their defenses and fired on a group of Ruhaald charging out of a small building. He cut one down before Mathias and another Marine finished the rest off.

Hale looked for more enemies...and saw the base of the energy wall. A low wall of coral-like material stretched across the bottom of the wall, thick nodes dotting the line at equally spaced intervals.

Hale switched his rifle to HIGH power and fired at a node. Hunks of coral crumbled from the impact and a section of the wall flickered.

"Fire on my target!" Hale slapped the Marine next to him and pointed to the wall. He shot the node again, and a narrow band of the energy wall faded.

A horn blast filled the air. The building the Ruhaald had charged out of broke apart as another scorpion tank emerged.

"Elias?" Hale whirled around and saw the armor bashing his spike against the damaged tank's forelimbs.

Hale turned to face the new scorpion as a cannon-tipped tail rose over its shields.

Light glinted off something between the Ruhaald tents and the scorpion shifted suddenly. Hale heard the thunder of heavy footsteps as a pair of armor soldiers charged into the open.

The Hussars arrived, lances in hand and cannons blazing. Vladislav launched himself into the air and sailed over the scorpion's armor. He thrust his lance into the sensor ball as he slammed onto the scorpion. He grabbed his lance with both hands and wrenched it aside, ripping through the scorpion with a metallic pop.

Adamczyk jumped onto the scorpion's back and grabbed the base of the cannon as energy coursed up and down the tail. He swung off the tank and twisted the tail to aim at the energy wall.

A searing blast struck the coral base and sent chunks of rocky shrapnel zinging through the air. A hunk the size of a coin careened off Hale's helmet and knocked him to the ground.

"On your feet, sir!" Yarrow pulled Hale up.

The energy wall now had a gap wide enough for two armor soldiers to fit through. Hale saw Firebase X-Ray in the distance.

"Out! Everyone out!" Hale jumped over the berm and ran for the opening. The two Hussars that killed the tank backed toward the wall, laying down a furious barrage of fire on any Ruhaald that moved.

Elias had his spike buried in the damaged scorpion's left shield. The tank lifted the forelimb—and Elias with it—into the air and tried to strike at him with its damaged tail. Elias slapped the tail away and tried to hit it with his rotary cannon. Bullets stitched a line through the sand toward Hale as the scorpion swung Elias around.

Hale dove to the ground and thumped against the coral wall next to the gap. He hit a button on the side of his helmet and activated his radio set.

"Steuben? Steuben, take the ambush element and withdraw to Phoenix. You copy?"

Hale waved to the Marines dragging the Ruhaald prisoner and a wounded comrade toward their new escape route.

"I must respectfully decline," Steuben transmitted. *"We just came down the mountainside to rescue you. The opening you*

made to the firebase is a better tactical option."

The flash of gauss weapons flared between the base of the mountain and the middle of the Ruhaald camp.

"Elias, we need to leave!" Hale aimed his rifle at the damaged scorpion's exposed flank and fired. The high-powered shot kicked an armor plate loose and a splash of liquid burst from the impact. Hale reloaded his power pack as Elias' duel continued without end.

The third Hussar, Ferenz, roared toward the scorpion, propelled forward by his treads, his lance secured against his side. Ferenz slammed the tip into the scorpion and knocked it onto its side. The Hussar rode the momentum of the impact and shifted his treads back into legs. He used the impaled lance as a lever and twisted the scorpion onto its back. Ferenz pounded the exposed underbelly with his cannons.

The scorpion twitched then went limp. Elias ripped his arm away from the embedded spike, leaving it buried in the scorpion's forelimb.

Fire from the Ruhaald slackened as the aliens retreated from the Marines and the armor.

The Marines with the prisoner ran past Hale and into the open ground between the wall and the firebase.

"They know we're coming?" Matthias stopped next to Hale and looked across the desert.

"I'm willing to bet they'll see us and realize we're not aliens," Hale said. "Do you have a better idea right now?"

"Nope." Matthias turned and limped through the breach.

Elias started toward the retreating aliens, but Ferenz grabbed him around the waist. The Iron Heart jabbed an elbow into Ferenz's helm. The Hussar held tight, dragging Elias toward Hale.

"Elias? What the hell are you doing?" Hale asked.

"*—me go! I'll kill every last one of them, you hear me!*" Elias' voice carried over the IR.

"*You're about to redline! You cycle down or you will answer to Carius for this,*" Ferenz said.

Elias stopped struggling. He backed toward the gap, taking potshots at the Ruhaald.

Cortaro grabbed Hale by the shoulder. Alien blood and dirt caked the gunnery sergeant's armor. Marines from the ambush team ran past them.

"All Marines accounted for," he said. "Can we get the hell out of here?"

Hale looked over at the other Hussars. Caas was with them, an arm missing and half her armor fire-blackened.

"Get moving, crunchy!" Vladislav called out.

"We'll cover you."

"Let's move." Hale followed Cortaro beyond the wall. Weapons emplacements around Firebase X-Ray slewed toward the gap. Hale breathed a sigh of relief as the big guns remained silent.

Hale's footfalls kicked up dust as he caught up to Matthias, who was barely moving faster than a walk with his wounded leg. Hale glanced at the blackened hole on the Marine's thigh. Red streaks of blood ran from the wound.

Matthias stumbled to the ground.

"Ugh...thirsty," he said.

"How bad are you hit?" Hale stopped next to him and pried away the armor plate on Matthias' leg. A glut of blood splashed into the sand.

Hale sucked air through his teeth. Matthias was bleeding to death. He found a shiny tag on the side of the pseudo-muscle layer of Matthias' suit and pulled. The tourniquet integrated into the muscles should have tightened to shut off the blood flow to the wound...but nothing happened.

"Suit's...messed up," Matthias said. His eyes fluttered beneath his visor.

"Corpsman!" Hale pulled an emergency tourniquet off Matthias' belt and wrapped it around the wounded Marine's thigh. He pulled it tight and pressed his hand against the wound as Yarrow sprinted over.

"What've we got?" Yarrow ran a line from his gauntlet to Matthias' helmet.

The clank of treads filled the air and Vladislav stopped a few yards away.

"Put him on," the Hussar said, slapping the armored skirt over his treads.

Hale and Yarrow hefted Matthias onto the armor. Yarrow jumped on and held onto the casualty. Vladislav took off in a cloud of dust.

Hale looked down at his hand. Bright-red blood dripped through his fingers and onto his boots. It was his idea to take one of the aliens prisoner. Now one of his Marines was bleeding to death and once he and the rest of his company made it to the firebase, they'd be backed into a corner.

The last Hussar backed out of the gap, his rotary cannon sending out a fan of bullets to dissuade any Ruhaald from following. Hale ran into a dried-out creek bed and made for the firebase.

The *bam-bam-bam* of an antiaircraft gauss weapon echoed through the valley. Flashes of light broke from the firebase and a white-hot tracer round zipped over Hale's head. He took a look over his shoulder and saw rounds impacting near the gap in the Ruhaald energy wall. Ripples broke across the barrier as rounds went wide and missed the break.

Hale lowered his head and ran faster. The defenders within the mountain would cover their tactical withdrawal across the desert.

A tall metal door, its surface heat warped and pockmarked with craters from alien weaponry, stood ajar. Cortaro and Steuben waved Hale over to the opening, which grew wider with each heave of an armor soldier as two of them pushed and pulled it open.

Hale ran through the opening and slowed to a stop within a maintenance bay the size of a basketball court. Hale bent at the waist and ripped his helmet off. He gulped down oil-tinged air and felt rivulets of sweat pour down his face.

Taking a deep breath, he stood up and found his Marines sitting along the walls. They were all caked in dirt, their armor singed by energy weapons, and many bore smears of Ruhaald blood.

Lieutenant Jacobs stood over their prisoner, which had its head buried within its arms and rocked back and forth over the wide tail curled beneath its body.

Hale took out the voice box he'd recovered off the dead alien that nearly executed Nickel and offered it to the prisoner, who didn't seem to notice. Hale tapped the box against the alien's chest plate. A single black eye peeked through the many tentacles the thing used for fingers.

It reached out slowly, stroking Hale's wrist and hand before taking the box. It clutched the translation device to its chest.

"My caste will pay dearly for my return, but only if I am alive," came from the box.

"We don't know you." Hale shook his head. "Don't know your planet, your needs, but you sure don't look like you breathe our air. How long will your suit keep you alive?"

"Up to nine full rotations of this planet…if the power systems are recharged. Less than a full rotation otherwise. I will tell my pod of your fair treatment. There will be no blood debt if I am returned unharmed."

"Jacobs, you like calamari?" Hale asked the lieutenant.

"In a cioppino, maybe. Better if it's breaded, fried and paired with my granny's marinara sauce."

"Why don't you get our prisoner secured. Share more of your granny's seafood recipes if it causes any trouble. Got a lot of hungry mouths to feed tonight."

The Ruhaald's feeder tentacles went berserk.

"I assure you my species' resemblance to cephalopods does not—"

Jacobs took the voice box away and grabbed the prisoner beneath its armpits.

"Excuse me," came from behind.

An army corporal flanked by two doughboys stood a few feet away. The doughboys snapped to attention when they saw Hale's face.

The corporal, a line of sutures running down his face and a patch over his left eye, squinted at Hale.

"Huh, well that's funny," the corporal said.

"I'm looking for a Lieutenant Bolin," Hale said, "Corporal…"

"Montes, sir. The lieutenant's in the aid station. Follow me."

There was a bang of metal on metal as the front door slammed shut. All five armor soldiers had made it inside. Elias, his armor stained to reddish-black by alien blood, slammed a fist against the door. His shoulders heaved up and down, as if he was breathing heavily. Two of the Hussars grabbed him by the arms.

Hale saw the armor's IR channel active on his forearm screen, but didn't tap in. He had enough problems, and the armor could handle their own. He hoped.

****

The aid station had seen better days. The ceiling had partially caved in, breaking the light bars and exposing the bare rock above. An auto-doc robot hung from the wall, its optic suite smashed beyond repair by fallen masonry. Wall lockers once full of medical supplies had been ransacked. A glass medicine case was riven by spiderweb cracks.

Hale stepped around a gurney holding a sheet-draped body, the smell of dried blood and spilled urine wafting from the corpse.

The captain found Mathias around a plastic partition. He lay on his side, stripped from the waist down except for a small towel for modesty. Dried red foam covered his injured thigh and bags of fluid ran into his arms.

"Believe it or not, sir," Mathias said, raising his head slightly, "I'm doing pretty good." The Marine's words were slurred, a testament to whatever painkillers Yarrow had given him.

"Yarrow's a good sawbones." Hale touched Mathias' shoulder. "He's patched me up more than once. You get some rest and we'll get you evacced soon as possible."

Assuming there is a way out of here.

"The doc gave me something…good." Mathias grinned a little and closed his eyes.

Yarrow stuck his head around the partition.

"Sir, a second?"

Hale nodded.

"Mathias is stable. Artery in his leg had a small cut. That tourniquet you got on him saved his life. I can have him up and around in a few more hours, got to let the nu-skin set. Bolin…" the corpsman continued as he glanced over his shoulder, "he's touch and go. The firebase lost their medics in the initial attack. His soldiers did what they could, but not enough. I need you to keep him distracted while I work on him. I'll lose him to shock if I put him under."

"Fair enough, let me see him."

Yarrow pushed the screen aside. Bolin lay on a gurney, stripped of his armor. His legs ended just below the knees in a mess of blood-soaked bandages. The lieutenant's chest rose and fell with a slight wheeze.

"Is that him?" Bolin asked weakly.

Hale grabbed a stool and sat next to the head of the gurney. Bolin's skin was deathly pale, his cheeks sunken. Hale looked at the man…and all he could see was his brother, Jared.

"My God." Hale put his hand on Bolin's forehead. "What happened to you? How did you get here?"

Confusion washed over Bolin's face. "You're another one," he said. "Thought our line was spread out over the planet. What's your name?"

"Hale. What do you mean, 'another one'? Don't you recognize me?"

"You're the original? I thought he was gone."

"I'm Ken Hale…and you're not my brother Jared."

Bolin strained his neck up. Hale saw him looking at a sheet propped up over his waist, blocking the view to his severed legs.

"What're you doing, doc?" Bolin asked. "Feel you tugging down there."

"Keep him distracted," Yarrow whispered into Hale's earpiece.

"You know who Ken Hale is, right? Why do you look like him? Did Ibarra clone him?" Hale asked as he pushed gently against Bolin's forehead and laid him back against a sweat-soaked pillow.

"Officially, we're Jared mark twos. After the Toth fight on Hawaii, Ibarra studied the battle and the doughboys that survived. Ken Hale organized the beach defenses, had a bunch of doughies following his lead. Doughies connected to Ken performed better than others. Braver, better shots, smarter even. I never heard why, but then Ibarra changed the doughboys' programming to come off the assembly line keyed to that Hale as their leader. Then the proccie tubes pumped out a bunch of Hales. All in the name of efficiency."

"So you're a clone? Do you think I'm your brother?"

Bolin grimaced and the scent of fresh blood filled the air.

"Not a clone. I've got my own life before all this. Grew up in Nevada. Fought off the Chinese incursion on the Aleutian Islands before joining the Saturn colony. Ibarra changed up my face and vocal cords before I left the tubes. Ghost bastard promised to give me my looks back after the war's over. There are thousands of mark twos through the system, all leading doughy units. Hell of a job."

Hale sat back, a cold lump in his stomach. Relief, sadness, a torrent of emotions ran through his mind. The badly wounded man before him wasn't his brother, but his brother was truly gone. Light-years away on a colony that would never come under threat from the Xaros.

"So you know the guy?" Bolin asked. "I see him

every time I look in the mirror. He a good man?"

"Better than me...what happened to you?"

"Forgot to duck. Still came out better than the others in battery three. Wait...if you're here, are the squids gone? Should have asked sooner but things are a bit fuzzy right now."

"I'm here with some help, just not enough to break out of this mess. Again, why are the Ruhaald attacking this firebase and the doughboys? This isn't happening anywhere else."

"Damned if I know," Bolin said. "One minute we're fighting the Xaros, next my outer line of bunkers is screaming about those squid-looking bastards attacking. They killed all the doughboys they could find—had a couple reports of them taking human soldiers captive. Their fighters hit the firebase hard. They put up that energy wall during the air attack, seen their transports coming and going since then."

"They demand anything?"

"One transmission." Bolin looked over to a pile of armor in the corner and then the soldier's eyes glazed over. His head fell against his pillow.

"Damn it." Yarrow stood up, blood covering his hands and knees. "His blood pressure is plummeting. I need you to strip off your sleeve right now."

"What happened?" Hale reached under a shoulder pad and unsnapped the link to his right arm. The armor plates fell to the ground and he peeled away the sleeve of pseudo-muscles and environmental shielding.

"Too much blood loss." Yarrow raced to the disordered supply station and dug into a locker. "You're O-, he's AB-, he needs a liter from you."

The corpsman ran over with tubes and needles.

"Your green blood cells, the ones keyed to your DNA to ward off alien infection, might be an issue down the line." Yarrow slid a needle into Bolin's arm. "But if I don't do this right now, he *will* die. No one's ever studied if the presence of green blood cells will cause an acute hemolytic transfusion reaction. Probably because only our team and the *Breitenfeld*'s sick bay ever got the green blood cells."

Hale offered up his bare arm and looked at Bolin. In his mind, he knew the man that needed his help was little more than a stranger, but his heart ached to see his brother suffering.

****

Hale flexed his bare arm as he left the aid station. His other hand held a water bottle to his lips. The captain grabbed on to the wall, steadying himself as a wave of dizziness overtook him.

"You are unwell." Steuben grabbed Hale with his four-fingered cyborg hand and helped steady the Marine.

"Just a little woozy. Happens every time I give blood. Don't normally give so much at once." Hale finished his bottle and tossed it into a bin. "What's the situation?"

"The firebase has four functioning defense emplacements, sixty-seven doughboy augmentees and nine soldiers, none over the rank of corporal. Power reserves will last for another twenty hours—less if there's another fight. Munition reserves…" Steuben tabbed a claw tip on his forearm screen then touched Hale's. A spreadsheet scrolled over Hale's display.

"The firebase has one good fight left in it," Hale said. "Access tunnels?"

"All the connected nodes were collapsed. Standard protocol when a position was in danger of being overrun. The prisoner is asking to speak with you."

"Let's walk and talk." Hale took a tentative step away from the wall and went down the hallway, his coordination out of step like he'd had one drink too many.

"Is this a normal human reaction to exsanguination?"

"Normal donations are about half a liter. Corpsman took twice that from me. The Red Cross used to have cookies and juice waiting for people who donated. The only thing Yarrow gave me was a shot to boost my red-blood-cell production…wait…Jenkins. Jenkins needs—"

"Sergeant Jenkins is on his way to provide plasma for Matthias. I took care of it."

"Thanks, XO." Hale smacked dry lips and propped himself up against a wall. "I think Yarrow got more than a liter."

Steuben reached into a pouch and pulled out a candy bar.

"This is named for your fourth planet. I do not see the connection."

Hale wolfed the treat down and took a long sip from a tube connected to his suit's water packs.

"Where did you get that?"

"Cortaro found a cache of such confections while invoicing supplies. He said it was a lure for some sort of an animal. What species eats something with so little nutrition but so many harmful preservatives?"

"Pogie bait. I don't know…how about when this is all over I take you snipe hunting?"

"Are snipes worthy prey?"

"Yes, very tricky animals. Taste incredible but you can only hunt them at night. I'm feeling better now. Tell me what we've learned from the Ruhaald prisoner."

****

Caas dragged a power washer across the bay to where Elias' armor sat against a wall. The once off-white slabs of composite aegis armor were stained with layers of gore from Ruhaald soldiers.

She stopped a few feet away and checked the readings on the side of the tanks.

"What are you doing?" Elias asked.

She let off a test spray against the deck.

"Carius made us suffer if we neglected our equipment. He found a speck of oxidation in my double barrels and nearly sent me to the infirmary with dehydration after an entire night of touching the wood line at Fort Knox. Did that ever happen to you?" she asked.

Elias' helm tilted slightly.

"More than once."

"I know we're on Earth and Carius is stuck on Mars, but look at you. You can't do this yourself, thanks to your condition. So here I am. Do you have any idea what you smell like? Low tide and…your canine's flatulence."

Caas aimed the nozzle at his helm.

Elias kicked out and knocked the tank to the ground. The hose went flying out of her hands.

"This is who I am," he said. "Let the enemy see the monster."

"No," Caas said as she marched over and kicked Elias in the shin, "you are no such thing. Do you remember when we met? Monsters don't feed hungry little girls. Monsters don't scare the piss out of bullies so orphans can live without fear."

"Let me have this. It is all I have left."

Caas clicked her beak several times and let out a trill.

"Do you know the story of High Lord Yiir? Of course not, you were never a Dotok child. Yiir was a beast of legend. Tall as a giant, stronger than twenty men. Crushed every opponent that dared stand against him. Yiir conquered almost an entire continent on Dotari and led his undefeated army to a wide river separating him from the last free kingdom.

"He charged into the river and got up to his knees before he stopped. For all his victories...he couldn't cross the river. His soldiers asked to help, to join their hands to his and cross the river *together*. All Yiir had to do was humble himself, admit that he needed others to complete his task…but he refused.

"Yiir demanded the gods part the river or he would destroy every temple in his domain. He continued on and drowned."

"This great leader couldn't swim?" Elias asked.

"His armor was too heavy. Do humans not understand allegory?"

Elias tapped fingers against his knee, then shifted forward.

Caas backed up, wondering whether Elias was about to put an end to her bothersome presence.

Elias held a hand to her, mimicking the time he offered her a food ration years ago. The fingertips were black with congealed blood.

"Help me cross the river," Elias said.

Caas righted the pressure washer and sprayed the stain clean.

****

The Ruhaald sat in a corner of an empty barracks room. Its tentacles writhed over a small plastic model of an armor soldier posed with cannons extended and rail gun ready to fire. It held the model up and turned it over in the light from a failing light strip in the ceiling, flickering every few tens of seconds.

Hale burst into the room and strode toward the Ruhaald, his hands balled into fists and a sneer on his face.

"What's your name?" Hale thrust a finger at the prisoner.

"Shu'ul! Call me Shu'ul," the Ruhaald said, ducking behind its hands. "I cannot communicate my scent pheromones through this box. Forgive me."

"Why are you attacking us?"

"It cannot be helped. Your slave sect murdered the scion. A new scion must be chosen and that cannot happen until the offending sect has paid the blood price. The warrior brood is going mad with aggression hormones. It cannot be helped. It cannot be stopped."

"This dead scion is why your ships are hovering over every human city, threatening to nuke us if we fight back?"

Shu'ul dropped its hand to the side. The wide black eyes focused on Hale one at a time.

"I wasn't told why this occurred. The decision came from the queen. We do not question her orders."

"Your people kidnapped three of my Marines. Where are they?"

"I do not know. I am a pilot breed, not a locus, not a decision maker. Are you a high born? You look like most of the rest."

"Every human being is a decision maker."

The feeder tentacles within Shu'ul's helmet went still.

"How do you get anything done?"

"Listen to me. We need to stop this bloodshed. There was some sort of misunderstanding with the doughboys and your…scion. His death was an accident. The doughboys are designed to attack anything not human. Someone along the line failed to warn you about the doughboys or prepare us for your arrival. This is war, and sometimes shit happens. Does that translate to you?"

"We excrete waste. I do not see how this will restore the warrior brood's biology to equilibrium."

"Wait…so when the scion was killed, it sent the rest of his troops into some sort of a rage?"

"The new scion will rise from those who extract the blood price. They will not stop until the last of your slave sect in this area is dead, their end witnessed by—" a blur of wet ticks and pops came out of the voice box "—then there will be peace."

It held up the plastic armor figurine. "What subspecies is this? They are…incredible."

"They are armor, but they are human. Most of them. I don't accept that we have to kill each other for this situation to end. Tell me another way to resolve this."

"The scion will rise. Then it will end. Our biology does not negotiate. It is not all humans that must die, only your slave sect."

Hale's gauntlet buzzed in quick succession. An urgent message needed his attention.

"Keep it." Hale brushed his fingers toward the figurine and left the room.

CHAPTER 7

Ordona double-checked the new code inject he'd spent the last many hours perfecting. Working the mélange of Toth, human and Qa'Resh programming languages was taxing, but not much of a challenge for his considerable intellect. The leadership cadre hadn't chosen him for this mission by accident.

He considered the new code to be sublime, yet simple. Achieving control over the Crucible in the next few minutes would be a real boon to his compensation arrangement when he returned to his home world. A nice bonus could elevate him to a new home in volcanic caves closer to the centers of power. His spawning-pool siblings would be most jealous.

Ordona unfolded a silver needle from his arm and extended it to press a holographic button.

He floated back and swung around to watch the probe as his program took root.

The air around the probe became hazy, then the top third skewed to the side at an ugly angle. The lights snapped off, but the panels arrayed around the probe glowed white-hot. Sparks erupted off the panels, ending the pyrotechnics with small flames along the edges of the ruined holo emitters.

The probe returned to its normal shape and the lights slowly returned to their former luminescence.

Ordona whirled around and checked his computer logs. The error was obvious. He'd sent the malicious code into the local energy distribution net and not the probe's source code. He double-checked the last commands to see where he'd gone wrong. He checked his video logs and watched his needle reach for the correct execution key…and saw the button move, replaced by an access file that created the cascading failure.

The Naroosha resisted the urge to lash out and wreck his already damaged equipment. The conclusion was obvious…and should have been spotted sooner. There was another hacker at play.

Ordona summoned new equipment from his starship. Knowing there was another actor within the probe made things difficult, but not impossible. He made a mental note to leave the details of this incident out of his final report.

****

Walking through the desert was a lot easier if one never became hungry or thirsty, Torni decided. The miles came easy when her limbs never grew tired and her "feet" were free from the worry of blisters. Her Strike Marine training involved many treks through uneven terrain under the burden of a heavy pack and rifle. The many "gut checks" weeded out those who lacked the mental and physical stamina demanded by the Atlantic Union's elite void-borne rapid-action teams.

While Torni's physical concerns were largely moot, the isolation of the Arizona desert weighed on her mind. The highway had cut off miles ago, leaving her to meander through mesquite trees and tumbleweeds sent into motion by an encroaching storm front. The abject emptiness unnerved her. She'd grown up in Sweden, never too far from civilization and where there was a village in every valley.

There was no sign of humanity. No powerlines, no garbage, not even the distant sound of airliners or delivery drones.

"Most of the planet is like this," she said. "It's like our entire existence was forgotten in the blink of an eye. And now I'm talking to myself. Great."

A pack of coyotes moved through the brush, keeping a respectable distance from her. She remembered stories of the first builders from the Titan fleet returning to Phoenix. The local predators had gone several generations without exposure to humans. All workers had to have armed guards after the third brazen attack by wild dogs and coyotes. Children had been evacuated from the city until electrified fencing and armed patrol robots were put into service.

She didn't know if the pack stalking her knew better than to attack a human.

"What does scent tell them? I wonder. A nice fat meal? Inedible metal? Talking again. Time to stop." Torni took her attention from the coyotes and checked the sun's location in the sky to reorient herself.

Worrying about the wildlife was pointless. They'd find they made a huge mistake if they attacked. The occasional snake sightings meant nothing, not when she lacked flesh and blood vulnerable to venom.

Clouds moved across the horizon. Torni did a double take when she saw a mountain lying flat across the sky. Not a mountain…a ship. Not a human ship for sure, the angles were all off and her brief experience with the *Breitenfeld* in the skies over Takeni taught her that human ships weren't designed to hold a position that close to the ground.

"That's got to be over Phoenix, but what the hell is it? How long was I out?" Torni hurried forward, stretching her legs into a jog. She'd heard the American folk tale of Rip Van Winkle as a child and hoped she wasn't in a similar story.

At least she had a guidepost now. Wandering around the desert for years would be something of an embarrassment if she ever met up with her Marines again.

****

Torni ducked beneath the thorns of an ocotillo tree and found a car-wide scar across the desert floor. A fire-blackened swath stretched for almost a hundred yards into a ravine. Several nearby shrubs had burnt down to nubs, and black smoke wafted in the strengthening breeze.

The city was a few miles away. Everything looked still and peaceful beneath the alien ship. The triangle-shaped fighters orbiting the ship had shown no interest in her as she made her way closer to the largest remaining city on the planet.

Torni looked down the abused path, then back to the city.

"Not like I'm in a hurry." She turned and followed the trail to the ravine. Below, a single Eagle lay crumpled against the rocky side of a muddy creek bed. A mound of dirt covered the cockpit.

Torni ran over, feeling the heat from engine fragments broken around the crash site. She skidded to a halt next to the cockpit and knocked over a hunk of broken wing embedded in the fuselage.

Wiping dirt from the cockpit, she uncovered glass riven with cracks. A small section was whole, and Torni got a decent look at her face. The left side was canted the wrong direction, like she was a Cubist painting made real. She pressed her hand against her cheek and realigned her features.

Torni brushed more dirt away. The canopy was so full of cracks it looked like it was covered in frost. She had no idea if the pilot was alive or dead as she rapped her knuckles against the glass.

She waited a few seconds and took a step back. While prisoner of the Xaros, she'd witnessed her own death several times. The thought of opening the canopy and being so close to another corpse filled her with dread.

The pilot was dead. There was nothing she could

do for him.

She turned around and heard a fist bashing against the canopy.

"Hey! Hey! Is someone out there?"

Torni spun around and tried to jimmy the canopy open. When that didn't work, she melded her fingers between the metal seams and used her prodigious strength to rip the canopy free of its hinges, then she tossed the broken glass aside.

The pilot held his hand over his face, blocking the sun as he tried to look at Torni. His right shoulder was badly dislocated, that entire side of his flight suit torn and bloody.

"Thank God," the pilot said. "I crashed. It was dark. I thought I died and was in purgatory but everything kept hurting so I thought maybe I was alive."

"How bad are you?" Torni turned aside, hiding her hand from him until it reformed.

"I can still move my feet and hands. Neck's fine. Everything just stings like a bitch when I do move," he said. "You got a name, pretty lady?"

"Later. Your radio working at all?"

"You think I didn't try that? Xaros hit me good, fried everything but the hydraulics. Why do you need a radio? You can't be out here alone too."

"My…my Mule crashed a few miles away. Only survivor. You're lucky I found you. I'm going to get you out, make a litter and get you to Phoenix. OK?"

"Or sit in this seat until I die of blood loss or dehydration? Fine by me."

"What's your name?" she asked as she unbuckled him from the cockpit.

"Greg Harrison, assigned to 10th Defense Wing out of Maricopa. You?" His face twitched with pain as she slid her arms beneath his knees and back.

"How many drones did you shoot down during the fight?"

"What? I know I got at least nine before the—" Harrison let out a wail as Torni lifted him out of the cockpit. His right leg dangled at an obscene angle, badly broken. She set him down as gently as possible amid a torrent of profanity from the pilot.

"Pain is good," Torni said, "means the damages isn't too bad."

"None of what I said was directed at you." Harrison grimaced and laid back. "I got to get your name. I'm taking you to a steak dinner. I know a guy who knows a guy who knows a guy that can get actual booze. You like whiskey? I'm a whiskey guy. Oh, what I wouldn't give right now for a shot…"

"My name…my name is Torni." She dragged a section of wing away from the crash, then went back to the cockpit for the straps.

"Torni? Like from that movie? What're the odds?"

"What movie?" She ripped the straps off then reached under the seat for the medical kit that was part of the ejection suite. The red plastic box came free with a tug. She opened it and found a can of disinfectant/analgesic spray.

"You haven't seen *Last Stand on Takeni*? I thought the big admiral made sure everyone saw it. Shame about what happened to that sergeant with your name. People ever ask if you're related to her? Can't be. She was true born—most everyone's a proccie these days." Harrison's head wobbled from side to side.

"Greg? You OK?"

"Just dizzy."

Torni ripped the sleeve off his good arm and wrapped a fluid pack around his inner elbow. The pack stiffened, immobilizing the joint, then sent a needle into his veins and began flooding his system with a cocktail of drugs and hydration fluids.

"Keep talking to me. Where you going to take me to dinner?" She ripped open his pants and sprayed the synthetic skin across oozing gashes down his leg.

"There's a guy named Vinny, little hole in the wall place. Doesn't take script for payment, only gear. He owes me a couple meals after I found him a spare armored bodysuit. Ah…is that supposed to be so cold?"

"I need to put a splint on your knee." Torni reached back and saw a long shadow stretch across the ravine. It traced back to an armor soldier that had its arm cannons leveled right at her.

"Get away from him," boomed an oddly accented voice from the suit's speakers.

Torni raised her hands and got onto her knees.

"What's the problem? He needs medical attention," Torni said. Could the armor know what she was?

"Your infrared scan matches ambient temperature. You're either a corpse…or Xaros." The arm cannons clicked as rounds loaded into the breaches.

"I'm not either of those." Torni got to her feet slowly. "Don't shoot. You'll hurt him. Let me step away and I can explain all this. Somehow. How long have you got?"

"Hey, tin man! You leave my girl alone!" Harrison shouted.

Torni sidestepped away from the wounded pilot. A direct hit from the large-caliber cannons could crack a drone into pieces. Torni didn't think she'd fare any better, not in her weakened state.

The armor advanced toward her quickly, its cannons aimed with deadly intent.

"Xaros killed my parents." The armor slammed an open hand into Torni's chest and lifted her off the ground, its fingers wrapped around her torso. It slammed her to the ground in a cloud of dust.

"You murdered my world and now you come to take our new home from us." The armor lifted its other arm overhead. The fist retracted, replaced by a diamond-tipped spike.

Torni struggled against the mighty weight pressing her to the ground. Her arms lost their human appearance and reverted to the undulating patterns of a drone's surface.

"Leave Torni alone!" Harrison threw a rock that bounced off the armor's helm.

The arm went a bit higher, then froze.

"There was a Torni…on Takeni. Saved me and my sister from the banshees," the armor said.

"We ran through the burning forest," Torni said. "We were all on fire by the time we made it through. There was a little boy…Ar'ri…and Caas. Standish and I got them back to the capital and I never saw them again."

The fingers in her right hand lengthened against her will. A burning ruby formed when the tips touched. She tried to pull her fingers apart, but her body had different ideas.

A massive foot from another armor soldier slammed onto her right hand, crushing the fingers. Bodel loomed over her.

"At ease, Ar'ri. I know this one," Bodel said. Ar'ri released his grip and sheathed his spike. Bodel slid his foot away.

Torni grabbed her crushed hand at the wrist. It took a moment of concentration to return to its normal shape.

"We didn't part on the best terms," Bodel said.

"Elias was trying to destroy Malal. I did what I had to." Torni stood up. She closed her eyes and forced her shell to mimic her old human form.

"What the hell kind of drugs did you give me?" Harrison asked.

"He needs help," Torni said.

"He'll get it." Bodel canted his head to the pilot. Ar'ri picked him up gently and carried him out of the ravine. "Picked up his emergency beacon. We were out looking for him. What are *you* doing here?"

"Trying to get to Phoenix. If you could give me a

ride, maybe explain what the hell's been going on, I'd appreciate it," Torni said.

CHAPTER 8

The crack of gauss weapons pounded through the passageway as the three Marines reached the stairs leading into the dome. Standish mag-locked his rifle onto his back and thrust his arms up into the hatch. His palms hit with a metallic clang. The hatch bobbled, but stayed closed.

"What the hell?" He pushed on the door again and managed to lift it a few inches. "It's not locked."

Panicked shouting and the rattle of a rotary cannon came from the other side of the entrance.

"We're not going to sit here while everyone else fights," Egan said, joining Standish beneath the hatch. They managed to lift it a few inches before dropping it again.

Bailey touched the other hatch...and lifted it with ease. She pumped her arm and sent the door flying open.

"I knew that." Standish took his rifle off his back and charged up the stairs behind Bailey and Egan.

Smoke rose from the flaming towers and coalesced into an ugly cloud against the ceiling. Doughboys and Marines fired over the battlements, ducking as short bolts of lightning struck the walls.

A pile of slain doughboys lay on the closed hatch door, jumbled with rectangular aegis shields almost the size of the soldiers that carried them. Each bore a circular wound through their helmets.

"Hey, what happened to them?" Standish asked.

"Hornets!" The warning came from one of the last intact towers and echoed across the battlements.

"What the hell are they talking about?" Bailey swung her long sniper rifle up and looked down her scope.

"I'm not sure," Standish said.

A shadow zipped across the ground. Standish looked up and caught a blur diving straight at Bailey. He slammed his hip against the diminutive Marine and sent her sprawling. The blur clipped Standish on the shoulder and spun him around.

What looked like a chrome-covered wasp slid across the floor, gouging tiny furrows as it came to a stop. Bulbous and misshapen eyes focused on Standish. Silver-tipped claws the size of daggers snapped out from the hornet's many legs. It rose into the air on a thrum of antigravity generators.

Standish swung his rifle up as it shot toward him so fast his eyes could barely follow. The hornet smacked into the barrel and ripped the weapon out of his hands. It lurched higher and snapped the rifle in half.

Egan fired on the Ruhaald attacker and missed as it danced from side to side, getting closer to Standish with each swoosh through the air.

Standish drew his pistol and tried to draw a bead on the hornet. An evil buzz rose through the air as the daggers stretched toward Standish and it dove on him.

A dark shape crossed in front of the Marine and he heard a metallic clang and a grunt. The doughboy in front of Standish stepped aside, revealing metal spikes from the hornet that had pierced through the aegis shield he carried. The spikes jiggled as a discordant buzz filled the air. The doughboy lifted the shield over his head and slammed it to the ground, on top of the struggling hornet, then he leaped onto the shield and jumped on top of it like a child playing on a mattress.

"Whoa, whoa! I think you got it," Standish said to the doughboy.

Onyx Twelve-Twelve pointed his gauss rifle at the shield and said, "No like!"

"I'm with you on that one, buddy." Looking at the remains of his rifle, Standish sighed. "Now how about we—"

A nearby barricade buckled inward as something smashed into it with the force of a runaway truck. Defenders along the wall opened fire on whatever was opposite the damaged wall.

Bailey ran a line from a battery pack on her hip to her rail rifle. Electricity arced up and down the twin vanes of the barrel.

"Don't think that's another hornet," she said.

Another slam battered the barricade aside and a scorpion tank charged through the breech. The scorpion's tail snapped over the shields and let off a torrent of lightning bolts that cracked over Standish's head and filled the air with the reek of ozone.

"Bailey? Anytime now!" Standish yelled.

The sniper grabbed Standish by the shoulder and nestled against his chest.

"Don't move." She raised her rifle and aimed it at the Ruhaald armor.

Rail rifles were designed as anti-materiel weapons, meant to knock out fortified positions and punch through vulnerable spots on well-armored void warships. Firing a fully charged shot from a standing position was strictly forbidden in training, given the injury rate to the shooters.

Bailey's rifle whined as the magnetic fields along the twin vanes accelerated a slug beyond the limits of the sound barrier. Thunder clapped as the bullet streaked toward the Ruhaald armor so fast it left a burning trail of air in its wake.

The recoil slammed Bailey into Standish. With no backstop of his own, Standish went flying and slammed into the ground so hard stars erupted across his vision.

He lifted his head off the ground and saw the Ruhaald armor—a giant chunk of one armored forelimb blown away and its tip-less weapon's tail spewing green liquid as it flailed in pain—running straight for him.

The enemy let off a squeal, leaped into the air, and arced straight down toward Standish.

Standish let out an un-Marine-like yell and rolled to the side. Darkness slammed around him and he bounced against something hard and unforgiving. He looked around and found himself surrounded by pulsating cables full of lambent liquid. He tried to get to his feet and found his foot caught in a mess of wires.

A ray of light opened ahead of him as a gap appeared. He caught a glimpse of doughboys and Marines firing on the scorpion tank. A gauss bullet sprang off the ground and bounced off his thigh as the gap closed.

"Ah, damn it!" Standish struggled to pull his foot free and accomplished nothing.

The walking tank shifted to the side, dragging Standish across the floor.

"Not. Good." He tightened his grip on his pistol, pointed at the morass of alien machinery and snapped off a round into a cluster of wires. The bullet bounced away and pinged around the enclosure.

"Not there." He found a slight bulge against the roof and fired again. The tank jerked like it had been hit with a live wire. Neon fluid poured onto Standish. The tank stumbled to the side as the concussion of an explosion shook the floor.

"If I don't get stepped on, I'll get blown up by my own Marines." Standish took a grenade off his belt and double-pressed the firing pin to activate it. He emptied his pistol into the sack and tossed the grenade into the flapping tear—then he threw his arms over his head and squeezed his eyes shut.

The grenade exploded with a *whoomp*. Standish felt a tidal wave of fluid slam into his body and send him tumbling like driftwood coming in to a beach. His world became a chaos of motion and green until he thumped into something.

Wiping slime off his visor, he found Onyx glaring

down at him. Standish looked at his body: green ooze covered every inch of him, sloughing to the side in thick gobs. He whined and tried to wipe the mess away.

"Standish!" Bailey ran over. She reached for him, then jerked her hand back with a look of disgust. "You...OK?"

The Marine tried to shake the goo off his hands. "Do I *look* OK?"

"We thought we'd have to take you home in a bucket. Glad you're...somewhat better than that," Bailey said.

Standish let out a miserable cry and looked around. None of the defenders fired as doughboys and Marines hustled around the barricades.

"Did we win?" he asked. "Oh God...I feel so yucky."

"Squids pulled back after you killed their tank," Bailey said. "Nice work."

"Can you get me to the reactor?" Standish sat up, accompanied by a slurping sound from the goo.

"What? Why?"

"To make me a towel, maybe? Wet wipes? A pressure washer? Something!"

"Stop being a wuss," Bailey said, but she helped him to his feet.

****

Hale, Steuben and Cortaro stood on a fire step running across the access bay and above the entrance doors. They peered through a foot-high firing slit to the Ruhaald energy wall, made whole since their escape. The image of a crude white flag played across the barrier along with slanted numbers reading "09."

"And the number is getting smaller?" Hale asked.

"Was '17' eight minutes ago," Cortaro shrugged.

"I do not understand the image," Steuben said.

"It signifies surrender," Cortaro said. "Maybe we gave them enough of a beating that they know what's best for them."

"No one surrenders while they have the high ground." Hale handed a set of binoculars to Steuben. "I watched plenty of shuttles come and go in the last few minutes. They're reconstituting their force behind the wall. From what I remember of my laws of land warfare class at Quantico, a white flag means 'we want to talk.'"

"You think those Ruhaald had the same class?" Cortaro asked.

"We know the Ruhaald have prisoners. It's not impossible that they asked around for some way to talk to us without getting shot in the face the second we saw them." Hale rapped his fingers against the firing slit. "We have comms with Phoenix yet?"

"Nothing yet. I've got Devins in one of the wrecked AA batteries trying to get an IR bounce back to the city," Cortaro said.

"Shall we speak with them? Or is this a trick?" Steuben asked.

"Trusting an enemy to honor a flag of truce depends on the enemy. The Chinese kept to the laws of land warfare. *Daesh* in Europe and the Levant, not so much," Hale said.

"We saw them murdering prisoners. I don't trust them," Cortaro said.

"It is a mistake to judge an alien culture by your own standards," Steuben said. "The Karigole do not kill those unable to fight, but we also do not take prisoners."

"You're not helping," Cortaro muttered.

A segment of the energy wall faded away. Hale heard orders snapped as the defenders readied their doughboys to fight.

"Hold your fire." Hale held up a hand as a single alien vehicle came out of the gap. It was little more than an anti-grav sled with a single Ruhaald driver in the front. Behind it were a half-dozen humans, all bound into a fetal position by silver cord. The barrier returned seconds later.

"First Sergeant?" Hale asked.

"If it weren't for the prisoners, I'd say this is a trap—shoot a couple rounds in the dirt to get them to turn around. But maybe they've got Bailey and Egan out there," Cortaro said.

"What about Standish?" Steuben asked.

"Oh. Him."

"Steuben?" Hale nudged the Karigole with an elbow.

"There is risk. Let me speak with them."

"They're expecting to negotiate with a human. It needs to be me." Hale watched as the sled came to a stop in the middle of the barren plain between the firebase and the energy barrier. The Ruhaald driver—the wide-shouldered kind with two legs—stood up, held its arms wide, and slowly turned around. Hale took the binos, zoomed in, and saw this alien had a constellation of stars etched onto its breastplate.

"Unarmed and kind of a big deal by its flair." Hale handed his gauss rifle and pistol over to Cortaro. "Have Thibodaux cover me with his rail gun. Anything goes wrong, don't risk coming for me."

Hale touched the sacrificial dagger he'd taken from the Ruhaald when he rescued Nickel and left it on his belt. He'd worn it during the smash-and-grab; there was a decent chance the Ruhaald would recognize it. If he'd learned anything from negotiating with the Toth, having some sort of reputation helped his bargaining posture.

"Your instructions are received," Steuben said.

Hale grabbed on to a ladder leading up the firing stoop and slid down. One of the Hussars yanked the reinforced door open wide enough for Hale to squeeze through. He stepped into the dry heat and marched toward the stopped sled. The Ruhaald paced back and forth, its helmet locked on Hale.

"Steuben," Hale said into the IR, "you said you received my instructions about not trying to save me. You understand what I mean? If this is a trap, you let it play out and take charge of the firebase."

"Standish shared the human parable about the value of asking for forgiveness instead of permission."

"What did I tell you about listening to him?

"Conversations with him are most informative. Bailey attempts to teach me unique Australian insults and Orozco shares his favorite...what is the term? 'Put out lines'?"

Hale felt his cheeks flush with frustration.

"First Sergeant."

"I will engage in some wall-to-wall counseling the next time I have them in reach," Cortaro said.

Hale removed his helmet and locked it onto his hip. The smell of smoke lingered in the air.

Ten feet from the Ruhaald, he stopped. The Marine kept his stance wide, his weight shifted forward. The six prisoners on the sled didn't react to Hale's arrival. Their eyes were shut, pain writ across their faces.

"I am Tuk, Third of the Ruhaald Expeditionary force. I render appropriate greetings," the Ruhaald said. Its tentacles were balled into fists that banged against its armored legs and the front of the sled. It kept pacing, never taking its bulbous eyes off Hale.

Hale pointed to the prisoners. "They're in pain. You release them right now or I will rip your helmet off and let you choke on Earth air."

Tuk held up a hand and waved its many fingers in the air. There was a pop of air and the reek of ozone. The prisoners let out groans and opened their eyes. Some struggled against the silver cords, but they remained bound.

"The Ruhaald do not allow prisoners the means to escape or resist. We do not inflict pain without reason."

"But you'll murder prisoners in cold blood."

"The blood debt is not murder. Your slaves took our scion from the brood. There will be another!" Tuk slammed a fist against the sled and dented the hood.

"I wasn't there when your scion died. The one man that witnessed what happened said it was an accident. This blood debt is a misunderstanding, one I'd rather settle with words than bullets."

"The scion is dead. There is no misunderstanding. The brood mother demands I offer you *kitithrak*, a mercy for only the weakest of foes. Turn over your slaves, all those in the same brood as the ones that killed our scion, and we will spare your kind and return the ones I brought as a gesture of good faith." Tuk tapped tentacle tips against the top of its helmet and motioned to the Ruhaald knife on Hale's belt.

"You mean all the doughboys inside the firebase?"

A snarl came through the voice box on Tuk's armor. "All of them! Does this device not speak your words properly?"

Hale had no doubt what would happen to the doughboys if he did turn them over.

"I will pass on your offer to my commander," Hale said, pointing to the prisoners, "but I will take all of them back with me. Now."

"I will not return to my brood with nothing. You will commit to paying the blood debt now or the *kitithrak* is void."

Hale stepped to the side and pointed to a

redheaded captive.

"You see those spots up and down his face and shoulders? He's on the verge of dying from an allergic reaction to xeno-germs. We saw this sort of thing with the Toth—call it Kirk Syndrome. The rest won't last much longer but I have a doctor that can save them—but only if he can treat them right away." Hale put his hands on his hips.

"We will allow your doctor to render aid within our encampment." Tuk's shoulders hunched over, its eyes darting from Hale to the prisoners.

"They need long term treatment and I'm not going to send a doctor away for days. You leave these sick men and women with me or they'll all die because you were too pigheaded to listen. Then there will be another blood debt to pay. I don't know about you, but I want the killing to stop sooner rather than later," Hale said.

"I will not return carrying promises." Tuk straightened up.

"How about a prisoner exchange? I will give you Shu'ul, one of your…other kind. No legs."

"You may have the sick one."

"All of them, and I will take your demands to my higher headquarters. I'm a lowly captain, not allowed to make the big decisions."

Tuk's tentacles stretched out and wiped dust from its legs.

"Agreed. I give you ten percent of a rotation to surrender your slaves. After that we will take them by force and your kind will not be spared," Tuk said.

Hale touched his throat mic.

"Bring out the Ruhaald prisoner."

His earbud clicked twice.

"Are you a decision maker? A locus?" Hale asked.

"I have limited autonomy."

"Why did you betray us? You came as allies and helped win the greatest victory in the history of the war against the Xaros. We destroyed their leader, the General, and now you've got a knife to our throat. Why?"

"The scion knew, but then you murdered him."

"It was an…never mind." Hale looked back and watched a pair of unarmed Marines carry Shu'ul toward them.

"Put the navigator on the ground," Tuk said. Hale gave the Marines a slight nod and they tossed it forward.

Shu'ul rose up like a snake and slithered behind the larger Ruhaald.

The silver cords fell away from the human prisoners. They ripped their restraints away and scrambled off the sled, never taking their eyes off the Ruhaald as they put space between themselves and their former captor.

"Ten percent of a rotation." Tuk pointed a few tentacles at Hale. "Choose quickly. Choose wisely." It lifted Shu'ul onto the sled then jumped behind the controls. The aliens left in a cloud of dust.

One of the armor-less Marines, the one with a shock of wild red hair, rubbed at his face and neck.

"Sir? You serious about that Kirk Syndrome? I do feel a bit woozy, but I think that's just from the pain cords they were using," he said.

"Relax, soldier." Hale turned him toward the firebase and walked him forward at a quick pace. "Your freckles aren't Kirk Syndrome. In fact, there's no such thing as Kirk Syndrome."

"You were just bullshitting him?"

"Yes, now hurry and get behind those armored walls before it realizes I pulled a fast one."

****

Hale looked at the timer on his gauntlet. Two hours until the Ruhaald deadline.

"Think I've got it," said Devins, his company's last commo Marine. "There's a relay on Luna still up and running. All the ones on the dark side of the moon are off-line. Guess that giant flare we saw had something to do with that. You heard what that was, boss?" she asked from within an open closet full of dangling fiber-optic cables. Raw sunlight filtered through floating dust, glinting off the specks like they were made of gold.

"No, I was busy fighting for my life against Xaros drones and then the big one in red armor. Time is of the essence, Devins."

"Check…check." She took a grease pencil off her ear and made an X against a panel. "Not that one but the telemetry data's coming from one of these…" She unsnapped a data wire running to the hole in the ceiling and plugged it into a panel on the other side of the closet.

A green icon lit up on Hale's gauntlet.

"I've got a connection. Good work, Devins."

"Am I better than Egan?"

"Yes, but if you tell him I said that, I'll deny it." Hale cycled through channels and opened a line to Phoenix high command. He waited a full minute before General Robbins' face came up on his gauntlet.

"Captain Hale, I was getting worried."

Hale gave a rundown on everything he'd encountered since leaving Phoenix as well as the Ruhaald ultimatum.

"That's quite the offer," Robbins said. "The

situation hasn't improved in Phoenix, and there's still no contact with the surviving ships around the moon or with Mars command. I don't need you to make a tense situation any worse."

Hale felt a wash of fear spread through his chest.

"Sir, you can't mean…"

"Listen, son, the doughboys are an expendable asset. They are mass-produced like bullets. If the Ruhaald want them, let them have them. The entire garrison can be replaced within a day once we have the tubes up and running again."

Hale opened his mouth, but no words came out.

"You copy my last? Are we losing this connection already?"

Devins waved a hand to get Hale's attention. She jiggled the connection to the transmitter above and static washed across Hale's gauntlet. Once Hale had his eyes on her, she twisted a thumb up and down at him.

Hale looked at the general, then thought of the last words Bolin said to him. The Marine tapped a thumbs-down against his thigh, beyond where the video feed to Robbins could see it.

Robbins' image switched off.

"How long will this interference last, sir?" Devins asked. "Because I sure didn't hear anything about handing the doughboys over to be murdered. Nope. Not one word about that."

"Hold tight." Hale checked the timer on his gauntlet. There wasn't much time before the fate of the doughboys was decided for him.

****

Torni kept a grip on Bodel as she rode atop the armored skirt over his treads. As she looked up at the Ruhaald cruiser hanging over the city, she felt a surge of anger. Bodel had given her the rundown during the drive from Harrison's crash site: the aliens' aid during the Xaros attack, their subsequent betrayal and demands. The Ruhaald and Naroosha had rammed a knife into humanity's back, and now everyone beneath the occupation waited for the twist that would rain down death and destruction.

"Bastards," Torni muttered.

Bodel rolled toward Camelback Mountain, the massive doors already open.

Torni felt a strange vibration through her shell as they neared. They passed a work detail of construction equipment removing tons of rock from the road leading to the main entrance. The blasted remains of a rail cannon emplacement directly over the big doors filled her with dread. There had been one hell of a fight here.

Bodel rolled into the open bay and slowed to a stop. Torni jumped off, the vibration growing stronger. Soldiers and technicians repaired the interior, which looked like a hurricane had hit it.

"What's wrong?" Bodel asked.

"There's something...some kind of energy. I can't explain it," she said.

Bodel pointed to a blackened patch on the floor.

"The General died right there. His armor survived. It's all under that tarp, white garbage truck."

Torni took a step toward the truck and ripples broke out over her shell.

A mechanic with a toolbox in hand froze mid-step when he saw the display over Torni.

"You didn't see anything. Keep moving," Bodel said.

The mechanic nodded and walked off with a renewed purpose to his steps.

"The armor is...I don't know...messing with me," she said. "I don't exactly have all the ins and outs of this drone thing down. What happened in orbit damaged something. Not sure if I can ever fix it. Did you kill him? The General?"

The Xaros master was one of the last things she saw before her biological death. The memory of the being's touch made her want to crawl beneath a bed and hide.

"Elias got the killing blow. I helped," Bodel said.

"Elias. Is he still angry with me for pulling Malal out of his hands? I ask because he's big and might rip my limbs off for fun."

"Probably, but I'll see that he leaves you alone. You're on the side of the angels now. Stay there."

"Where is he? And Hale? Kallen?"

Bodel's hands balled into fists. He transformed back into his walker configuration and stomped off.

"Something I said?" Torni's shoulders drooped. *What am I supposed to do now?* Lafayette was gone. The Crucible occupied. She was legally dead and no longer a Marine. If her shell malfunctioned again, she'd end up eating a gauss bullet before she could explain that she was a Xaros drone, but a friendly one.

Torni bowed her head and folded her hands in prayer. *"Fader vår som är i himmelen helgat varde ditt namn—"*

Wind rushed into the bay, blowing a cloud of dust into the air that cut visibility down to mere feet. Torni heard the thump of landing struts against metal. Light rippled within the cloud and a Mule took shape next to

Torni as its cloak fell away, the words *Gott Mit Uns* emblazoned on the hull.

Those in the bay watched in stunned silence as the ramp lowered. Durand came down, removing her helmet and gloves. She stopped when she recognized Torni.

"I heard you were dead. You look good," the pilot said.

"What're you doing down here? Does Valdar have a plan to deal with the Ruhaald?"

"Of course he does. It's Valdar. The man always has a plan. In fact, I'm down here to find Hale and his bunch of killers. I'm going to take them up to the Crucible, ruin some squids' day. Maybe make a pit stop along the way, cause some trouble. You interested?" Durand asked.

"I'm up for that. Mind if I hang out in the back until we're ready to leave?"

"Suit yourself." Durand pulled a pack of cigarettes from a pocket and lit one.

"Aren't you going to go find Hale?"

"I just landed a Mule in the middle of a garage. I figure all the very important people who might know where Hale is are on their way down here to scream at me." She took a deep drag and closed her eyes in ecstasy. "I will wait."

CHAPTER 9

Steuben jumped off the firing step and landed into a roll. He used his forward momentum to bring him to his feet and strode across the bay. Three suits of armor sat in their travel configuration, their breastplates open, exposing the fortified wombs within. The Karigole sniffed at the air, detecting an unusual chemical.

Three men in skintight bodysuits sat in a semicircle. Each held the tip of an oversized lance, the other end gripped by the armor. One of the men squeezed a bit of clear oil onto a cloth and rubbed it along the tapered point of the lance.

"What is that?" Steuben asked.

"Do you ask about the *kopia*?" a dark-haired man asked. "Our lances?"

"Perhaps the *obcy* wonders why we dismount and

lose our synch to do this?" a blond asked.

"Maybe he's never seen a Hussar outside the armor," a bald man said, winking at Steuben.

"The enemy could attack at any moment, and you are engaged in some manner of ritual?"

"In times past," said Vladislav, according to the name stenciled on his shoulder, "the *kopia* was a gift from the Polish king to his Hussars. Colonel Carius gave these to us when we earned our spurs after the Battle of Aurukun."

"Told us of the Hussars that saved Western civilization at the Battle of Vienna in 1683," Adamczyk said as he stood up and ran a cloth down the length of his lance.

"As if three *polski* wouldn't know about that day," Ferenz snorted.

"The Marines keep to their own history," Steuben said. "Your kind are more…fragmented. I saw the Smoking Snakes fight on Takeni. I've fought beside the Iron Hearts. None of you are the same."

"Bonding with the suits is…different. We aren't mere crunchies that throw on power armor and flail around the battlefield. We are armor." Vladislav hit a fist against his chest. "We choose our lineage. Forge our names in battle."

"Do you think Carius will let us add wings to our armor? After that charge he'll have to," Ferenz said.

"He might, but where will we find the ostrich feathers?"

Steuben felt a low thrum through his boots. He removed a glove and pressed the bare flesh against the floor. The thrum picked up, teasing the outer limits of his hearing.

"Something wrong, *obcy*?" Adamczyk asked.

"You don't hear that?" Steuben pressed the side of his head to the floor.

The Hussars cocked their ears to the side, then shrugged.

"You may be death itself on the battlefield," Steuben stood up, "but I've met rocks with better senses. Suit up…something is awry."

****

Cortaro, fully armored and leading a team of Marines, stopped at the top of a short metal staircase leading to a long tunnel.

"There's nothing here, Steuben," the gunnery sergeant said.

Steuben pushed past a Marine and snarled.

"There," the Karigole said, pointing to a set of armored doors mounted on rollers at the end of the hallway, "how can you not hear it? Like the whine of those tiny insects that suck your blood."

"The only thing down here is the supply tunnel leading to bunker Alpha Two," Corporal Montes said in a loud whisper. "It blew after the squids overran the bunker."

"Wait…" Cortaro looked at a map of the tunnels running to and from the firebase, "did the men in that bunker collapse the tunnels, or was it done here, at X-Ray?"

"Uh…Major Paul was in the command center when that happened. She died when the squid fighters hit," Montes said.

"If you don't know, just say you don't know." Cortaro went down the stairs, his rifle trained on the sealed doors. "The last situation report in the logbook we recovered from the command center listed this tunnel as impassable."

"There's something beyond those doors." Steuben strode past Cortaro and went to the metal slabs. Steuben touched his hands to the door, then pressed his ear to it and slammed a fist against the door.

"*Madre de Dios!* You trying to tell them we're over

here?" Cortaro backed up.

"There is at least ten feet of broken rock on the other side of this door. Many voids. That sound...I've heard it before." Steuben tapped his gauntlet. "Caas, is this familiar to you?"

"That's a vibro-cutter. My father worked the mines on Takeni. I used to help, know that sound anywhere," the Dotok woman said over the IR.

"I still don't hear anything," Cortaro shrugged.

"It's stopped." Steuben put his ear against the wall again. "Thumping, they're clearing by hand now."

"Fine, I believe. It's got to be the squids, right? How long until they break through?" Cortaro asked.

"Ninety minutes until the deadline. The captain needs to know about this."

****

Cortaro, Steuben and Hale huddled around Elias in the entrance bay. The three looked to Hale as he swiped map panes across his gauntlet.

"OK," Hale looked up "here's my plan. Elias, you can break through a few feet of loose rock, right?"

Elias chuckled.

"Elias breaks through the cave-in and the armor

clears our path to bunker Alpha Seven. We load the wounded onto the Hussars and we haul ass to the next supply tunnel running under old 87 to Phoenix."

"We're not going to get back in the next hour, sir," Cortaro said. "Won't be hard for the squids to figure out where we've gone."

"That's why you're going to rig the…nineteen kilos of denethrite explosives in the supply sheds to blow this place once we're clear," Hale said.

"That's not enough for the entire firebase, but I'll do what I can," Cortaro said.

"And if the route is blocked from the bunker? We will be trapped in a very narrow barrel, like fish," Steuben said.

"It's a risk we have to take. Going overland is not an option," Hale looked up to the battlements. Wind whistled through the firing slits, sending tufts of sand into the chamber.

"Storm's coming," Cortaro said. "Could be good for us. Doubt those squids know how to function when they can't see more than a few feet in front of them."

"Weather is just as cruel to both sides. Lot to do. Not a lot of time. Move out and draw fire," Hale said.

CHAPTER 10

Stacey hated the conduit room. The pale-white squares with thick black lines of separation played tricks on her eyes, seeming to merge and wander apart of their own volition whenever she made the mistake of looking at them for too long. Whether it was some optical illusion or a side effect of the process that sent her back to Earth, she wasn't sure.

Traveling via conduit was…disconcerting. She'd spend some amount of time, ranging from minutes to hours, floating in a white void, trapped with nothing but her thoughts to keep her company. Eventually, the dark lines of the conduit room would appear along with her ability to move. There'd been trips where she could have sworn she saw the lines, only to have them fade away. Some nights she woke in a cold sweat, the memory of the squares racing through her mind.

She thought the others meant to send her back to Earth, but they'd sealed the door behind her after throwing her in with all the grace and care of a bar bouncer ejecting a rowdy drunk. She was up to her fortieth hour in confinement, assuming the mental coping tricks she'd learned from e-mails traded with Elias were working. He hadn't responded to any of her messages since she helped Malal recover a codex of the entity's research. She couldn't really blame Elias for cutting her off, not when he'd seen firsthand the trail of dead laid by Malal's actions.

The armor soldier fought sensory deprivation by visualizing old anime movies in his mind. Stacey preferred memorized talks from Technology, Education, Design symposiums. She'd dreamed of giving a speech to the groups when she was a little girl, but the Xaros put an end to that wish.

The room had to have some sort of temporal distortion field to it; in the last twenty hours of mind games, she'd yet to feel hungry, thirsty or tired. It was possible she'd messed up her count, jumbled the playlist in her mind. The room was playing tricks on her—had to be.

Stacey recalled a TED talk where she'd sat in the front row: her grandfather discussing his grand vision for Saturn colonies. The sound of applause in the darkness…the click of Ibarra's cane as he came from behind the curtain…

The door opened with a hiss. Stacey's head snapped up and she saw Wexil walk into the room, two other ambassadors behind him.

The Vishrakath looked at her and motioned for her to get up, like he was summoning a domesticated animal.

Stacey returned a hand gesture that might not have translated well.

"Why am I not surprised that you're behind all of this?" she asked.

"Earth survives." Wexil's patrician nose rose slightly with the words. "The Xaros were defeated, thanks to the Ruhaald and Naroosha fleets *I* allowed to join the battle. Don't think that your begging at Congress meant anything of substance."

"Can Vishrakath actually reach up and pat themselves on the back? I don't know what you really look like. Maybe you're just a giant sphincter full of teeth." Stacey kept a veil of contempt over her words, hiding the thrill she felt that Earth may have truly defeated the invasion force.

"The Xaros were defeated, then the Naroosha and Ruhaald seized control of the Crucible and the skies over your world. They will rain down enough nuclear bombs to render Earth's surface uninhabitable to a microbe for the next million years...if I so choose." Wexil clasped his hands behind his back and strode toward her.

"Why? Why would you do this? We are *allies*! Earth's fleets would have gone to the Ruhaald's aid—to anyone's aid—and fought the Xaros. How could the Qa'Resh and the Alliance have authorized this?"

"Listen to me, child, the Alliance is dead. After the Qa'Resh allowed your little expedition to save the worthless Dotok, and after the Qa'Resh aided you against the Toth...it was obvious to myself and many other ambassadors that our union was a fraud. We joined this Alliance to stand together against the Xaros, not play favorites and risk everything for the sake of those who will be little more than footnotes in the annals of history."

"Bull. You've been angling to control Bastion since before Pa'lon ever arrived. Humanity had to trade all but a few hundred thousand souls to get that Crucible. You think we'd pay that price and just let species far from the fight decide our fate? I hope you burn in hell."

"We decided to send the probe that worked with your namesake to create a fleet strong enough to beat the Xaros before they completed the Crucible. The only reason your race survives is because those 'far from the fight' decided your loss would benefit that whole. Instead of thanks you give us insubordination and work behind our backs with the Qa'Resh. But such concerns are past us."

Stacey got to her feet, her legs and back surprisingly pain-free, given how long she'd sat in the corner.

"Hardly. You need the Crucible to fight the Xaros, to attack their home world, their Apex. You saw the report from the Marine taken prisoner by the enemy. The Crucible is a fragile thing. All it takes is one solid hit from the hundreds of macro cannons around the solar system to blow it into toothpicks. Don't think we'll let you take over our…world…why are you smiling?"

Wexil chuckled. "You thought you could keep Malal on Earth, force our hand into sending you aid. We lose the Crucible, we lose Malal, we're back at square one against the Xaros. Yes, you had leverage over us. *Had.* That all changed once the Naroosha ship returned from Earth."

"You have Malal? Here?"

"We do. It is a most intriguing creature. I don't know why the Qa'Resh kept it—and the bargain you negotiated—hidden from the rest of us. I had to smuggle in Toth malicious code over the course of centuries to adjust my personal AI in order to dig out those details from the Bastion mainframe."

"Listen to me. You don't know what the thing is. What it's capable of. Anthalas. The Jinn. You need to hand it over to the Qa'Resh before it gets loose and—"

"The Qa'Resh are locked away in their crystal city. They are of no significance. The secret to constructing jump gates is being distributed to all races loyal to me, all courtesy of Malal. I know what it wants, and only the Vishrakath can give it to him. There is only one piece missing from defeating the Xaros: procedurally generated humans. That is where you come in."

Stacey's jaw clenched.

"The Ruhaald and Naroosha forces were enough to seize the orbitals, but the procedural-generation facilities are buried beneath your mountain cities. The cost of extracting the technology and raw materials would be excessive. You will go back to Earth, under guard, and convince your people to hand over what we need without delay. Do this, and we will return your home world to you and then our association will be at an end," Wexil said.

"You're going to make yourself an army to fight the Xaros, aren't you? But they won't be proccies with free will—they'll be brainwashed slaves. You'll feed them into the grinder to spare the lives of your precious Vishrakath."

"Many more races than just mine will benefit from the procedurals. Do I sense reticence? This was the plan from the beginning, the plan you and your grandfather agreed to, with a slight modification to stop your kind from saying 'no.'"

Stacey's hands balled into fists.

"You've thrown everything Bastion and the Qa'Resh worked for right out the window so you could be the one that pulls the strings?"

Stacey had an epiphany. The protective force fields were still down.

She swung a punch that hit Wexil's jaw with a crack. The ambassador stumbled back, sputtering and waving his hands in shock.

Stacey had never done well during her combatives courses at Officer's Candidate School, but she'd passed the training. She kicked Wexil in the knee and sent him to the floor with a yelp, then she slammed an elbow against the side of his head with a satisfying thump. She raised a foot to crush his fingers when one of the other two ambassadors that had arrived with Wexil grabbed her from behind and pinned her arms to her sides.

The attacker kicked her feet out from under her and twisted her around. She landed facedown on the deck, the weight of the other pinning her to the ground.

Stacey tried to wriggle free, butting her head backwards, trying to connect to anything. The grip stayed strong, and Stacey stopped struggling. She'd save her energy for her next chance to lash out.

Wexil sat up and ran a hand down the side of his face…which had a crack running from the temple to his jawline. The Vishrakath touched the wound gingerly, then scowled at Stacey.

"If you will not convince your people to cooperate," Wexil said as he got up and put a heel to her throat, "then I will have the Toth do the job for me. They have their foibles, but they will honor a contract."

Wexil turned and left the conduit chamber.

The ambassador pinning her to the ground left her on the floor. She waited until the others left before pounding one of the hated white tiles in frustration.

****

The center of the great Congress on Bastion was a giant stone dais with a diameter slightly wider than a football field. Hexagon-shaped pillars a few feet across made up the entire dais, forming ridges around the circumference from the flat top down to the deep darkness below.

Ambassadors had theorized as to the dais' origins for several centuries. Was it a relic from the Qa'Resh home world? An interesting geological construct from a lost planet? Created solely by the crystalline entities with some unknown association to their opaque ways of thinking? There were many questions, but never any answers from the Qa'Resh.

Before the mutiny, only the Qa'Resh ever appeared on the dais. Now, a single occupant stood there still as a statue, his head against his chest, within a shielded hemisphere at the center.

Malal.

An ambassador pod hovered over the lip of the dais and floated toward Malal. It stopped a few yards away and a few inches over the bare stone. The dark glass dome over the pod lifted up.

Wexil stood up and smoothed over his black tunic before taking a gentle step onto the tightly packed stone rods. There was not a single grain of sand beneath his foot. For all the centuries he'd attended Congress, none had ever set foot onto the dais. This was the place for the Qa'Resh, not the others.

He looked up, admiring the beautiful light coming down from an unseen source. Such marvelous engineering, too bad the Qa'Resh would never share the secret to the construction.

Wexil hefted a box from the pod and carried it with both hands to Malal's prison. He set it down, then took a small device from a pocket. With a click, the shielding around the ancient entity faded away.

The Vishrakath ambassador waited a moment for a reaction. When there was none, he cleared his throat. Still nothing.

"Malal?"

Malal's head snapped up and his featureless face twisted toward Wexil.

"Release me," Malal said, the words generated by vibrations in his omnium shell.

"In good time," Wexil said. "There is much to be done."

"My bargain is with the Qa'Resh, not you."

"The Qa'Resh are not to be trusted. They spent thousands of years trying to organize an opposition to the Xaros, and instead of abiding by the will of the very body they created, they chose to protect a new member. A race that should never have been contacted, let alone inducted to the organization. A race that acted beyond our council, broke our decrees."

"The humans," Malal said.

"The human issue broke this grand alliance apart.

For those truly willing to work toward the greater good and defeat the Xaros, there is a future. A future that you and I will create." Wexil raised his arms to the grand silence around them.

"I have a price."

"It will be paid in full—by the humans, no less—either on Earth or with what we prepare for you." Wexil bent over and opened the box. Dozens of data crystals glittered in the light.

"That is not all I require." Malal opened his arms and lifted a foot off the ground. His chest rippled aside, revealing a spherical device made up of thin strips of metal, a dark light held within.

"The governor remains until your end of the bargain is complete. We know what you are capable of. None of us are fools."

"You betrayed the humans and the Qa'Resh. I have been around this galaxy since before the Vishrakath first crawled out of your jungles and looked at the skies in fear. The humans are vicious and deadly. The Qa'Resh…cunning and patient. Poor traits for your enemies to have."

Wexil shook his head. "The feral humans will be taken care of shortly. They will survive as pliant servants or not at all. The Qa'Resh are irrelevant, exiled within their city. As for their cunning, they thought they could hide the *gate* you seek."

Malal's form reknit itself. His face became more defined, a mirror of Wexil's features.

"You found the place..." Malal said, floating around Wexil. "You know where I can finally have my apotheosis?"

"We do." Wexil removed a small tile from his other pocket. The omnium metal glowed faintly as script jumped from the surface, changing, depending on how the light struck it. "A small token from the site. A recreation, naturally, but I'm sure you recognize the craftsmanship. In fact, we found it long before the Qa'Resh ever did. When they failed to mention its discovery to us over a thousand years ago, the Vishrakath knew our hosts were not the benevolent beings they made themselves out to be."

"Where is it?" Malal reached out to Wexil. His fingers nearly touched the ambassador's face, but the governor within Malal's chest glowed and the entity's fingertips melted before they could caress Wexil.

Malal withdrew his hand and the drooping fingers reknit themselves.

"In time. First, you will share the knowledge you retrieved from the laboratory—construction plans for our own jump gates. Omnium reactors are nearly complete in many systems. Once we have our own gates and massive fleets of human-crewed ships—compliant humans with no thought of surviving the battle—we will end the Xaros threat once and for all. Then, and only then, will we pay your price," Wexil said.

"A grand plan. One that will not play out for…centuries?"

"The Xaros will plod toward inhabited worlds, but they are slow to traverse the void. We may lose some members of my new alliance—the Ruhaald, the Naroosha—but what is the loss of a few more races when the rest of the galaxy will be saved? We will have our counterattack ready long before the Xaros can threaten those who truly matter."

"You mean the Vishrakath."

Wexil shrugged. "Survival of the fittest."

"I make my pacts in blood, but you have none. Here, your soul is cold." Malal held a hand out to the box full of crystals. One leapt out and landed in his palm. Strands of light crept into the crystal.

"What do you mean about my blood?" Wexil looked down at his hands, confused.

"Irrelevant. This requires my concentration." The definition in Malal's face faded away.

Wexil pushed the box closer to Malal then backed

away and reactivated the force field. He turned in place, looking over the entirety of the Congress. Ambassador pods stretched into the darkness. It all belonged to him now. Eventually, the entire galaxy would belong to the Vishrakath.

CHAPTER 11

Elias waited in front of a pair of metal doors in his travel configuration. His torso shifted from side to side like he was a prize fighter about to make his entrance to the ring.

"Five minutes until the deadline," Hale said from beside the doors.

"Let me go," Elias said. "The enemy's leaning forward in the saddle, ready to attack. Better I break through than wait for them to blow the doors. You crunchies won't do well if that happens."

Hale looked down the tunnel, packed with soldiers, Marines and doughboys. The freed prisoners wore what they could scavenge from wall lockers and the dead. None were fully armored for battle but they carried rifles. Hale's motley crew was filthy, tired and pissed off.

At least they're motivated to get the hell out of here, he thought.

"First Sergeant, explosives set?" Hale asked.

"Trip wires and timer good to go," Cortaro said. "I agree with Elias, sir. I don't want to be here when the squids decide it's time for us to pay up."

"Elias. Go."

The Iron Heart rammed his fingers into the seam between the doors and shoved them aside. Rocks the size of Hale's head tumbled down around Elias. Bright light shined through the gaps from the other side of the cave-in. Hale's mouth went dry as he realized just how close the Ruhaald had come to reaching the gate.

Elias reached back then punched a boulder, knocking it into the tunnel like a cork out of a champagne bottle. His treads lurched forward as he batted rocks out of his way.

High-pitched clicks came from beyond the barricade. Truncated bolts of lightning zapped through the gates and hit the opposite wall with a hiss. Hale swung his rifle around the opening.

Elias had a squirming Ruhaald in each hand. He swung one into the ceiling, killing it in a splatter of gore. He smacked the other against the side of the tunnel, crushing its helmet. He twisted his body around and beat the alien against the other side then threw the very dead alien down the tunnel and charged forward.

Shots from the Ruhaald energy weapons ended seconds later.

"Clear!" Hale waved to his charges and they clambered over the rocks and into the tunnel.

Hale went the opposite direction until he came to Vladislav at the back of the access way. Lieutenant Bolin lay strapped to a litter atop the armor plates over the Hussar's treads.

Bolin opened his eyes and reached for the Marine. Hale gripped the man's hand and touched his head.

"Hey, we're getting out of here," Hale said.

Bolin nodded slightly. Tiny black dots marred his face like a constellation. Hale saw more of the marks on Bolin's hand.

"You take care of my boys. They're dumb, smelly, but they're loyal," Bolin said. "Loyalty…it has to go *down* the chain of command more than up. Right?"

"You know your Patton. I'll bring them home, I promise."

Bolin squeezed Hale's hand.

Yarrow jumped onto Vladislav and held his gauntlet over Bolin's chest. The corpsman looked at the readings, then to Hale. Yarrow, his hand blocking Bolin's line of sight, nodded toward their escape route.

Hale took the hint and headed back.

"Sir, I need to get him to a surgical facility," Yarrow sent over IR. *"He's slipping away. Can't say that in front of the patient."*

"Don't you lose him."

"Your lips, God's ears."

Steuben stood at the entrance holding a smashed piece of equipment that looked like it had once been an oversized bullhorn.

"A Dotok stone burner, after Elias ran over it," Steuben said.

"You enjoy being right about everything?" Hale asked.

"We could use another. Digging through your planet's regolith with my bare claws is inefficient and slow," Steuben said.

"Good point. Keep your eyes open for one."

The last of the Marines passed by and into the tunnel. Hale slapped them on the shoulder, calling a few out by name as they went. Caas filled the entrance and nodded to Hale. The armor would bring up the rear.

Hale and Steuben took off at a jog, broken light strips providing spotty illumination as they went. The captain saw something dangling from the ceiling near a sparking light and slowed to a stop.

Viscera dripped from a Ruhaald corpse smooshed against the ceiling like a bug against a car windshield. One intact arm dangled from the rest of the remains, a Dotok stone burner wrapped in the tentacles.

Bile rose in his throat at the thought of touching the gooey remains of the alien, but that device would prove useful.

"Steuben, lift me up. I think I can—"

Caas reached over Hale's head and plucked the stone burner out of the Ruhaald's death grip. There was a slurping noise, and the body fell off the ceiling and landed with a wet plop between Hale and Steuben. Dark liquid splattered on Hale's visor. He backed away, wiping furiously against his faceplate.

"Ah…man." Hale fought to keep his last tube of nutrient paste in his stomach.

"Is it functional?" Steuben asked Caas.

"Haven't seen one in a while…the buttons aren't in Dotok but the power cell and oscillation ring are intact. Should be good," she said.

"Caas, what is with Elias?" Hale pointed to an armless Ruhaald body on the other side of the tunnel. "This isn't like him."

"We all grieve differently. You're holding up the

Hussars. Now, you want to get moving or you want to grease my treads?"

Hale raised a hand in surrender and took off down the tunnel.

****

The inner chamber of Firebase X-Ray was deathly silent. No curt commands from sergeants, no grunted responses from the doughboys that called the place home. The once ever-present whine of hydraulics had ceased hours ago.

Half-eaten food rations and overturned ammo cases littered the floor.

The only orderly object was a large case in the center of the chamber. There was no trash within four feet of the case, as if what was inside repelled garbage. A small piece of orange paper was stuck to a recessed handle in the middle of the case.

Sparks erupted around the heavy doors, flaring like a sudden fireworks display then fading away. One of the doors leaned back, severed from the hinges that connected it to the frame.

It tilted over and slammed to the ground, kicking loose paper into the air.

The scorpion tank that dislodged the door swept the tail-mounted cannons across the room, then backed away from the entrance. As dozens of Ruhaald soldiers rushed into the room, teams broke away and raced down the connecting hallways.

A pair of taller aliens, both their bodies under strain from the hormonal imbalance caused by absence of their scion, stopped next to the case.

"If the humans aren't here, then where are they? How could First Tuk let them escape?" one asked.

"The search has just begun. Wait until we've swept the entire compound before we alert the First. This will knock him out of the contest. The mantle will be mine for the taking," the other said.

"Not if I find the humans first…What does that say?" The first gestured to the note on the case. "Do you know their symbols?"

"The speaker cubes translate words, not images." The second leaned closer to the note and examined it.

Had either of the Ruhaald been able to read English, they would have seen the words SURPRISE ASSHOLES! Both alien soldiers were too well disciplined to open the case and trigger the trip wire to the denethrite explosives in the case and rigged around the firebase. But when the timer counted down thirty-seven seconds later, what the Ruhaald could or could not understand was rendered moot.

****

The tunnel shook as the force of the blast rumbled through the earth like a sudden quake. Hale slammed his back to the wall and looked up, hoping the last thing he saw wouldn't be the ceiling caving in, ending all the lives under his charge.

A wide crack cut through the ceiling and a few hunks of dense clay fell through. Hale took a tentative step away from the wall and allowed himself a sigh of relief.

Caas, following on his heels, revved her treads impatiently.

"Captain, need you to the front," Cortaro said over the IR.

"Balls," Hale said and took off at a run.

At the tip of the column, Elias idled next to a slight bend. His aegis shield bore a smoking crater in the center. Cortaro crouched behind the shield, his rifle pointed down the tunnel.

Hale slid to a stop.

"They're in the bunker," Elias said. "Heavy weapons trained down the tunnel. I might get ten feet before the shield fails."

Hale swallowed hard. If the armor couldn't get through, the rest wouldn't stand a chance. And there was no way back.

"Rail cannons?" Hale asked.

"I saw energy shielding before they opened up on me," Elias said. "Thibodaux's toy can't get through."

"I heard that!" came from a Marine farther down the line.

"If I use my rail cannon in this confined space, the overpressure will kill you all," Elias said.

"I bet the enemy's on the radio right now, screaming for backup," Cortaro said.

"If we cannot go through the obstacle, then let us go around it," Steuben said, hefting the stone burner and pointing to the ceiling.

"I'm no miner," Hale said as he backed away from Steuben, "but digging up isn't a smart idea, right? How much earth is overhead?"

"Two meters," Cortaro said.

"We're six feet under, great. Won't all of that come tumbling down on our heads?" Hale asked.

"Not if I disable the safety protocols." Steuben tapped three buttons and a low whine filled the air. He angled the wide circular muzzle toward the ceiling and leaned away. Air shimmered between the stone burner and the ceiling like haze over fire.

As the ceiling disintegrated, layers of aegis armor stripped away, revealing light-gray clay mixed with rocks. Loose soil spilled into the column rising through the ceiling. The dirt flowed up the stone burner's beam and dissipated into nothing. A tear in the ground opened up and Hale saw a dark sky, run through by streaks of tan.

Steuben shifted the beam aside and gnawed away at the opening, making it wider as he swept it around in a spiral motion. The device cut off, but the whining noise grew louder as it oscillated in Steuben's hands.

Steuben hefted the Dotok equipment back, then hurled it at Elias. The armor ducked and brought his shield up as the device sailed over his head.

The burner exploded, spraying Elias' shield with shrapnel and sending tiny razor-sharp fragments bouncing off the wall. Hale felt something ping off his armored pauldrons.

Elias lowered his shield and turned his helm to Steuben.

"Really?" the armor asked.

"I will now ask for forgiveness," the Karigole said.

Elias rolled toward the opening and folded his treads back into his legs, then he jumped up and grabbed on to the edge of the hole. Hale watched as Elias' heavy sabatons vanished up through the hole Steuben made. Loose dirt billowed through the hole and poured through the tunnel like a ruddy fog.

"Storm's here," Cortaro said. He went to the base of the hole and looked up. "Brought plenty of ammo and food, no rope."

A thunderclap broke through the air. A wave of compressed air traveling from the bunker slapped Hale off balance and left his ears ringing.

"Elias!" Hale ran to the opening.

The Iron Heart bent over the top, his rail-cannon vanes glowing red hot as they slid over his shoulder and onto his back. Dark-red whiffs of sand swirled around the soldier like he was a demon rising from the fires of hell.

"I took care of the bunker. Get up here." Elias stepped away from the hole.

"Alley-oop," Cortaro said, lacing his fingers over a braced knee.

Hale got a running start and planted a foot in Cortaro's hands. The gunnery sergeant lifted as Hale jumped off, the combined strength of two power armor suits sending the captain straight up.

Hale got an elbow over the lip of the hole and hauled himself out and into a sandstorm. Wind whistled over his helmet, blasting his face with grit and flakes of sand. Elias stood a few feet away, his helm nearly invisible in the gloom. The sky was a deep-brown abyss. There was no light, no mountains, no way to tell one direction from another.

He thought of the pocket dimension the *Breitenfeld* found itself in after leaving Anthalas, remembered standing on the edge of the flight deck beside Sergeant Torni and feeling a deep emptiness in his soul.

"Compass is shot," Elias said. "We'll get precisely jack and squat for comms in all this."

"Don't be so pessimistic. Strike Marines, we adapt and overcome." Hale had to raise his voice over the storm. He looked at a map screen on his gauntlet. The bunker was a little over a hundred yards east of old Highway 87, which Hale knew had been rebuilt since the Xaros scoured the Earth's surface clean.

Hale looked around and saw smoldering fires in the distance, a low yellow smudge against the blowing sand.

"Elias, that the bunker you destroyed?"

"No, it's a Girl Scout cooking fire. Yes, that's the bunker."

"Turn on your floodlights. I might have us a way home." Hale faced the fires, made a sharp left turn, and started walking. He'd learned basic land navigation in the forests of Virginia, and one of the first skills that came with that training was to learn his pace count. One of the hardest tests was to navigate at night.

Hale counted each time his left heel struck the ground. Every forty-third step meant another hundred meters. He glanced over his shoulder at Elias and saw a cloud of diffuse white light around the Iron Heart like a beacon.

After his ninetieth step, Hale stopped. The sandstorm had grown so thick that he could barely see his feet. The light from Elias faded to nothing with each gust of wind. Hale felt utterly alone and had an urge to abandon his idea and run back to Elias.

"No, not stopping here." Hale took another ten steps, then his foot pressed against something solid. He bent down, wiped sand away and uncovered black glass.

The Ibarra Corporation patented a road surface that doubled as solar panels long before Hale had been born. Everything Ibarra built on Earth since the Xaros invasion ran off solar, and using Highway 87 as a resupply and power route was exactly the kind of synergy Ibarra was known for. Hale'd found the road that ran to and from Phoenix.

Turning toward Elias' beacon, Hale pointed to the

right, toward the southwest and to Phoenix, then he laid his rifle on his foot, the muzzle pointed to the right. He took a small flashlight off his belt and unleashed a powerful beam. He pointed it toward Elias and chopped his hand in front of the beam as a signal to everyone climbing out of the tunnel. All they had to do was walk toward his light.

A few minutes later, Steuben emerged from the sandstorm.

"Your planet," the Karigole said, putting a hand on Hale's shoulder, "I'm starting to hate it."

"Is everyone out?" Hale asked.

"The armor allowed us to use them as ladders. The rest will be here soon."

"Direct everyone to my right. Tell them to keep their feet on the road and it'll get us back to Phoenix." Hale waved to a line of Marines coming through the storm.

The hulking shadows of doughboys came next, each with a hand on the armor of the bio-construct in front. One broke away and grabbed Hale by the arm.

"Sir! No leave!" Nickel shouted.

"I'm fine, Nickel. Get back with the rest."

The doughboy shook his head vehemently.

"Dark. Nickel stay."

Hale wondered if the doughboy meant that Nickel would protect Hale from what lay in the darkness, or that Hale would protect him.

"Fine, big guy, just stand still." Hale jogged over to a Hussar and told Ferenz how to get back to Phoenix.

"Sir?" came a plaintive wail from the darkness.

Hale finished his conversation with the armor and found Nickel, standing right where he'd left him.

The doughboy grabbed Hale by the hand, enveloping it with meaty paws.

"Sir no leave." Nickel tightened his grip.

"Keep your feet on—umph." Hale tried and failed to pull his hand away. "Just keep your feet on the black glass road and we'll make it home."

Hale started walking. One hand on his rifle, the other with Nickel.

****

The sandstorm had died down, leaving the night sky starless beneath a sheen of dirt streaking across the sky. Hale kneeled with one knee on the black glass, nervous as he checked over his suit's systems. Visibility had increased, allowing Hale to see Elias and Caas at the front of the formation and the rest of the column.

A rocky hill rose just beyond the road, the slope disappearing into the dusty air. By his map, Hale knew the hillside extended into more uneven terrain and hilltops. That terrain feature meant they were near another vital part of Phoenix's defenses.

Weiss and a pair of lower-ranked Marines walked a few dozen yards off the road, digging the toes of their boots into the dirt.

"Find anything yet?" Hale called out to Weiss.

"We ain't found—" Weiss looked down. He kicked a tuft of sand into the air, then bent over and lifted a handle camouflaged as a coarse rock up on a hinge.

"That'll take us straight to Phoenix," Hale said. He waved to Elias and pointed to Weiss.

The Iron Heart rolled over to the Marine and opened a pair of heavy doors, their outer layers disguised to look like the desert floor, leading to the tunnel Hale and the rest of his team had used at the beginning of their mission.

"Wounded first," Hale said to the Hussars.

The dust storm abated as the three armor soldiers rode down the ramp. Hale made out the distant lights of Phoenix, a wan glow on the horizon. He directed the rest of the column into the tunnel and stood up.

Keeping an eye on the nearby hills, Hale tapped a

finger against his rifle as he waited for the Marines and soldiers to make their way off the road.

Out of the corner of his eye, he caught movement along a hilltop. The captain raised his rifle and looked through the scope. Stones tumbled down a rocky outcrop, and the hair on the back of Hale's neck stood up.

"Steuben, you see anything up—"

A lightning bolt struck out from the hillside and hit the road. A geyser of broken glass and rock knocked Hale off his feet and sent him tumbling through the dirt.

"Ambush!" Hale stopped his roll and saw the hilltop alive with Ruhaald weapons fire.

Another massive bolt streaked overhead and impacted between the doughboys as they scrambled for cover.

There was only one tactical option when caught in a close ambush. Hale charged up the hill, firing from the hip.

An alien raised himself over the hilltop and took aim at Hale, but a gauss bullet fired from behind Hale and blasted it off its feet, sending its energy rifle bouncing down the bare rocks. Hale kept moving, his boots propelling him higher up the hill with each step.

He snapped off a high-power shot that exploded a boulder and silenced part of the alien firing line. Hale looked back and saw a dozen doughboys racing toward him. Flashes of light from gauss rifles crept toward the base of the hill. The soldiers and Marines had joined his hasty attack on the ambushers, a dangerous move but a better option than sitting in the open with no cover.

He snatched a grenade from his belt and lobbed it into the air. It bounced on the trailing side of the hill with a muffled boom. His rifle quivered, ready for another high-powered shot.

A massive Ruhaald energy cannon rose over the hilltop. Hale swung his rifle around and took aim.

He didn't see the jagged bolt of electricity coming, but he felt it when it hit his chest. Searing pain stabbed through his body and sent him to a knee. His left arm refused to move, but he managed to take poor aim on the cannon by sliding his rifle along his knee.

Hale pulled the trigger and the recoil knocked him into the dirt. He saw flaming debris burst into the air—his last shot must have connected. Hale tried to sit up, but his suit refused to budge. His UI went fuzzy, a slew of error icons crossing his visor before the entire thing shut off with a blip. He felt something grab his ankle and pull him over exposed rocks.

He managed to get his chin up. A Ruhaald had him and, within seconds, had pulled the Marine into a gap between the hills and into a gully.

A heavy alien boot kicked Hale in the side hard enough to flip him onto his side against a rock wall. He tried to move, but his power armor held him like a vice.

Clicks and pops of Ruhaald language flooded Hale's ears. A many-tentacled hand clamped over his helmet and hauled him into the air. Hale saw nothing but an alien palm and felt his feet dangling in the air.

A roar filled the air and Hale fell to the ground. The Ruhaald that held him backpedaled, fumbling for a pistol on its hip. The concussion of a doughboy rifle slapped the air. The alien slammed against the rocks, its torso blown open by Hale's rescuer.

Nickel stood over Hale, rocking back and forth as his bulky rifle spat death.

Light from the muzzle flashes glinted off a Ruhaald helmet looking down over the top of the gully.

"Nickel! Nickel, look up!" Hale shouted, desperately trying to move an arm and touch the doughboy.

An alien jumped down and landed on Nickel, deflecting his next shot into the wall and blowing rocky shrapnel into the air. Nickel fell against the wall, struggling to swing his weapon to bear against the alien pressed against him. The Ruhaald stabbed a blade down into

Nickel's shoulder, piercing the armor and earning a pained grunt from the doughboy.

Nickel dropped his rifle and ripped the alien away with his uninjured arm, then he swung a haymaker. His massive fist hit a jagged rock sticking out from the wall and shattered it, and the blow continued into the side of the Ruhaald's face, knocking the alien's head clean off. A spray of blood shot out from the severed neck and Nickel kicked the body aside.

"Sir?" Nickel grabbed Hale by the chest and shook him. "Sir OK?"

"I can't move, Nickel. I need you to carry me."

Nickel, his face a mess of bleeding cuts and split lips, nodded. The doughboy glanced to the side, then shot to his feet. He raised his good arm over his head and beat it against his chest, bellowing a war cry.

A bolt of lightning struck Nickel in the side. He backpedaled, his hand against the smoking tear in his armor. Another bolt hit him in the chest, knocking him off balance. A third shot sent him to his knees.

"Sir…" Nickel crawled forward, blood dripping from his lips. "No hurt."

Nickel fell over Hale, shielding him with his body.

Hale heard the thump of heavy footsteps, then Nickel was pulled away.

Tuk popped Nickel up onto his knees. Nickel looked at the alien with hate-filled eyes and struggled weakly.

"Tuk, stop!" Hale shouted.

The Ruhaald took the ceremonial blade off Hale's armor, then held it into the air.

"No! Take me! Take me!"

Tuk slammed the blade into Nickel's skull and, after a second, pulled the knife away and let the doughboy fall to the ground. The Ruhaald wiped blood from the blade across his armor, then pointed the tip at Hale.

"We will have our scion."

The snap of gauss fire filled the distance.

Tuk tapped the dagger's hilt twice against his chest, then turned and ran off.

Hale twisted his head to Nickel. The doughboy lay motionless, a pool of blood seeping into the dirt around him. The Marine reached over, then collapsed to the ground. The din of battle faded away minutes later.

Steuben rolled Hale onto his back.

"Captain? Say something."

"Help him."

"There's nothing to be done." Steuben looked aside and said, "Get his feet." The Karigole grabbed Hale beneath his shoulders as he and another Marine lifted him up.

They carried Hale down the hillside. Dead doughboys lay where they died, crumpled against rocks, many still holding their weapons. The smell of burning plants and spilt blood hung heavy in the air.

Pain grew against Hale's chest, digging through muscle and bone like a slow-moving talon. Hale's breathing became shallow and his vision darkened. He closed his eyes and fought against the pain assaulting his body, and the ache spreading from his heart.

****

The aid station beneath Camelback Mountain smelled of iodine. Yarrow adjusted a lamp over his captain's chest and clicked his tongue as he looked over the wound. Hale, naked from the waist up, sat on a gurney. Yarrow sprayed disinfectant across the swatch of burnt flesh on Hale's chest then the corpsman peeled open a patch of synthetic skin and stretched it across the wound. Hale, his head turned to the side, didn't seem to notice.

"Second- and third-degree burns, a cracked rib." Yarrow kneaded his fingertips along the edges of the patch. "Your armor took the brunt of that hit. The electricity fried your power systems. Better that than you, am I right?"

"Who else did we lose?"

"They targeted the doughboys," Cortaro said from the other side of the small curtained-off exam area. "Minor injuries to soldiers and Marines."

"How many did we lose?"

Cortaro folded his arms across his chest. "All of them. They followed you up the hillside before the rest of us even realized what was happening. Squids cut them down before most could reach you."

"And Elias? Caas?"

"They got in a scuffle with scorpion tanks. By the time that fight was over, the rest of the Ruhaald had fallen back to waiting shuttles."

"How's the pain?" Yarrow held up an auto-injector. "I can give you something that might leave some of the sting," he said, holding up a second auto-injector, "or something that won't let you count to ten for a few hours."

Hale sat up, his brow furrowed.

"Where's Matthias? Bolin?"

"Matthias is in surgery. He'll be fine," Yarrow said. He swallowed hard and glanced at Cortaro.

"I'm sorry, sir." Cortaro stepped aside and opened the curtain. There was one other lit exam room, the shadow of a laden gurney cast against the flimsy walls.

"No…" Hale struggled to his feet and slapped Yarrow's hands away when the corpsman tried to hold him back. He ripped the other curtain aside and found Bolin, eyes closed, mouth slightly agape, chest still.

Hale went to his brother's double and braced himself against the gurney, his arms trembling.

"He…we lost him two hours ago," Yarrow said. "I don't know if it was from shock, the stress of the evac or…"

"My blood," Hale said.

"The transfusion was a risk. I take full responsibility for this," Yarrow said.

"No. I'm the commander." Hale touched his chest. "My decision. My responsibility. It's my fault he's gone. I'm the one that killed him." Hale gave Yarrow a dirty look. "Why am I learning about this now?"

"I told him to keep it quiet," Cortaro said. "You were fighting to keep it all together. Word about the lieutenant would have been poison, and you…I know who he looks like, sir. This isn't something you should have dealt with in the middle of all the chaos."

"Yarrow. Leave." Hale pointed to the door.

The corpsman jabbed an auto-injector against the back of Hale's neck and left the room.

"I failed him." Hale touched Bolin's face and gently closed the dead man's mouth. "All of that…for nothing."

"No, sir, not for nothing. You saved the rest of the firebase. Another two dozen men and women are alive right now because you led them out of darkness. You understand that?"

"He's gone. He's gone forever." Hale lowered his head.

"Sir, tell me why we left Phoenix and risked everything for a firebase full of soldiers and doughies."

Hale sat on a bench, wincing as he put weight on an arm.

"We don't…we don't leave people behind."

"If you knew that we could not have brought them all home, would we have gone?"

"Of course."

"What if we only brought one back?"

"Worth it," Hale nodded slowly.

"That's right. You led on that mission because of who we are. Did it because of who we are. Don't abandon anyone to the enemy."

Hale made a pained laugh. "I left Torni behind."

"No, she chose to save civilians over herself. She made the same decision you would have. This is war, sir.

You can do everything right and still lose. As time goes on, you'll kick yourself, you'll struggle. But when it's time to close your eyes and sleep at night, you'll know you did everything you could have."

Cortaro grabbed Hale by the shoulder. "You're a fine officer, sir. I'd follow you through the gates of hell."

Hale gave him a slight smile.

A shadow passed over Hale. He looked up and found an open pack of cigarettes in front of his face.

"You could use this," said Durand, clad in her flight suit.

"Marie? How did you get down here?" Hale looked from her to the cigarettes.

"We cheated. Have a smoke, it cost three months of pay for your Standish to find this pack of Gauloises." Durand gave the pack a little shake.

Hale took one out and pressed the tip against a small dark patch on the side of the pack to ignite it. He took a deep drag and coughed. Looking down at the patch of synthetic skin over his chest, he shrugged slightly.

Cortaro shook his head when Durand repeated the offer.

Durand blew smoke out of her nose and leaned on the wall next to Hale.

"You look like shit," she said.

"Nice to see you too."

Hale took another puff and gave a satisfied grunt.

"There must be a very good reason for you to be here and not on the *Breit*," Hale said, "and for you to come looking for me."

"*Ouais*." Durand tapped ashes into a biohazard disposal box. "Valdar has a plan. It sounds like a suicide mission to me, but…" Her shoulders made a very Gallic shrug. "Naturally, he wants you in on it."

"Tell me."

Durand laid out the scheme.

Hale burned his cigarette down to the filter and snuffed the ember out against his body glove.

"When do we leave?" Hale got to his feet with a wince of pain.

"Your Karigole friend is getting everyone else loaded up. So, as soon as you're dressed," Durand said, "but the window for this to work closes in maybe six hours. *Vite vite*."

"We need a hacker." Hale looked at Cortaro.

"We know someone who knows someone. I'll take care of it. Meet you at the flight line." Cortaro hurried away.

"Hey…" Durand looked at Bolin and frowned. "He looks like your brother."

"It's complicated." Hale pulled his bodysuit over his exposed chest and zipped it shut. "Those bastards have Standish, Bailey and Egan. I'm not going to lose them too. Let's go."

CHAPTER 12

Standish scrubbed his breastplate furiously. Shaking his head at the effort, he drew his Ka-Bar and ran the point into a crease, removing a congealed mass. He, Bailey and Egan sat beside the omnium reactor. Egan snored softly, his chin against his chest.

"I'm going to smell like low tide for the rest of my life," he muttered.

Bailey, sitting on a stack of ammo boxes, sucked on a tube of nutrient paste. She smacked her lips and held the tube out to Standish. He opened his mouth and accepted a mouthful of the deep-red substance.

"Tomato soup? That's new." He spritzed his armor with an alcohol solvent and ran a cloth over his legs.

"Nah, cherry pie." Bailey squeezed the last of the paste into her mouth and tossed the empty into the omnium receiver. There was a flash as the garbage transformed into moldable energy.

"Why don't we just make me some new armor? Armor not despoiled by a Ruhaald septic tank," Standish said.

"Because the thing's making bullets and aegis plates. We're not going to put the rest of us at risk so you can smell like a rose," Bailey said.

"This thing can make anything you put into it?" Standish looked at the scanner box in the center of the reactor.

"Think so. Why?"

Standish's eyes narrowed as an idea came to him.

"No," Bailey shook her head. "Absolutely not."

"You don't even know what I was going to suggest."

"I know you, you thieving lout."

"*Alleged* thieving lout."

The lamp over the workstation blinked rapidly. Standish gave Egan's feet a gentle kick. The Marine came to with a snort and grabbed his rifle.

"Ghost boy wants you," Standish said.

"What now?" Egan got to his feet and sniffed the air. "Dear Lord, light a match."

"Ask him if this smell will come out!" Standish

shook his brush in the air.

Egan went to the lamp and put his helmet over it. There was a brief conversation before Egan set his hands onto the control station and shook his head.

"Well?" Bailey asked.

"Either of you heard of a neutron inhibitor?" Egan pecked at the keyboard and the omnium reactor hummed to life.

****

The long, heavy box Standish carried by a handle forced him to walk lopsided behind Egan, who had the other end.

"Amazing how long these hallways get when you're carrying something heavy," Standish said.

"Almost to the bunker, quit complaining," Bailey said from ahead of the other two Marines.

"I hated ammo-box drills during Strike selection," Egan muttered. "'We'll never do this in the field,' they said. 'This is just a haze,' they said."

"Here." Bailey stopped and reached up to grab a ring welded to a hatch on the ceiling. She stretched but managed only to brush her fingers against the metal.

"Bollocks," she said as she stepped aside and

Egan grasped the ring and slid the hatch open.

"Sorry, Bailey, you must be this tall to ride the space-war ride," Standish said.

Bailey gave him the finger as she climbed up Egan and into the bunker. She lowered a hand and helped guide the box through the hatch.

"Don't bump it," Egan said. "It's precision equipment."

"That does what, again?" Standish jumped up and floated into the microgravity and hard vacuum of the bunker. He glanced through the firing slits and saw a glint beyond the dome. A segment of a Naroosha silver ship passed like a shark's fin between the Crucible's thorns. He swallowed hard as the enemy vanished.

"Something about forcing free neutrons to decay within femto-seconds and making nuclear explosions impossible." Egan slid open a panel and tapped on a keypad.

"Oh, that all?" Standish edged away from a body that had come unmoored. "So we just flip a switch and leave, right?"

"Ibarra's worried the enemy could find the source of the dampening field. He wants us to stay with it and activate it on his signal," Egan said.

"What? You're telling us this *now*?" Standish

asked. "How long are we supposed to sit out here waiting for them to find us?"

"You've got a hot date, Standish?" Bailey asked.

"Egan turns that thing on and it becomes a giant 'kick me' sign, correct?"

"Ibarra said he'll arrange a distraction. If we don't do this right, a bright-white flash of light may be the last thing every man, woman and child on Earth ever sees." Egan gave the case a gentle pat.

"No pressure. That neutron thing sounds like radiation—we gotta worry?" Standish's hand brushed past his crotch.

"You have any free neutrons in you?" Egan asked.

"I don't know, do I?"

"Movement." Bailey crouched next to a firing slit. All around the Crucible, Naroosha ships left their refuge amongst the thorns and glided toward the moon.

"That our signal?" Standish asked.

"No." Egan watched as a small light on the base of the IR transmitter flickered on and off. "You'll know it when we see it."

CHAPTER 13

Stacey ran her hands against the rounded corners of the conduit room, searching for a seam or gap between the panels that might lead to a way out, a weapon, anything to make some manner of progress out of her confinement.

"Bet they could flip a switch and send me home," she said. "What're they waiting for?"

The door slid open and a pair of ambassadors armed with dead crystal spears entered, the points leveled at her.

"Did you destroy the trees in the atrium to make those?" Stacey put her hands on her hips and shook her head.

"No weapons on Bastion," a cherub-faced man said.

"So here we are, the pinnacle of technology in free

space, armed like savages. Can your AI convey irony?" Stacey slid one foot back and half turned her body from the armed men. Fighting unarmed against spears wasn't something she knew how to do and she knew any such contest would end badly for her.

Pa'lon stumbled through the door, his hands bound together with strips of cloth, his elbows wrapped tight against his sides. Wexil kicked his knees out and grabbed the Dotok by his collar.

Pa'lon stared at the floor, his shoulders low.

"What is this?" Stacey asked.

Wexil gave the Dotok a rough shake.

"They came to me," Pa'lon said, "and offered to spare my people if I returned to Earth and helped secure the proccie tubes. I told them I've been to Earth. I've seen the homes humans built for the Dotok and how our militaries trained to fight as equals. I told them that Hawaii resembles lost Dotari. They promised me my own island, protection from the Xaros. I told them that I've been to Earth, learned human customs and courtesies. Then I told Wexil, as the humans would say," he looked back to the Vishrakath, "shove that offer up your ass."

From the small of his back, Wexil took a sharpened bit of metal with a cloth-wrapped hilt and set the blade against Pa'lon's neck.

"I grow tired of this," Wexil said to Stacey. "You will return to Earth and do as I demand, or I will kill him right here, right now."

"God damn you!" She started toward her old friend but stopped when the guards shook their spears.

"Stacey," Pa'lon said calmly, "you saved us. You and the *Breitenfeld*. There is a debt. Don't trade my life and damn your future. Don't do it."

Wexil twisted the blade, letting light glint off the edges. "Your decision. Lose this one and leave the fate of Earth to the Toth, or help make our inevitable taking of the procedural technology a bloodless affair."

Stacey thought of the countless billions her decision would doom to slavery and death—of Earth subjugated—and weighed that against the life of her friend and what little integrity she had left.

"No," she said. "I'll never help you, Wexil."

"As you wish…" The Vishrakath drew the knife back then slashed it against the side of Pa'lon's neck.

"No!" Stacey reached for her old friend as he seized up.

Wexil shoved Pa'lon to the ground.

Stacey slapped a spear aside and swung a fist at a shocked guard. There was a flash and Stacey felt a thump against her chest. She looked down and saw Wexil's knife embedded just below her collarbone. There was no pain…or blood.

"What the…" Stacey touched the hilt to make sure it was really there.

"Why isn't she dying?" one of the guards asked.

Crimson light filled the conduit room. The blare of an emergency claxon stung Stacey's ears.

Wexil looked up and said, "It can't be."

"What? What is it? Yours is the only functioning AI. Tell me!" a guard demanded.

Wexil flicked his fingers in the air and a holo-field appeared. Several wormholes had opened in the void high above Bastion. A tide of dark objects emerged from glowing portals, all converging on the station.

"It's the Xaros," Stacey said. "They're here."

"Impossible…" Wexil backed away, then ran from the room.

The guards tossed their spears aside and followed. The door slid shut before Stacey could take two steps after them.

The pulsating lights and claxon continued. She turned her attention to the knife in her chest, grabbed the hilt with both hands and pulled the blade free. Instead of a gut of blood, there was a glimmer of silver within the tear in her tunic. She probed the cut with her fingers and felt the sting of ice when she touched the wound.

She jerked her hand back.

"Pa'lon?"

The Dotok had a knee bent beneath him, one hand over the side of his neck.

"I should be dead," he said.

"Me too." Stacey lifted his hand away. A slash of silver ran along his neck beneath split skin. "Dotok aren't made of…this."

"Neither are humans." Pa'lon scooped up a spear and bashed the butt against the door. The shaft broke after the third strike.

Stacey grabbed the knife off the floor and poked the point against the meat of her palm. She pressed, but felt no pain as the tip pierced her flesh. Twisting the knife slowly, she saw a glint of silver beneath her skin. She yelped and tossed the weapon away.

"What is this, Pa'lon? What did they do to us?"

"Our energy is better spent trying to get out of here. Other questions can wait." Pa'lon grabbed the knife and pressed the blade into the seam running around the door. He used both hands to try to wedge the blade home—with little success.

A deep thrum filled the air. Stacey felt the floor vibrate in tune as the sound grew stronger. She'd felt this before, when a drone had chased her through the Crucible's halls.

"Oh no…"

A dent appeared in the roof as something slammed against it. The dent grew larger as blows beat against the ceiling.

Stacey picked up a spear, considered it for a moment, then tossed it aside.

Pa'lon put an arm over her shoulders.

"Humans and Dotok stood against the Xaros on Takeni, and won. We fought side by side on Earth, and won. This may be the end for you and me, but the alliance we formed will live on. I'm glad we were friends," he said.

"I always wanted to die in bed surrounded by fat grandchildren. With you here…almost as good." Stacey took Pa'lon by the hand.

The ceiling ripped open, the haze of the gas giant's upper atmosphere blending against the star-speckled void. A pair of crystalline tendrils tipped with leaf-shaped pads reached into the conduit chamber and wrapped around the two ambassadors' waists.

Stacey didn't have time to scream before being jerked out of the room. Her world went upside down several times before she landed in a narrow trough made of glimmering crystal. Pa'lon was with her, looking as confused as she felt.

The tendril still around her waist tightened.

+You are well.+ The Qa'Resh's words pulsed through her mind.

Stacey looked up and saw the raw void overhead. Bastion shrank slowly as the Qa'Resh flew away. The mass of Xaros spread across the sky like a great murmuration. Beams of coherent light struck out from the station, ripping swaths of destruction across the Xaros.

The enemy coalesced into constructs the size of dreadnoughts. Red beams lashed out, silencing the defenses in seconds. Stacey had run through enough simulations of Earth's defenses to know Bastion wouldn't last long.

"What is this?" Pa'lon touched the shelter made up of the Qa'Resh's body.

"This is one of our hosts. They're normally quite shy," Stacey said.

+Extraordinary times. Extraordinary measures. We thought we could end the dispute with Wexil and his confederates. We failed.+

"How are we…" Pa'lon began, raising a hand over the Qa'Resh's side, "…we're in vacuum right now. Where are we going?"

+Maintaining biospheres for over a thousand notus in a single station was logistically impossible. The Bastion solution allowed an ambassador's consciousness to inhabit a simulacrum body with no biological or environmental needs. It was simple, elegant, and it worked—until now.+

"Wait...I'm not *here*?" Stacy pressed her hands against her side. "But I've been eating, drinking...everything."

+All biological processes were simulated. The details would have been revealed once the lack of aging in your true body was undeniable. The other Ibarra-designate insisted on withholding the information. He said you would take the information poorly.+

Stacey fell onto her rear end. Her fingers touched the knife wound in her chest.

"Did you know?" she asked Pa'lon.

"I knew I didn't age while I was here. The AI told me our bodies aged incredibly slowly while on Bastion, an energy field that slowed cellular decay. The AI said Bastion preferred ambassadors that could serve for long periods of time, given the difficulty in creating ambassadors that could go through the conduits...but if these aren't our real bodies..."

A cloud of deep-orange gas enveloped the Qa'Resh.

+Those ambassadors who could not accept the simulacrums were told a more acceptable explanation. The translation AI prevented unauthorized disclosures.+

"Another lie from my grandfather," Stacey said. She pressed her face into her hands, not knowing what her skin actually touched.

"You're taking us to your city, Qa'Resh'Ta, aren't you?" Pa'lon asked.

+Correct. Ninety-three percent of those on Bastion have escaped through the other conduit chambers. You had no chance of survival, which we found unacceptable.+

They passed through the cloud bank and into a canyon, the walls made of thick bands of gas the colors of sunset, the base a deep blue punctuated by lightning bolts. In the center floated a great city of crystal spires.

Stacey lifted her head up. She felt a teardrop frozen against her cheek and wiped it away.

"What now?" she asked.

+This world is untenable. We must leave. Devise a new strategy.+

"The Xaros came through wormholes—wormholes not bound to Crucible gates. Do you understand what that means? No place in the galaxy is safe," Stacey said.

+We know.+

The Qa'Resh'Ta looked like the inside of a geode. Towers of sparkling crystal soared around them as they flew toward the city center. Other Qa'Resh flit between the spires, all heading the same direction.

They swooped into a wide park dotted with the same blue-white trees that had graced Bastion. Their rescuer set them down on a wide hill covered with spindly blades of ivory grass.

"This is…" Pa'lon said, turning around, his mouth agape as he took in the city, "something extraordinary."

"It's all over," Stacey said. "The Alliance. Bastion. Every world stands alone. The Xaros will find us down here. It's only a matter of time."

A Qa'Resh flew toward them, its tentacles bound together behind its glittering bubble of a body, and came to a stop a few feet away without so much as a rustle of air. The tentacles drooped to the hilltop and deposited a swirling mass of omnium metal shaped like a man. The Qa'Resh flew straight up without a sound.

Stacey backed away as Malal's form solidified, its face a featureless mask. As it ran fingers over the thin blades of grass, shoots of white traveled up his arm.

"Ah…home," Malal intoned.

"Who is that?" Pa'lon asked.

"Not a friend." Stacey looked for any kind of cover, the presence of a Qa'Resh for protection, but the three were alone in the center of the alien city.

"That's...him, isn't it?" Pa'lon stepped between Stacey and Malal.

"Cold souls, so dim next to flames." Malal's face twisted up at an angle that would have snapped a person's neck.

High above, Qa'Resh congregated in the air, forming ever-wider circles with their bodies.

"What're they doing?" Stacey asked.

"The bargain remains. My aid in exchange for my price. I will not have it here, so we are leaving." Malal's head snapped toward her.

"How are...oh..." Stacey gripped Pa'lon's arm as a blazing point of light formed in the center of the Qa'Resh formation and spread out into a white plain. Stacey closed her eyes as the wormhole engulfed them all.

CHAPTER 14

Yarrow double-checked his gauntlet to the number stenciled on the concrete wall of a civilian bunker. The corpsman, still in his power armor with a rifle slung over his shoulder, wiped grime off his face then looked himself over. He scraped a bloodstain off his boot then twisted his head around to look down his back.

"You look like a warrior. Accept it," Cortaro said.

"They're going to see me like this. This isn't how I thought my homecoming would go. Or that there'd ever be a homecoming like this…I don't even know what to say to them." Yarrow checked his reflection against a window.

"Son, I did my hellos and good-byes with my wife and kids too many times when I was growing up in the Corps. My youngest didn't recognize me after I came back from Borneo, hid behind a chair every time I came in the room. Took her a month before she called me 'daddy' again." Cortaro's mouth tugged aside.

"Good old days had family support groups and chaplains to smooth out all the reintegration bumps. We don't have time for the perfect solution. You understand what we need in there?" Cortaro asked.

"This isn't…" Yarrow looked at his hands, then shook his head.

"I know." Cortaro put a hand on Yarrow's shoulder and gently pushed him toward the door. "We'll make this right when it's all over. You have my word."

Yarrow hit a button on the doorframe and the entrance slid open.

The civilian bunker held nearly a hundred people, all grouped into tiny family knots near cots piled high with backpacks and suitcases. Most clustered around screens mounted on walls and support pylons, watching news reports of the occupation force in the skies over their heads. Every civilian turned to the open door and stared at Yarrow and Cortaro as they entered.

Yarrow searched the room, looking for a lavender-haired woman and her—their—little girl. He found Lilith on a cot near a pylon, staring down at a data slate. Next to Lilith, curled beneath a blanket, lay a tiny figure.

A very un-Marine-like sense of panic filled Yarrow, making each step closer feel like he was walking through clay. The sound of his heavy boots caught Lilith's attention. She did a double take between him and the data slate, then set it aside carefully.

Yarrow tried to speak, but only unintelligible sounds fell from his mouth.

"You're back?" Lilith stood up, wringing her hands over her stomach.

"No. I mean yes. I'm here, but…"

The blankets stirred and a little girl sat up. She looked up at Yarrow with sleep-filled eyes, her hair a mess.

"Daddy?" she squeaked.

Yarrow knelt down in front of her. He raised his right hand and offered it clumsily to the girl. She looked at his hand like it was an alien thing.

"Your name is Mary, right?"

She nodded.

"I'm Jason Yarrow, your father."

"Mommy said you were away fighting the monsters. That's why you couldn't be with us."

"That's right. I wanted to be here, but the jump engines needed years to recharge and this thing named Malal put us all—"

Cortaro cleared his throat.

"But I'm back now. For a little while, at least."

"What's going on out there?" Lilith asked.

"That's one of the reasons we're here, ma'am," Cortaro said. "You can hack a Bastion probe. We saw you do it on Nibiru. We need your help. We need you to come with us. Right now."

"Wait just a second." Lilith raised her palms to Cortaro and glanced at her daughter. "I can't just leave her. There are other Akkadians who know the coding better than me. Nabua over on Okinawa. Even Digan in Hawaii."

"Okinawa was wiped out by the Xaros, nothing left but a smoking hole," said Cortaro. "We don't have time to reach Hawaii. You're our best hope, ma'am."

"You just waltz in here and expect me to leave our daughter behind and go-go-go where?" she asked Yarrow.

"Lil, honey, this isn't what I planned. This situation is…not good for us," Yarrow said.

"Mommy has to leave too?" Mary asked.

"No." Lilith crossed her arms over her chest.

Cortaro stepped closer to Lilith and touched her arms.

"Ma'am, you look over at those screens and you'll see a couple Naroosha and Ruhaald ships in orbit. A few hours from now, the Crucible will open up and hundreds more ships will arrive. They will take what they want from us and then they will destroy everything left behind." Cortaro looked at Mary, then back to Lilith. "We have a shot at stopping this from happening. For it to work, we need you to come with us. Help get the Crucible back under our control so we can win this fight and free the skies. We'll protect you and we'll bring you back to her as soon as possible. So I need you to find someone to look after your little one—right now—and grab whatever you need to hack into a probe. You understand?"

Lilith wiped a tear away. "I have my brother in here. He'll watch her."

"Go get him." Cortaro let her go and turned to Mary, who was touching her father's face.

"Hey, little Mary?" Cortaro asked.

"You're Cor-ta-ro," she said. "You were mean to Daddy in the movie."

"I still haven't seen it," Yarrow shrugged.

Cortaro tapped his rank stenciled onto his chest. "This means I don't have to be nice to Marines, but I'm always nice to smart little girls like you. Mary, do you know what a hero is?"

"They do brave things, like save the Dotok from monsters."

"That's right. Your mother and father have to

come with me. I need them to be heroes. I need you to do a brave thing and let them come with me," Cortaro said.

Mary's lip quivered. "But Torni was a hero. She didn't come back."

"Both your mother and father will come back. I swear it," Cortaro said.

Mary's eyes widened. Her bottom lip pouted on the verge of an out-and-out bawl.

Cortaro jabbed Yarrow with an elbow.

"We'll come right back," Yarrow said. "We just have to go up to the Crucible and fix a computer."

"Mommy fixes computers all the time," the little girl said, composing herself slightly.

"It'll be just like that. In fact, she's fixed another computer the exact same way before. Except there were the Toth—" Yarrow caught another elbow from Cortaro "—so much easier this time. We won't be gone long."

"Little one," Lilith said, returning with a middle-aged man in tow, "you're going to stay with Uncle Yeshua until we come back."

"Can we go home after that? I don't like it in here," Mary said.

"Yes, darling, and your daddy will come live with us too." She turned her head to Yarrow. "Right? All of us. Together."

"Of course! I've been meaning to talk to you about all that."

"Grab your stuff." Cortaro clapped his hands twice. "Need to get her to the armory."

Lilith picked up a small cloth bag beneath her cot and gave Mary a tight hug.

"Want to give your daddy a hug?" Lilith asked.

Mary backed away, shaking her head.

Cortaro's lips pressed into a fine line as he saw Yarrow's heart break a little bit.

"Kids are kids," he said, pulling the corpsman to his feet. "She'll come around. Don't force it. Now get moving, both of you."

He hustled them toward the doors. Lilith stopped and looked back at her daughter. She put a hand against the doorway, refusing to move another step.

"What if something happens to us?" she asked. "Who'll take care of her?"

"Miss, you're doing this for her. Take a look. Remember that she is what you're fighting for—her future. I am about done being patient and understanding. Get moving before angry Cortaro comes back."

"He's serious, Lil," Yarrow said.

Lilith turned away, crying.

****

Torni stood off in the wings of the landing pad built into the side of Camelback Mountain. Marines loaded a pair of armor soldiers, both contorted into their compact configuration to fit into the cargo space, into Durand's Mule. Two more suits of armor waited on either side of the void craft.

A woman in power armor, her lavender hair in a tight bun, accompanied Yarrow through the landing pad. She walked stiffly, almost waddling. Torni let a smile spread over her face. She'd always found green Marines in power armor terribly funny.

She concentrated on her left arm, smoothing over the warped sections of her shell. Irregularities in her appearance came without her noticing, and the more she tried to adopt a perfect human form, the more often they arose. Easing into the swirling fractal surface of her drone form would be easier, but doing so while surrounded by busy Marines and armor was a good way to get shot.

Maybe Malal can fix this. If I ever see him again, she thought.

Torni spotted Hale at the end of the Mule's ramp, engaged in a one-way conversation with another Marine. Her body mimicked a deep breath and she walked over, the metal deck groaning beneath the enormous weight of her steps.

"Sir, I see captain's bars on you. They look good."

"Torni…" Hale backed up a half-step. "Haven't seen you for a while. Been busy?"

Torni debated telling Hale about producing the portal weapon, destroying most of the Xaros fleet and disfiguring the dark half of the moon, and nearly dying while injecting a kill command to the Xaros superweapon that formed after the General's demise.

"Same old, same old," she said. "You?"

"Just another day in the Corps." Hale chuckled, then his face contorted with pain.

"Sir?"

"Fine…" Hale said, taking a shallow breath through his teeth, "just…what's wrong with your face?"

Torni touched her cheek and felt deep folds, like it was compacted by unseen forces. She ran a hand over her face, smoothing it out like a sculptor working in clay.

"Things don't work the way they used to. I can do my part in this mission though. No worries."

"Captain," Steuben came down the ramp with long strides, "the armor is loaded and secure. We're ready." The Karigole looked at Torni and bared its needle-sharp teeth.

"Your scent is...wrong. I mean no offense," Steuben said.

"That's Lafayette's hand," Torni said, "his eye."

"Do you know where my brother is? I've not heard from him since the battle with the Xaros ended."

"You don't...know. Lafayette took the *Scipio*. Jumped it to the surface of the sun and opened a portal to destroy the Xaros fleet with a flare. He's not...he's gone. He told me to say something to you. *Shol mar cul.*"

Steuben recoiled, as if she'd punched him in the stomach.

Torni reached out, her fingers extending into talons against her will.

Steuben caught her by the wrist with his mechanical hand. He pulled back, then ran his flesh-and-blood hand from the metal over his skull and eye down his true face.

"You will not speak those words again, abomination. Understand?" Steuben's hand went to the sword hilt on his belt.

Torni nodded.

Steuben backed up the ramp and vanished into the Mule.

"What did you say to him?" Hale asked.

"I don't know. Will he be alright?"

"No idea. We all grieve differently," Hale said as he took his helmet off his belt and locked it over his head with a click. "Good to have you with us again, Marine."

"It's good to be back. Whatever way I am…here."

"See you on the high ground." Hale went off the ramp.

Torni looked at the top of the Mule and willed an antigravity field into being around her feet. She floated over the Mule and landed next to the upper gauss defense turret. The Chinese woman in the ball was halfway through a cup of ramen noodles. She froze when she saw Torni land, her fork half in her mouth.

Torni kept her form but let her shell revert to its natural color, a swirling mass of black fractals over a gunmetal-gray exterior. She gave the gunner a friendly wave.

The gunner looked at her noodles in terror, then set the steaming cup aside.

CHAPTER 15

Keeper surveyed what remained of the Congress. Hundreds of drone boreholes peppered the massive dome like a star field, letting in light from the binary heart of the system. Several of the ambassador pods floated aimlessly around the dais, trailing smoke and rolling slowly.

It flexed the deep-black armor surrounding its photonic body. Assuming a corporeal form was a risk, but the threat from this Bastion was too great to leave to the drones. Even then…being in the presence of a species other than the Xaros filled Keeper with an atavistic sense of revulsion.

+I feel defiled,+ Keeper said to the Engineer, who'd chosen to encase his photonic form inside thick plates of armor orbiting around a star, mimicking the initial construction of the Apex.

The Engineer held a humanoid body in front of it as quantum scan lines performed a subatomic vivisection of the inert form.

+You are a purist,+ the Engineer said. +That is why you cannot learn.+

+The others may never know of this, but you willingly pollute yourself to learn these mongrels' technological cantrips. We were pure and perfect before we left our home. There is nothing more to learn.+

The Engineer boiled the body into a fine mist, then annihilated it with a flash.

+We still do not have the answer to the ultimate question. The escape from inevitability. The cold nothing at the end of all things,+ Engineer said. +That is why the others agreed to preserve remains of dead civilizations. Some may have stumbled across the answer during our travels, and that decision has proven fortuitous.+

+What do you mean?+

The Engineer's body vanished in a flash and reappeared over the center of the dais. A wide beam swept over the ground and a time echo of Wexil and Malal appeared. Malal's image was nearly whole, showing where it had stood for so long. Wexil's apparition swirled around Malal, marking where the Vishrakath had moved through time and space.

+The one in the center is Malal. Its omnium body links to several artifact sites across occupied space. There is evidence of an ascension. Its species found an answer to the question. They defeated oblivion. They found a way to transcend death itself,+ Avarice tinted the Engineer's words.

+The drones found no trace of Malal,+ Keeper said.

+In this instance, what is missing is more telling than what is here. There are quarters for three thousand nine hundred twenty-seven ambassadors. Taking into consideration those that escaped through the conduits or were cleansed by the drones, there are three species unaccounted for. Our attack was too bold, rushed. The General would not have made this mistake,+ the Engineer said.

+Spare me your excuses.+

+Then there is the matter of the missing Qa'Resh city. The drones are searching through the gas giant now, but I would wager we will not find it. Malal could not use their conduit to flee. The Qa'Resh escaped, and they took Malal and the missing ambassadors with them.+

+We will find him. He will share the secret to the ascension or he will be in agony until the last star fades to ice,+ Keeper said.

+But where would they hide?+

+Far from us. Do we know which ambassadors the Qa'Resh escaped with?+

+No. The data cores ejected into the gas world. That knowledge is lost. Pity. But the memories remain.+ The Engineer sifted through the time echo, expanding the aperture until the pod Wexil used came into view.

+Markings on this primitive vessel assign its use to the…Vishrakath. If this one spoke to Malal, it must be important. The important members of a group are always the first to survive, if they abide by our standards. The ambassador's quarters speak of a unique physiology. I can find the home world. Once I do, we will go there in force and learn of Malal's whereabouts.+

+You will parley with the unclean and soil your being? The others will cast you out, no matter what you discover.+

+Once we have what we need, there is no reason to suffer the Vishrakath's continued existence. All of this remains our little secret. Doesn't it, Keeper?+

CHAPTER 16

Torni kept a hand magnetically locked to the top of the Mule as it rose through the atmosphere. The Karigole cloak cast the world beyond a small bubble in gray scale. To her, the Earth looked lifeless without the vibrant blue of the distant Pacific Ocean and the tan hues of the desert stretching beyond Phoenix.

Bodel and Ar'ri hung from mag locks on either side of the dorsal turret. Torni had spent many flights as a gunner, but never with a pair of armor riding along like remora eels. Despite the unexpected passengers, the gunner kept her eyes glued to Torni holding on close to the rear edge.

The sight of an unsuited Marine holding on by her fingertips while the Mule passed into near vacuum must have looked like something out of an old horror show.

That the engines weren't firing on full blast must have added to the strangeness.

"This is taking forever. Why are we riding anti-grav shunts and not blazing toward the target?" Ar'ri asked.

"Cloak can't hide extreme temperatures," Bodel said. "It can mask anti-gravitons. If we hit the afterburners, the Ruhaald might come looking to find out why there's a heat flare coming out of a whole lot of nothing."

"I knew that." Ar'ri shifted against the hull, causing a slight wobble.

"Sit. Still." Durand's stern command came over the IR.

"Yes, ma'am," Ar'ri said.

"Coming up on your target. Stand by."

Torni sat up and peered around the turret. The Ruhaald ship, miles long and shaped like a fat arrowhead, hung in low orbit. The Toth shielding formed a cradle beneath the ship, warping light in and out. Lines of fighters orbited the central axis, a gap several stories high and full of weapon emplacements and fighter bays. She looked for a command bridge, but no possible targets stood out.

"Where we going to tell her to drop us?" Ar'ri asked.

"Pilot picks the spot. Try dictating things to the ones behind the stick and you'll find yourself looking at a very long walk home," Bodel said as he cycled rounds into his forearm cannons.

The Mule flew over the upper half and slowed to a relative stop next to a slight ridge dotted with semiopaque hemisphere.

"Assault element, disembark," Durand said. *"Good hunting and Godspeed."*

Torni cut the magnetic field generated through her fingers and slipped off the Mule. She fell gracefully and touched down on the *Forever Tide*. The hull felt thick and dense through her feet. The two armor soldiers landed with noticeable thumps.

"The goal is *not* to be noticed the second we arrive," Torni said.

"We are fifteen-foot-tall suits of armor. We are not subtle," Bodel said.

"Look up," Cortaro said through the IR. Torni did so and saw no trace of the Mule except for a slight distortion in the star field. A package appeared out of nowhere, heading straight to Torni. She caught it with ease and gave a quick salute to whoever could see her through the Mule's cloak.

"Keep your eye on the Crucible for the signal," Hale said.

"We'll be set in a few minutes," Torni said. "Tell Standish and Bailey I can't wait to see them."

The channel crackled with static. The Mule had already moved beyond IR range. She slid her rifle onto her back and molded her shell around it into a holster. Control over her drone body had improved, but she still had to concentrate to maintain her human visage and she had no confidence in her ability to revert to full drone form and fly.

Torni opened the pack and removed a spool of burn wire and an adhesive tube. She glued down the tip of the wire and stretched out several more feet. Setting a breach hole for an armored Marine didn't take long. Setting a hole for armor would take significantly longer.

"You were on the *Naga*?" Ar'ri asked.

"I was. Hull is different. Interior will be different. Elias says the Ruhaald fight more like us than the Toth," Bodel said.

"We're supposed to find this Jarilla. All we've got are pics from the meeting he had with Valdar. The only way I can tell them apart is from armor markings."

"So?" Bodel asked.

"What if he's in there and he's not wearing armor?"

"You just think of this?" Bodel asked.

"It's been bugging me since Hale briefed the mission."

"Why didn't you say something sooner? We could have pinged the *Breit* for more information."

"And question Hale in front of everyone? I can't insult him like that."

Torni pressed another segment of burn wire into a dollop of adhesive, then shook her head.

"Ar'ri, is this some sort of Dotok culture thing?"

"Junior ranks don't question orders in the Home Guard. Colonel Carius gave us training briefings on Mars, and it seemed like a bad idea to ever question him," Ar'ri said.

"Everyone that's earned their plugs knows that," Bodel said.

"If I'm supposed to…what does a Ruhaald look like outside their armor?" Ar'ri asked.

"Really, Ar'ri? We get away from Hale and suddenly it's time to play twenty questions?" Bodel said.

"I ask because I think one's looking at us." Ar'ri pointed to one of the small hemispheres rising from the hull. Within, a Ruhaald swimmer with large red eyes and a tapered head stared at the trio. The alien's feeder tentacles moved very slowly.

"Torni…" Bodel slowly twisted his forearm

cannons toward the observer.

"Three more segments," Torni said, stretching out another length of cord.

"What do we do, shoot it?" Ar'ri asked.

Bubbles erupted from the Ruhaald's mouth.

"There is no denying a bullet to the face," Bodel said. "That thing starts yelling that there's a bare-skinned human and a pair of giants on the hull and the others might not believe it right away." The armor raised a gigantic hand off the hull and waved to the Ruhaald.

"Breach line is set." Torni clamped a small remote detonator to the wire and crawled away, gripping the hull with magnetic fields she projected through her hands and knees. "Bang is ready, then we clear."

The Ruhaald ducked down, reappearing a moment later. The eyes went wide and a torrent of bubbles came through the feeder tentacles.

"I think that's a different one," Ar'ri said. "We're in trouble."

"Fire in the hole!" Torni flattened against the hull and clicked the detonator.

She felt the hull's temperature rise as the white-hot cord burned through the outer layer and sank into the *Forever Tide*. Against a human ship, it should have taken less than a second for the cord to breach the hull and ignite the air within, blasting the sliced hull segment out like a cork from a bottle of champagne. Torni counted to five, then glanced over at the breach site.

Did I screw up? she wondered.

The hull rumbled. Bubbles rose into the observation blisters all around her.

"Uh oh." Torni gripped the hull tighter.

The hull plug popped out of the breach and went hurtling toward Earth. A geyser of water burst through, freezing to snow and hunks of ice almost instantly. Ruhaald came out with the flood. Torni watched their arms and wide tails flailing about as the flood carried them into the void.

The hull split away from the breach as the explosion of water ripped out a larger hole. The tear made straight for Torni. She tried to roll back, but a hand remained stuck against the hull. She yanked hard and ripped up a section of armor plating.

The rip surged forward as a new glut of water poured forth.

The hull beneath Torni lifted up and went tumbling away, propelled by an escaping fluid. Torni felt something grab her ankle. She looked down and found Bodel with a death grip on her leg.

"Let it go!" he shouted.

Torni felt her body shell stretching between her anchor and the raging water battering the hull plating she gripped in her hand. Torni squeezed her eyes shut and thought of a sun-drenched meadow in Sweden.

The magnetic lock cut away and Bodel slammed her against the hull.

"Sorry," he grunted.

"That was…" she said as she sat up and shook her distended right arm until it took on its natural shape, "fine. This is fine."

The geyser slowed to a trickle, then to a flurry of ice particles.

Ar'ri jumped into the hole and Torni followed.

The tank had become an ice-rimmed cavern. Ruhaald swimmers lay bunched against the deck, frozen and dead.

"What the hell kind of ship is this?" Ar'ri asked.

Bodel spied a long yellow strip beneath the sheen of ice. He stomped down, breaking open a door to an air lock.

"The kind full of hostiles," Bodel said. "We need to find Jarilla or this queen of theirs."

"Doesn't seem to be a map anywhere," Ar'ri said.

"They're not going to put a high-value target in the outer edge of a ship. One good hit and you see what could happen. They'll be in the center and probably well protected," Torni said.

Bodel ripped the doorway free.

"Can't give them time to recover and coordinate," he said. "Less talk, more killing."

****

A holo panel next to Ordona lit up with a surge in signal traffic between Ruhaald ships. So long as they did not interfere with his tasks, he did his best to ignore them. The spike in messages between the ships—and one ship in particular—drew his attention.

Ordona lifted a tool arm and flicked a cutting blade over a holo panel.

The face of a Ruhaald walker, not Jarilla, appeared in front of Ordona's vision slit.

"Explain," Ordona said.

"I render—"

"Explain!"

"We've been boarded! Not by humans, some manner of mechanized bipeds and-and a Xaros! The Septon is…indisposed. Can you send help?"

"How did humans reach your vessel? They did not use this Crucible to travel there. I'm sure of that."

There was a crack of glass and a gout of water splashed behind the terrified Ruhaald.

"We don't know! The rest of our vessels are too far away to reach us by the time the humans reach the queen. You must do something!"

"Hardly. Order your ships to release nuclear weapons on the following targets: Phoenix, Bern, Capetown. Tell the boarders you will destroy another city every two minutes until they surrender. I will send Naroosha ships to destroy the *Breitenfeld* and the rest of their surviving ships. Inform Septon Jarilla that I am most disappointed in him."

Ordona sent the command to assault the human fleet transiting behind the moon with as much passion as turning the lights on and returned his focus to the vexing probe. He lifted work arms up…then paused.

How *had* the humans boarded the *Forever Tide*? A Xaros drone was impossible. He'd witnessed the kill command take place and seen every last drone in the system disintegrate. The Crucible had video files of a drone masquerading as a human working with Malal and a Karigole.

The Karigole. The designs for their cloaking devices had spread through the Alliance when the species was first integrated to Bastion. The technology was discredited after a Karigole centurion using cloaks was nearly wiped out attempting to capture a Xaros drone. Disrupting the cloak with a wide-spectrum lepton pulse was pitifully easy.

Ordona sent a command to a Naroosha cruiser.

****

Gor'al walked behind the stations on the *Vorpral's* bridge, glancing at screens and asking questions of his crew as he passed. Once, the room had been the chamber for the Council of the Firsts, the assemblage of Dotok leaders on Takeni. On that lost world, the ship had landed in the widest canyon on the planet and became the first "permanent" settlement. The Xaros arrival and some engineering solutions had brought the void ship back into the cold vacuum where she belonged.

It had taken years of effort, but the Dotok finally had a warship to call their own.

"Captain?" His communications technician rapped knuckles against the side of his chair to get Gor'al's attention. "There's a fluctuation in the neutron cage that human spirit ordered us to build."

"It's time." Gor'al leapt onto the raised circular platform where his command chair waited for him.

"Announce the battle. Helm, ahead at best speed. You know the route. Radio, get me Valdar."

The clacking of wooden sticks filled his ears as the ancestral call to battle went through the ship's IR. Warning lights blinked as the ship's atmosphere was withdrawn into armored tanks. Gor'al looked over his bridge crew, making certain they had their helmets on before he donned his. The human insistence on fighting in full vacuum had some merit, a tactic Gor'al learned to appreciate after losing a ship to the Xaros early in the fight to save Takeni.

"This is Breitenfeld,*"* Valdar's voice came through Gor'al's helmet. Some of the younger Dotok took to the infernal gauntlets with their screens and millions of distractions. Gor'al preferred the old ways of simple voice-to-voice conversation.

"We have the signal. Ibarra is ready for the final gambit," Gor'al said.

"Cubes are in the void. The rest of the fleet is yours. The captains know their role and will follow your orders. Gott mit uns.*"*

"Cod mittens to you too, *Vorpral* out." Gor'al cut the channel and pulled a holo projector arm up from the side of his chair. Light wavered in front of him, then resolved into the dark side of the moon. Icons for all the human ships accelerated ahead of the massive *Vorpral* while the *Breitenfeld* fell back.

Gor'al opened the command channel to his senior officers and asked, "Engines, can you stoke the fires a bit more?"

"I have one generator at 110 percent of safe capacity and another operating on a steady feed of prayer and expletives. Do not ask for more," his chief engineer said. The female was sufficiently "salty" as Chief MacDougall had once called her.

"Your service is noted." Gor'al felt the steady press of acceleration as their speed increased. The destroyers raced ahead, each trailed by a small icon, and crossed the threshold over the Earth-facing side of the moon. The distance between the different classes of ships would only grow wider as the moon's gravity lent more velocity to the slingshot maneuver.

"*Vacaville* has eyes on the Earth and Crucible," the assistant captain said from his seat just below Gor'al's right foot, "telemetry data coming through. The lead ships will enter weapons' range of the Naroosha ships in…six minutes."

Plots for the Ruhaald ships over the Earth popped onto his holo; none had moved since the *Vorpral's* last orbit around the moon. Gor'al tapped a fingertip against his armrest. The Ruhaald hadn't taken the bait to interdict the ships on course to the Crucible.

"No movement from the Ruhaald," the gunnery officer said from the seat below Gor'al's left foot. "Shall we send a small provocation?"

"We miss and it'll strike the mountains. Friendly fire is never appreciated, no matter the intention," Gor'al said. "Ready the alert fighters. Remind Bar'en *not* to shoot the Crucible. Again."

"Transmission from the Crucible," the communications officer said, "from the Naroosha."

"This will be interesting. Give it to me." Gor'al waited a moment, then a small square with a flat red line running through the middle appeared in his holo.

"Your violation is noted." The red line warbled with the words. "Three cities are marked for immediate destruction. Any ship that does not return to lunar orbit immediately will be destroyed and another settlement will be bombarded at random every two minutes until all your ships are destroyed…starting with Hawaii. That is the only location housing Dotok, according to records. If it is not, we will get to the others in due course."

Gor'al thought of his children and grandchildren—the youngest born just weeks ago—living within Mauna Kea. He believed the Naroosha would carry out the threat, but he chose to trust that Valdar and Ibarra had found a way to save the many innocents at risk. If not, this offensive would be futile.

"Naroosha commander," Gor'al said, "this is your first, last, and only chance to surrender unconditionally. I have little preference to your decision, but I do look forward to mounting a burned fragment of your hull in the mess hall, and your skull in my quarters, if you choose to fight."

The channel closed.

"A fight it is." Gor'al shifted his holo view to Ceres and the Crucible as the *Vorpral* came around the moon. Engines flared, breaking the ship free from orbit and sending it straight toward the jump gate.

The Naroosha ships crept out of the thorns and moved very slowly toward the approaching fleet, keeping the Crucible behind them. Gor'al's beak clicked in annoyance. The Naroosha would make sure that any missed shots directed at their ships would strike the jump gate. If the plan devised among the Dotok, human and Ibarra were to work, the Crucible had to remain intact.

The lead destroyers cut their engines and continued on at a steady velocity. Gor'al had never cared for human tricks, preferring a stand-up fight with the *Vorpral's* many energy cannons donated by the Toth. But if this one worked…

"*Vacaville* executing the Tumbleweed Maneuver," the assistant captain said. "I still don't know what a 'tumbleweed' is."

"Some sort of plant near Phoenix, I've heard," the gunnery officer said.

Gor'al stomped a foot and startled the two chattering officers back to focusing on their jobs.

The icons for the destroyers veered away from the Earth as their speed slowed. The icons just behind each ship continued…on a course straight through the center of the Crucible.

"All ships report payload separation," the assistant captain said.

The cubes full of IR-guided missiles streaked toward the Crucible, each trailed by the carbon-fiber cables that had once been fixed to the stern of each destroyer. The human crews had worked in brief stints to attach the weapons during their transit around the dark side of the moon where the Naroosha and Ruhaald weren't able to observe their efforts. Transferring the cubes—smaller than the one used by the *Breitenfeld* against the Toth—from the cruisers to the destroyers had been nerve-wracking to watch, but the void sailors had accomplished the task, losing only one cube to the moon's gravity. It had impacted against the glassed surface, shattering the base of a crater.

Gor'al checked the Earth and noted a distinct lack of heat flares from exploding nuclear weapons.

Torpedoes ejected from the cubes like wind-blown spores off a dandelion. The weapons continued unpowered for several seconds until crewmen aboard the slower frigates and cruisers established an IR connection and steered the torpedoes toward the Naroosha ships.

"Come on…pick your target," Gor'al said to himself.

The Naroosha ships pulled away from the Crucible. The edges of their spiral-shaped ships glowed blue. The weapon's edge of nine ships grew brighter than the others. Lances of coherent energy shot out and annihilated all nine of the torpedo cubes before they'd finished releasing their cargo.

"Captain, the *Vacaville*—"

"Yes, I saw." Gor'al watched as the guided weapons accelerated toward the Naroosha ships. At the same time, the destroyer squadron maneuvered toward the Crucible on a perpendicular attack vector toward the enemy ships.

Gor'al's fingers gripped the armrests as the torpedoes angled toward the nearest spiral ships. The destroyers closed, seconds away from effective range on the rail cannons.

Three of the Naroosha ships shot toward the torpedoes, their weapons' edges pulsating with energy. Bolts of energy no bigger than the IR-guided weapons fired from the ships like sparks off a live wire. Torpedoes exploded in quick succession as the bolts hit home. The sailors controlling the weapons began slaloming the torpedoes, dodging the incoming fire…but slowing their pace toward their targets.

Naroosha ships launched a flurry of shots at individual torpedoes, leaving the weapons no place to run. A handful of torpedoes survived, all cruising along without guidance past the enemy vessels.

"So much for that," the gunnery officer said.

"Wait." Gor'al leaned closer to the holo. One of the missiles came to life and looped around, screaming toward a Naroosha ship's engines. It slipped between a pair of thrusters and exploded. Engine cowlings went tumbling through space in a muffled flash. The stricken ship lurched up, then shattered into a blossom of flame.

A second Naroosha ship broke in half as a second torpedo came to life and struck the thin central axis.

The third ship tilted forward onto its prow. The weapon edge unleased a thin wave of coherent light that disintegrated the last of the fallow torpedoes and the broken fragments of their fellows in an instant. The ship went tumbling forward, cracks growing up and down the silver hull until it came apart like a mirror breaking in slow motion.

"Tricks," Gor'al said, "everyone has tricks. The humans, the Naroosha. Everyone's too good to get into a stand-up fight." He opened a channel to the fighter leader waiting on the deck. "Bar'en, did you see that Naroosha ship overload?"

"I did. The attack dissipated within range of our gauss. We'll watch for that. You ready to let us loose?"

"Patience, or you'll end up like the torps," Gor'al said and closed the channel.

"Destroyers engaging," the assistant captain said. "*Manticore* frigates on approach. Still several minutes before we join the battle."

Gor'al considered egging his engineer on but decided all he'd get was a tongue-lashing.

The flash from rail cannons rippled off the destroyers. Ruhaald ships let off pinpoint bolts and annihilated each and every shot from the human ships.

"Their point defense is better than we anticipated," the gunnery officer said. "We'll have to close to almost knife-fighting range to make a hit."

"Helm?" Gor'al asked.

"As you like, Captain," the young officer said from the conn. "I'll get us so close even those low-list gunners couldn't miss."

"Enemy descending...they're taking cover within the thorns," the gunnery officer said.

The *Vacaville* led the rest of the destroyers lower. Gauss flak guns opened up on the Naroosha ships. Gor'al couldn't tell if the weapons had any effect yet. A brief stab of blue energy shot across the Crucible's thorns where the destroyers hunted the Naroosha.

The *Vacaville*'s icon went deep red—destroyed. More flashes of light—like the path of fireflies in the night sky—and the entire squadron was gone.

Enemy ships on the other side of the Crucible maneuvered into a cluster of four. Their weapons' edges grew brighter and each ship fired a beam that combined at the head of a pyramid. A blue column of power wreathed by lightning lanced through the void and struck the *Barcelona* amidships. The beam bore into the aegis armor with enough force to knock the ship off course. The armor plating failed and the beam cored the ship, exploding out the opposite flank. The cruiser lolled onto its side, engines dead.

Another group of Naroosha ships fired, severing the *Copenhagen*'s prow clean off. Crew and shattered decks fell out of the ship and into the void.

"Conn! Fire all starboard maneuver thrusters the next time the beams combine." Gor'al flicked a pair of switches on his armrest to open a channel to his ships' captains. "This is Gor'al. There's a delay before the beam forms. Use it to—"

Gor'al slammed to the right as the *Vorpral*'s thrusters overloaded. A blast of blue light washed through the view ports around the bridge.

"It missed!" the gunnery officer shouted.

Gor'al felt the ship decelerate.

"Hope you're happy! Generator two just melted!" came from the engine room.

"Guns, target a single ship in the next group preparing to fire," Gor'al said.

"But, sir," said the gunnery officer, twisting around to look up at his captain, "one miss and we'll hit the Crucible."

"Then aim true. We're a giant, slow-moving target right now. Fire at will. Bar'en, launch all fighters immediately."

"As you like. We might die on the way to the Crucible, but if we sit here waiting around, I like our chances even less," Bar'en said.

"Why are the good ones always so difficult?"

Gor'al muttered as he reopened the fleet-wide channel. "All ships, get close and kick those bastards in the teeth. The *Vorpral* will get to the fight eventually. I challenge you not to leave anything left for us to mop up."

Lights dimmed and Gor'al felt a shiver through his seat as the Toth energy cannons opened fire.

Valdar…we really need you right now, he thought.

****

Lieutenant Mathias limped through the main gates of the Camelback Mountain fortress and slowly made his way to a group of soldiers and Marines gawking up at the sky. The compression splint on his wounded leg made his gait awkward and each tug on the pink scars beneath the webbing made him nervous that he'd reopen the wound, but the medics were adamant that he was fine to walk around.

"What is all this?" he asked the group.

"Look, sir…" A soldier pointed up toward Ceres where the flash of void combat raged around the Crucible.

Mathias watched in awe for a few moments, comparing his small part of the conflict as an officer leading Marines to the titanic forces battling away.

No wonder the navy officers don't seem impressed when I brag about my Marines, he thought. His gaze went to the Ruhaald ship overhead, half-hidden by high clouds.

"Everyone inside. Now!" Mathias used his command tone, reserved for combat and when his instructions were not to be questioned. His technique wasn't as good as First Sergeant Cortaro's, but it got people moving. "Those squids aren't going to be happy about whatever the hell's happening around the Crucible."

Mathias had managed to limp back to the doors when he heard a whistling sound overhead. A dark streak hit the side of the mountain, knocking flakes of rock and dust into the air. A metal oval the size of a Xaros drone bounced down the mountain…and straight toward Mathias.

He shuffled to the left, but the object took a crazy bounce off a boulder and kept its collision course. The Marine went right, but the thing seemed dead set on smashing into him. Mathias threw himself to the ground and threw his arms over his head.

There was a rumble of crushing rocks and a billow of dust over Matthias. He looked up and found the oval, its light-green surface battered and covered in the same script he'd seen on Ruhaald armor.

A soldier in power armor grabbed Mathias

beneath his arms and hauled him to his feet.

"Keep moving, sir. My sensors are going nuts with radiologic warnings. Thing's full of plutonium, but my Geiger counter isn't redlining," the soldier said.

"If that's a nuke, then why didn't it go off?" Mathias limped faster.

"You want to be out here when it does?"

"Must. Go. Faster."

CHAPTER 17

A Mule could fit eight fully armored Marines comfortably. The Strike Marine Corps cared nothing for comfort, so the ten Marines, Lilith and the pair of armor soldiers strapped to the deck found space wherever possible.

Hale fought for elbow room against the bulkhead and checked the telemetry feed from the Mule. Steuben sat next to him. The Karigole hadn't said a word since learning of Lafayette's death. He'd spent the entire flight staring at his mechanical hand, opening and closing a fist one finger at a time.

"Steuben, how you holding up?" Hale asked his XO over a private channel.

"Lafayette's *gethaar*, you would consider her his mother, was nearly ready to see him again. I spent years speaking of his virtues, his bravery in the fight to rescue them from the Toth. One of the others just gave birth to a new *gethaar*, a sure sign of good fortune for the clan. She spent a day meditating before an open flame and said the spirits were ready to welcome Lafayette from his time in the outer darkness. Surviving the Xaros attack would mean our ancestors blessed the Earth for our future."

"He was a fine soldier. We would never have beaten the Xaros or the General without him."

"His spirit lingers," Steuben said, touching his cybernetic eye.

"What does that mean?"

Steuben didn't answer.

"Gall, how much longer?" Hale asked over the shuttle's IR.

"You ask me again and I will turn this ship right around…nine minutes. Coming up on the outer rim of the Crucible now."

Hale switched to his team channel.

"Alright, Marines. We have one mission in here: deliver the payload to the command center and regain control of the jump gate. Some of you know our payload; some of you don't." Hale pointed to Lilith, who gave a nervous wave. "She is a civilian. Don't expect her to move or act like a Marine."

"I still don't have a gun," Lilith said.

"Secondary objective is to find our three brother and sister Marines captured by the Ruhaald," Hale continued. "What little we know about the enemy comes from Ibarra. Ruhaald troops are in the station. Also an unknown number of Naroosha are present."

"Gauss bullets work just fine on the squids," Lieutenant Jacobs said. "What do we use on the Naroosha? What do they even look like?"

"Not like us, not like the squids…" Hale's cheeks flushed with embarrassment. "Just shoot anything not dressed like us."

"I was going to do that anyway," Orozco said.

"How long will it take her to regain control of the station?" Jacobs asked.

Lilith's head bobbed from side to side. "It depends on the number of code fissures in the quantum state generators. Assuming they're using Toth protocols, it might be between—"

"As long as it takes," Hale said. "We don't have any plans for tomorrow."

"Hold on back there," Durand announced. *"One of the silver ships just came through the spikes and is moving toward the center."*

"Anyone know what'll happen to us if it opens a wormhole?" Cortaro asked.

"Something tells me we don't want to find out," Hale said. "Gall, can you—"

The Mule rocked back and forth like a boat over rough seas.

"We lost our cloak!" Durand shouted.

"Damn it." Hale unbuckled his restraints and grabbed a handle overhead. He swung himself up and into the cockpit.

The Crucible loomed beyond the glass, the dome of a command center straight ahead. Gigantic basalt spikes shifted against each other, revealing and hiding Naroosha ships on the other side of the jump gate's outer edge. Durand kept her focus on the command center and increased the Mule's velocity. In the co-pilot's seat, Choi Ma worked frantically over the control panels.

"What happened?" Hale asked.

"The field shimmered during that turbulence or whatever," Choi said. "Now it's gone, but the emitters are still functioning. Get that lizard friend of yours up here. Maybe he can fix it." She slapped the side of a monitor and swore with words Hale didn't know.

Tiny motes of light flashed across the dome's surface.

Durand banked the Mule to the side and dove. Hale mag-locked his feet to the deck and grabbed on to the back of Choi's seat before the maneuver could toss him against the wall.

Energy bolts snapped across the Mule's nose.

"We were supposed to land you on a thorn, let you cut your way in under the cloak." Durand angled the craft up and hit the thrusters. The Mule shook as it accelerated toward the command center. Durand jinked the craft from side to side, dodging fire from the armed bunkers over the dome's surface.

"I am open to suggestions!" she shouted.

One of the thorns connected to the dome broke away, revealing an opening half as wide as the *Breitenfeld*'s flight deck.

"It's Ibarra," Hale said. "He got us an opening. Can you land there?"

"Probably," Durand said. "We have to cut our velocity. But if we slow down—" Light flashed over the cockpit and the Mule lurched to the side with an impact Hale felt through his feet.

"Starboard engine malfunctioning," Choi said, "rerouting power to the maneuver thrusters."

"Landing now…maybe not." Durand slapped a button and the Mule jumped up as thrusters across the ventral side flared into action.

Hale felt blood run from his head and swell his

toes.

The momentum shifted as the Mule lined up with the entrance to the command center. Durand activated the dorsal thrusters and Hale fought to keep the contents of his stomach in place.

"Landing gear off-line!" Choi shouted. "All hydraulics are out."

"Fils de pute," Durand muttered as she hit the retro-thrusters and guided the Mule through the opening and into a semicircular room little bigger than the maintenance bay where the General met his demise.

Durand kicked the tail around and the port wingtip hit the deck. Sparks flew off the contact for a half second as the Mule screeched across the room. The wing collapsed and the Mule slammed onto its side.

Hale kept his grip on Choi's seat, but the handle broke away with a snap as Hale fell against the side of the cockpit with a crash.

Metal groaned as the Mule slid to a painful stop a few feet from the command center wall.

Durand leaped out of her chair and straddled Hale.

"Are you hurt?" she asked.

"Fine." Hale tossed the broken handle away.

Durand reached down and slapped Hale across

the helmet.

"This is why you stay strapped in your seat, idiot! So you don't go bouncing around my cockpit like a pinball."

"Why don't you two just get a room?" Choi asked as she unstrapped.

The Mule tilted slowly, falling back onto its belly and stopping suddenly at a forty-five-degree angle.

Durand frowned at Choi, then the Frenchwoman's jaw dropped open.

"The turrets! They didn't retract!"

"Mei!" Choi struggled out of her seat.

Durand fumbled out of the askew cockpit and Hale followed close on her heels.

Mei was inside the dorsal ball turret, slamming her hands against the reinforced glass hatch that should have opened into the cargo area. Elias' compact bulk covered the hinges and more than half the hatch; he'd slid loose after cargo straps tore apart in the rough landing. It was impossible to open the turret hatch.

The entire Mule's mass pressed against the ventral turret. Cracks grew across the hatch as Mei screamed for help.

"It'll crush her!" Choi said.

"Open the ramp and cut the rest of the straps

when I say so." Hale ran over Caas and to the ramp, where Orozco and Weiss worked furiously with hand cranks to lower the ramp.

"Jacobs, Yarrow, push Elias through on my word." Hale grabbed a carry handle on the far end of Elias' rectangular configuration—a handle meant for an exo-lifter many times stronger than Hale's armor—and jerked Elias a few inches toward the ramp with a grunt.

"Rest of you shirkers get off your ass and help!" Cortaro shouted. More Marines braced themselves against Elias.

"On three!" Hale commanded.
"One…two…heave!"

The Marines pushed Elias toward the half-open ramp, sliding along the straps still holding him against the Mule's canted deck. Steuben slammed a hand against the end opposite Hale and shoved forward.

Elias shot forward and knocked Hale back. The captain fell out of the Mule and went stumbling against the molded sand floor. Elias slid out of the back and angled down, straight for Hale.

Hale rolled to the side and avoided the soldier's crushing bulk. He grabbed the carry handle again and pulled Elias clear of the Mule, then he looked around the empty room. The scars of the Mule's rough landing were nearly gone as the Crucible repaired itself. Elias lay near a wide doorway, the basalt slabs shut.

Orozco fired up a cutting torch and severed the hinges on Mei's hatch. He ripped the hatch off and pulled the Chinese pilot free seconds before the turret collapsed in an explosion of reinforced glass. The Mule slammed to the deck.

Mei had her arms and legs wrapped around Orozco's torso. Her head shook violently when Choi tried to pry her away. Orozco cradled Mei's head against his shoulder and whispered to her. Hale heard lilting Spanish words through his helmet.

"She live?" Elias asked.

"She'll be fine." Hale pulled a lever on Elias' armor to unlimber him from his compressed form. He reached over Elias' rotary cannon and got a hand on the second handle when the doorway opened.

A hallway full of Ruhaald troops greeted Hale, their rifles aimed at the Marine. Wet clicks filled the air.

Hale pulled the second handle then raised his hands in surrender.

"Elias?"

"Get down." Elias' arm shot out from the side of his boxy shape and snatched an alien off its feet. The soldier bashed his captive into the alien next to it then swung the alien back like a club, knocking Ruhaald off their feet.

Elias sat up and dangled the struggling Ruhaald in the air, then dug his fingers into the alien's body. The Ruhaald popped like a balloon, spraying dark fluid and lumps of gore across the stunned assault party.

"I. Have. Come." Elias' other arm struck out and crushed another alien. He unfolded his legs and stood up. He pointed a bloody hand at the survivors. "For you!"

The Ruhaald backed away frantically. Most dropped their weapons as they turned and ran away.

"Pussies," Elias said as he pulled Caas from the Mule. The armor swung his helm toward Hale, still on the ground. "What are you waiting for? An engraved invitation?"

"Right, right." Hale pulled Caas' levers and went to the Mule. "Everyone ready to move out?"

Durand handed pistols to her Chinese crew.

"We are coming with you." Durand hopped off the ramp and looked over the wrecked Mule. "I've had worse landings," she said with a click of her tongue.

The boom of gauss cannons echoed off the walls. Elias had gone after the fleeing enemy, Caas right behind him.

"You want to live through this?" Hale asked

Durand. "You keep the armor between you and the enemy."

"Well, thank you, Mr. War Hero." Durand chambered a round in her pistol. "I would never have figured that out."

"These two need a room," Mei said.

"Marines! Follow me!" Hale waved an arm over his shoulder and ran toward the battle.

****

Enemy contact reports from the Ruhaald charged with defending the command center played across Ordona's holo-fields. A relatively small number of humans had breached the command dome, but among the attackers were a pair of mechanized soldiers that the Ruhaald failed to counter.

Ordona's hails to the *Forever Tide* went unanswered.

The Toth malicious code would require another hour to fully co-opt the probe's systems. Given the rate of the human advance across the dome, he estimated another nine minutes before they were at his door.

Ordona ordered the remainder of his Ruhaald troops to fall back to the inner ring of defenses and considered his options.

The mission must succeed, he thought. *I willed my compensation to my spores. They will advance even if I do not.*

He opened a channel to an underling, the one experimenting with the procedural generation crèche.

****

Jarilla wiggled a leg into his armor and sealed it tight over the appendage. The suit sucked in water from the bridge floor and filled his suit with the life-preserving fluid.

The human assault had come while he was in communion with the queen, the worst possible moment as it took him several crucial minutes to extricate from her embrace and leave her enclosure.

At first, he'd thought the humans had managed to strike the swimmer's living quarters with one of their rail cannons. Such a vulnerable area would have been evacuated and drained during combat. His lax standards had just cost the lives of hundreds of his crew.

Jarilla went to the partition between the walker and swimmer areas of the bridge and looked at the damage-control board. The boarders had cut a zigzag path through the ship, moving from deck to deck with terrifying swiftness. Each step brought them closer to the bridge.

"Mrixil," he called to the swimmer captain. The Ruhaald undulated over, panic pheromones leaking from its gills. "Prepare the queen's escape pod. I will summon the *Endless Depths* and it will recover her."

"She'll be vulnerable during the transfer. If the humans are on the offensive, the risk from their fighters or long-range weapons is too great to—"

"There is no human offensive!" Jarilla slammed a fist against the wall. "Their walking tanks are almost here. Get her to safety. Now."

"It will be done." Mrixil swam away.

Jarilla ran over to the communications station. "Get me the *Endless Depths*, and where are the sentries? I want every armed crew to fall back to the bridge. Nothing is more important than keeping her safe."

"The sentry team is down the passageway beyond the doors…but they're not moving," the comms officer said.

Jarilla drew a pistol off his thigh.

The doors to the bridge buckled as a massive fist slammed into them. One of the doors went flying as Bodel kicked it free. The door crushed the weapons officer and his cogitators. Bodel leveled his cannon.

"Nobody move."

"Forty percent complete!" Mrixil shouted.

"For the queen!" Jarilla charged toward Bodel, snapping off shots from his lightning pistol. The rest of the bridge crew abandoned their stations and followed their Septon.

Bodel ignored the hits from Jarilla's weapon and stomped a pair of Ruhaald into paste. He swung the back of his hand down and knocked the chief navigator against the partition.

Jarilla aimed at the thinner armor beneath Bodel's armpit and pulled the trigger. A human hand grabbed him by the wrist and jerked his aim high.

Torni, her shell swirling between fractals and her once-human appearance, looked at the Ruhaald with open scorn.

Jarilla struggled against her grip, surprised by her raw strength. His tentacle activated the pistol, unleashing bolts that stitched across the ceiling.

The hand around his wrist snapped into a fist, severing Jarilla's tentacles and sending the pistol to the deck with a splash. Jarilla's brief scream filled the bridge.

"Sixty percent!" Mrixil announced.

Torni reached back and her fingers extended into spikes. She slammed them into Jarilla's chest and pierced the armor enough to break the suit's integrity but not skewer the flesh within.

She hefted the Septon off the deck.

"You understand me?" Torni asked.

"I do." Jarilla jerked his head to the voice box on his shoulder.

"You tell those others to stop what they're doing right now and get on the ground." She raised her other hand toward the swimmer bridge. A ruby spark formed in the palm of her hand. "I won't ask twice."

"What are you?" Jarilla felt a spike press against his thorax.

"I am Sergeant Sofia Torni, Atlantic Union Marine Corps, and I am not here to make friends."

The spark grew into a jet of flame.

Jarilla gave her an insult that the voice box failed to translate.

Torni unleashed a disintegration beam that cut through the glass partition like it didn't exist and annihilated Mrixil. The liquid within the tank flash-boiled, killing the rest of the crew in seconds.

The Marine lowered her hand and looked at Jarilla.

"You will order your ships to lower their shields. You will order your ships to leave our skies and set anchor behind the dark side of our moon. Your ships so much as light a maneuver thruster without our express permission and the macro cannons across the solar system will blow you to dust. Don't think we're afraid to beat up the moon. I already wrecked it," she said.

"Your world is beautiful, and my ships are full of nuclear weapons. Ending my life will not stop us from poisoning—"

Torni walked toward the dark tank on the far side of the bridge, carrying the Septon like he was a plate of food in a restaurant. She extended her other hand toward the queen's tank, the burning mote of a disintegration beam ready.

"Who's in there? Someone important?"

"Nothing! Auxiliary fluid for—"

"Then it won't matter when I destroy it!"

The queen appeared from the inky depths. She was something out of a primordial nightmare, a massive cranium dotted with barnacles and feeder tentacles the size of octopus limbs. The true extent of her massive form faded into the darkness.

Torni's throat mimicked a hard swallow.

"What will you do if we surrender?" The queen's words lilted through Jarilla's translator. "Will you destroy us?"

"Your fate will be up to Valdar, people more

important than me. We don't kill those that surrender—I can promise you that," Torni said.

"Earth is the first habitable world we have ever visited," the queen said. Her tentacles touched the glass gently. "Look what we have wrought. A brave race is our enemy. Our allies betray us. Blood spilt for nothing."

"I am the wrong person for poetry." Torni tilted her head to Bodel and Ar'ri behind her. "They hate it even more than I do. Surrender. Now."

"We yield." The queen wiped tentacles across her eyes, each the size of the shield on Bodel's forearm. "Our ships will do as you command. Please spare the rest of my children from death."

Torni lowered Jarilla to the floor and withdrew the spikes from his suit. Water dribbled from the holes.

"Get on the radio. Do what you need to," Torni said.

The queen floated away from the glass.

"No!" Torni's hand flared red. "You stay right where I can see you. Things might get better between us, but right now you're going to learn what humans mean when we say, 'Trust but verify.'"

****

Yarrow led Lilith down the basalt-black hallway. She seemed content to keep her eyes on the ground but still shirked away from the sound of any and all gunfire. For a woman raised in a society with little to no concept of violence, Yarrow thought she wasn't doing half-bad.

Ahead, the two armor soldiers had stopped near an intersection. Short bolts of lightning from the Ruhaald hit the walls with a searing hiss. Enemy fire filled the cross section leading to a tall doorway marked CINC. Yarrow watched dozens of bolts cut through the air, and he knew it would be suicide to try to cross the last few yards to their destination.

The Ruhaald knew where they were going and seemed most determined to cut the Marines off.

"What now?" Lilith asked, clutching her cloth bag to her chest.

"We wait for the captain to come up with a tactical solution that doesn't involve running through that kill zone," Yarrow said.

"A 'kill zone'? You bring the mother of your child into a place with a 'kill zone'?"

"OK, Lilith, I think it was pretty clear that this wasn't going to be a walk in the park. Things are going pretty well, even with the crash landing and losing our one way off the Crucible."

"You mean we're trapped?" Lilith started to hyperventilate.

"No. No! Darling, look at me." Yarrow grabbed her helmet and raised her face to him. A Ruhaald bolt ricocheted off a wall and struck near Yarrow's feet. "I've gotten out of much worse places than this."

"Yarrow!" Hale shouted.

"Moving!" The corpsman took Lilith by the hand and led her forward, even as she tried to pull away from the torrent of fire zipping down the cross section.

They passed Lieutenant Jacobs, a bandolier of grenades in her hand. Orozco charged up his Gatling gun, one foot stomping against the ground like a bull reading a charge.

Hale ran to Yarrow and pointed to Elias. His shield unfolded from his arm into a circle.

"Jacobs will throw out concussion and smoke, stun the enemy position. Elias will block their fire and get us across in one piece. Ready?" Hale hustled them toward the edge of the hallway.

Yarrow felt the heat from passing bolts. Lilith tried to jerk her hand away from him.

"No! There is no way I can—" Yarrow wrapped an arm around her shoulder and twisted her away from the kill zone as Jacobs swung the bandolier around the corner.

A slap of air rattled his helmet and sent his ears ringing.

Hale grabbed Lilith up by the ankles and shouted to the corpsman. The command was lost to the whine but Yarrow understood his commander's intent. He clutched his arms around the squirming Lilith and carried her forward, past Orozco who unleashed the full fury of his Gatling weapon on the Ruhaald around the corner and behind Elias.

Elias sidestepped, keeping his bulk and his shield between the enemy fire and the three as they crossed the kill zone.

Yarrow heard the slap of hits against Elias' shield. A hunk of aegis plating broke away and bounced over Yarrow's feet. A lightning bolt caught Yarrow's toes and he felt like he'd just kicked a buzz saw. He limped forward and fell against the door to the command center, his right foot blackened and smoking.

"Jason!" Lilith shook the corpsman by the shoulders.

"I'm fine," he said through gritted teeth.

"How fine?" Hale asked.

"Can still walk on it, still shoot." Yarrow got up, keeping weight off the injured appendage.

Hale went to the door and tapped keys on a control panel. There was an angry buzz.

Elias rotated his shield against his forearm and used the damaged section as a firing nook. He leaned into the kill zone and let off a half-dozen shots from his arm cannon.

An electrical storm of bolts answered him, cracking the shield in half before Elias pulled away.

"Reinforcements," Elias said. "Looks like they're getting ready for a push."

"Let me use my breach charge," Hale said as he reached down to his belt and found a singed patch of armor where the explosive charge should have been. "Figures. Elias, rip open the door."

Elias let off a few blind shots around the corner.

"If I turn my back on them, this will get ugly real quick," he said.

"Ibarra!" Hale yelled to the ceiling. "Little help here!"

One of the doors to the command center jerked open. Hale and Yarrow swung around the opening, their rifles ready.

The probe hung in the center of the room at the bottom of a tiered amphitheater, a coral ring and dim force field surrounding the tear of light that made up Bastion's first envoy to the human race. Ordona floated near a bank of control panels, then whirled in place to face the intruders.

"I have this facility rigged to self-destruct," Ordona said. "You will throw down your weapons and submit to the Ruhaald. Now." He raised a mechanical arm, a thin finger pointed at a pulsating button.

Hale got his aim on the wide-shouldered machine. His finger tapped against the trigger.

The force field behind Ordona shimmered. A single word morphed against the wall of coherent light.

SHOOT

Hale hit the alien dead center. The suit wobbled to the side, then took another hit from Yarrow. Ordona let out a squeal then went to the ground as the containment suit's anti-grav failed. He tried to prop himself up, but Hale drilled a bullet through Ordona's bucket head and the encounter suit fell to the ground, red smoke churning from the wound.

"Switch to air tanks," Hale said, "no idea what that stuff will do to us if we breathe it."

"But what if I have to vomit?" Lilith asked weakly.

"Don't. You need to get the probe free right now, Lilith," Hale said. Yarrow tried to guide her down the tiers but had to stop against a broken workstation.

"Sir, I need to treat myself." Yarrow handed her over to his captain and sank to the ground. Grabbing his injured foot, he pulled it to his face. The armor toe was missing, but his toes were still there, albeit blackened and oozing blood. He sprayed nu-skin over the bare flesh and felt icy pinpricks jab his foot.

"So that's what everyone's always complaining about. At least there's no nerve damage," he said to himself.

A Ruhaald bolt sprang off the doorway.

"Hurry up in there!" Elias shouted.

Yarrow got up and limped down the tiers to where Lilith stood hunched over the bank of computer stations, her cloth bag open. The Toth computer she'd used on Nibiru connected to the coral ring around the probe and into the workstations.

Hale stood nearby, watching the other entrances.

"Jason, the Naroosha are using *Toth* injects into the probe's control prompts." Lilith shook her head in disgust. "I recognize some of the code. Code that *I* wrote!"

"What does that mean?" Yarrow asked.

"It means the Naroosha are—how do you say, 'script kitties'? Space-borne civilization can't even do their own trinomial quantum calculations…" Her fingers danced over the keyboard and the probe's shape smoothed over.

"Is she almost done?" Hale asked.

"Hell if I..." Yarrow's gaze went to Ordona. A panel had opened on the suit's back. "Did you see that open?"

A slimy tentacle with a clawed tip slapped onto a computer bank. A mass of pink tissue the size of a melon pulled itself up with a wet plop. Another clawed tentacle swung back.

Yarrow darted forward and snatched Ordona's true form up before it could strike Lilith. Tentacles scratched at Yarrow's face like he'd picked up a maniac cat. Yarrow slammed it against a workstation twice but the onslaught continued.

"Sir! Up!" Yarrow swung Ordona down then tossed it into the air.

Hale hit the alien with a single shot and the Naroosha leader broke open like a dropped egg. The remains splattered against the steps, fluid bubbling and popping as it evaporated, leaving behind a husk.

Yarrow wiped slime from his hands. "Is it dead?"

"It sure ain't happy," Hale said.

"Got it!" Lilith pumped a fist in the air.

The force field faded away and the probe rose into the air.

"All systems will revert to my full command in six seconds," the probe said. The ground shifted beneath

Yarrow's feet, sending him stumbling into a seat bolted to the floor.

"What's happening?" Hale asked.

A blue-white hologram of Marc Ibarra appeared between Hale and Yarrow. Ibarra stretched out his arms and cracked his neck.

"That was miserable," Ibarra said.

"Answer me," Hale said.

"Hale! My boy, I knew you'd come through. I had my doubts about your minions over in dome C, but they did OK." Ibarra looked up, as if listening to a faraway voice. "Jimmy just broke away the thorns the Ruhaald were hiding in and dumped them into the void. Now we're about to see something really special."

A holo of the Crucible appeared with a wave of Ibarra's hand. Naroosha vessels flew away from the outer ring. A whirlpool of light formed in the center of the jump gate.

"Front-row seats to the turning of the tide," Ibarra smirked.

The wormhole widened. The *Breitenfeld* burst forth and the Mars fleet followed.

****

Captain Valdar blinked away the afterimage from the wormhole transit. His vision cleared…and he saw a silver Naroosha ship dead ahead and closing fast.

"Helm!"

The *Breitenfeld* lurched down as the ventral thrusters sprouted to life. Valdar's vision went gray and his hands fell to the armrests, so heavy they were impossible to lift. The glowing edge of the Naroosha ship shot up and out of view.

"Cut…the…grav plates!" Valdar struggled to get through his clenched jaw.

The crush of artificial gravity vanished and Valdar felt a swell of blood through his head.

"Target acquired!" Utrecht announced. The ship's top rail cannons flashed with light as they accelerated shells the size of a full-grown man to a very small percentage of the speed of light. The recoil shook Valdar's chair like there was an angry man kicking it from behind.

The leading edge of a fireball cut through the upper third of the bridge's view ports. A spinning blade of silver metal slammed into the hull just beside the number one rail cannon. A hunk of wreckage the size of a Destrier transport was embedded against the ship's aegis armor. The inner edge still burned. Blue light on the outer weapon's edge flickered and died.

"Good shooting, guns," Valdar said.

"Got a priority target from the *Falklands*," Utrecht said.

"Bring us about and lay the guns." Valdar unbuckled his restraints and popped out of his chair. He got two steps toward the holo tank when his ship lurched aside. He felt a sharp vibration through the deck and stumbled against the tank.

"Minor damage to port armor plate seven," Ericcson said. "Dotok fighters moving to engage."

Valdar mag-locked his feet to the deck and brought the holo tank to life. Dozens of capital ships popped up around the Crucible, along with more and more fighters launching off the *Falklands* and *Waterloo*. He'd jumped his ship to Mars as Gor'al began the attack on the Naroosha ships. Once as many ships of the Mars fleet as his engines could carry formed around the *Breitenfeld*, he started knocking at the Crucible's proverbial door with the gate code over and over again.

Without the Crucible generating an open gate for Valdar, it would have taken almost an hour for the *Breitenfeld* to jump back to Earth with even a fraction of the ships now in a pounding match against the Naroosha.

Valdar had waited with zero patience for Ibarra to finally reassert control and open the gate as planned. Now it was up to him and the fresh ships to end the traitors' occupation once and for all.

The Naroosha ships had scattered away from the Crucible when the wormhole had formed and were off-balance, making them easy targets so long as Valdar could seize the opportunity.

The top rail cannons fired again. The rounds zipped away from his ship's location in the holo and intersected with shells from the *Falklands* through a Naroosha ship.

"Clean hit!" Utrecht announced.

"*Provo, Kingston,*" Valdar sent over his captain's channel, "concentrate your fire on the enemy at the Crucible's two o'clock. Condor squadrons six and twelve, drop torpedoes on the three ships moving toward each other…here." Valdar's fingers danced within the holo, relaying commands to several different units at once.

"Task Force *Vorpral*, where are you?" Valdar looked over the list of ships broadcasting an IFF signal. There were three *Manticore* frigates in the fight around the Crucible…and that was it.

No. This can't be. Valdar signaled a new IFF pulse, demanding every ship that could hear the call identify themselves immediately.

A distress call came from within the great thorns

of the Crucible. The *Vacaville* had crashed into a confluence of the basalt spikes.

"Sir, something odd's happening," Utrecht said. "Look at the enemy."

Valdar zoomed in on the nearest silver spiral and watched it nose over, blue light racing up and down the weapon's edge.

"Pull back!" Bar'en cut into Valdar's command channel. "They're going to blow. Pull back!"

"All ships disengage. I repeat, all ships—"

The tips of the Naroosha ships tilted toward the Crucible. A glut of destructive power the width of each ship spat out and struck the jump gate, the thorns glowing so hot they looked like the surface of the sun. Cracks broke along the axis, glowing lava red as they grew wider.

Valdar felt a lump in the pit of his stomach. Malal and his knowledge were gone. If the Crucible broke into a trillion pieces and disintegrated, the human race had a destiny with extinction.

The captain winced as the cracks jumped to spikes touching those struck by the Naroosha's attack. The cracks slowed…then came to a complete stop.

Nothing I can do but stop another hit on the Crucible, he thought.

"Why are my guns silent?" he asked Utrecht.

"All targets read as destroyed, sir." He double-tapped his screen and an image popped up in Valdar's tank. A Naroosha ship broke apart, shedding fragments of silver as the ship moved away like driftwood on the sea.

"Sir, communication from Septon Jarilla," the XO said, "they surrender. All the Ruhaald ships are broadcasting the same thing now."

"All ships, begin search-and-rescue operations." Valdar pointed to Ericcson. "Jarilla. Now."

Video feed popped up next to the Ruhaald ship over Anchorage. Jarilla, his head bent low, did not look into the camera. Torni, her shell alive with fractals, held a disintegration beam high and ready, aiming at something Valdar couldn't see.

"Captain Valdar," Jarilla said, "on behalf of my queen, the expeditionary—"

"You will eject every single nuclear warhead on your ships toward the sun. Immediately. Then you'll take every one of your ships to the L3 Lagrange point and anchor them so close together your hulls trade paint. You try to move an inch and every last macro cannon in the solar system will blow you to dust. Execute my instructions now, or I will let Torni Xaros-zap whatever she's looking at and then I will personally smash every last one of your ships into scrap."

When Jarilla didn't answer, Torni flicked the back of his helmet with her fingers.

"Immediately," Jarilla said.

Valdar cut the video with a swipe of his finger…and saw the transponder for the *Vorpral* between the moon and Ceres. He double-tapped the icon and heard the hiss of static.

"Captain Gor'al, this is Valdar."

There was a crackle in the static and nothing else.

"Ensign Geller, get scopes on the *Vorpral*. Tell me if we need to send search and rescue to the ship or not."

"Aye-aye, skipper," the navigator said.

"Valdar," came from the Dotok ship, "you took your sweet time getting back from Mars. Take lunch?"

"Gor'al? What's your status?"

"Yes, it's me. Took a good hit from the Naroosha, but the ship's held together. Our engines are out and we seem to be on a very slow crash course to Ceres. If you and some of your other larger ships could nudge us out of the way before that happens, we'd appreciate it."

"Roger, *Vorpral*, we're en route." Valdar stepped away from the holo table, went to the fore of the bridge and looked out onto the battlefield. Debris from destroyed human and Naroosha ships floated aimlessly through the void, electricity arcing over the silver fragments of the enemy's hull. Much of the fleet he'd sent to attack the Naroosha was gone, thousands of lives lost. The Crucible was damaged, to what extent he didn't know.

All for nothing, he thought.

The view shifted as the ship maneuvered toward the stricken *Vorpral* and the blue-white marble of Earth passed by.

"Captain Valdar? This is Hale," came through his earpiece. Valdar's head shot up, his malaise forgotten.

"Ken? Are you alright?"

"Everything's under control in the Crucible, or at least it will be soon. Ibarra says the damage to the station isn't fatal. It'll just take time for the place to heal itself. Some minor injuries to my Marines. We got lucky."

"I didn't ask that. I asked about you."

There was a pause lasting several heartbeats.

"I thought I found him. Jared. But…can I talk to you about it later, Uncle Isaac? It's a mess in here."

"It's a mess out here too, son. I'll see you soon."

"Hale, out."

Valdar's eyes went to Earth as it swept out of view. The day had been long, the victory bought with blood, but it wasn't all for nothing. Not by a longshot.

****

The flash of distant ship-to-ship combat faded away as the final few Naroosha ships died beneath the guns of the *Breitenfeld* and the Mars fleet. Standish zoomed in on a gray armored strike cruiser and saw *Gott Mit Uns* emblazoned in gold letters along her side.

"There she is," Standish said, grabbing Bailey and shaking her. "There's my girl. Told you she'd make it."

"Valdar's a good skipper," she said. "No way some bunch of cu—"

"Bailey?" Standish tried to look at her, but his head wouldn't turn. He struggled against his armor, which had frozen in place. Dead noise filled his ears and his visor UI vanished with a click, replaced by Marc Ibarra's hologram.

"Standish," Ibarra said, crossing his arms across his chest. "We need to have a talk."

"Mr. Ibarra! Real honor to meet you. Big fan of your work." Standish chuckled nervously and flexed his arms and legs in an attempt to regain control of his armor. His face went red with effort, then he smiled at Ibarra.

"Done? You've come across some rather sensitive information during our time on the Crucible. Information I need you to promise to keep confidential," Ibarra said.

"You mean the clones you're making of

Shannon?"

"They are not clones—they are re-creations. But the general public won't see it that way and that's why you need to keep your flapping gums shut about everything you saw in the crèche. We have an understanding?"

"No understanding, but we might reach an agreement." Standish jostled his eyebrows.

"Good. I'll release you—wait…what did you say?"

"You want my silence? I'm willing to give it. But first you need to accept my terms."

"You know I have complete control over your suit? I can use your boots to send you flying toward Earth and have you burn up on reentry. You're aware?"

"You've got that option, sure. But I don't think you're that kind of person. I have a business proposal for you. You give me what I want and you'll get what you want. Win-win."

"Son, I am Marc Ibarra. The richest man that ever lived. My corporation stretched from Mercury to Neptune. I used to overthrow governments on a whim and now you, a junior Marine with a spotty service record, want to make a *deal*?"

"Yes."

Ibarra's face grew larger on the visor until he was nearly eye to eye with Standish.

"I'm listening," Ibarra said.

CHAPTER 18

Hale half carried, half supported Yarrow out of the Crucible's control room. Yarrow hopped on his good foot, keeping his injured appendage out of Lilith's sight and an arm over the captain's shoulders.

"Jason, are you sure you're alright?" Lilith asked. She had her helmet off, and her nose crinkled at the smell of his singed toes.

"It's just a flesh wound. Nothing to worry about," Yarrow said.

Hale gave the corpsman a sideways glance, which Yarrow answered with a small shrug. Elias sat in the intersection where Yarrow had been hit, his shoulder-mounted rotary cannon sweeping from side to side over Ruhaald soldiers kneeling against the wall, weaponless and with their hands laced over their heads.

Cortaro stepped around Elias, followed by three more Marines.

"They gave up not long after you went inside," the first sergeant said. "One tried asking if they could keep their weapons, then Elias grabbed it by the bubble helmet and asked me if he could crush the negotiator's head."

"I'm still willing to do it," Elias rumbled.

"Damn, new guy," Standish said over Cortaro's shoulder. "You shoot yourself in the foot to get some more time with your baby ma—oh crap—is that her?"

"Standish?" Hale stopped in his tracks. "Where the hell have you been? No, I don't want you to answer that. Egan, where the hell have you all been?"

"Long story short," Egan said, "we were outside the omnium reactor dome when the Ruhaald surrendered, then Ibarra sent a Mule from the *Breitenfeld* to pick us up. Before that—"

"A tank ate me. All of me, not just the face. Then I killed it," Standish said.

"We saw where Egan was—" Standish jabbed an elbow into Bailey's shoulder "—we almost got put on trial for some squid tall poppy that carked it, but no worries."

"The Mule that brought you still here?" Hale asked.

"Parked next to one that's seen better days," Egan

said.

"Evac Yarrow to the *Breitenfeld* for treatment," Hale said, transferring Yarrow's weight to Standish. Then he looked over the many Ruhaald prisoners lining the walls. This was not a problem he'd anticipated.

"Mister Hale?" Lilith looked at him with big eyes. "Do you need me anymore? Because I could…" She waved her hand at Yarrow as he limped away. "I mean, you don't want me to—"

"Yes, go with him. Thank you for your service, miss. I'll get you back to Phoenix as soon as I can," Hale said.

She clapped rapidly and hurried after Yarrow.

Hale went to Elias and removed a glove. He ran his palm over his face, wiping away dried salt and grime left over from sweat.

"Elias."

"Hale."

"Hell of a day."

"It's not over. It will *never* be over," Elias said.

"Do you ever just…want a god damn shower?"

Elias, who'd been confined to his armor since the Crucible first fell into human hands, leaned his helm over a shoulder to give Hale a quick look.

"Sorry," Hale said.

****

Sunlight flooded the Mule as its ramp lowered. The snap of dry air stung Hale's nose. Yarrow and Lilith were out of their belts and halfway down the ramp before the captain could even get out of his seat. Hale stopped at the top of the ramp.

Yarrow, moving quite fast even with the aid of a cane, shuffled toward a little girl running across the tarmac to him and Lilith, who scooped Mary up and buried her head against the girl's neck. Yarrow reached them a few heartbeats later and wrapped both of them in his arms.

"There's something we might not see again," Cortaro said. "Family reunited."

"At least I brought someone home."

"Some promises aren't ours to keep. Glad we got Yarrow and her back in one piece, mostly. Would have hated to explain the other outcome to that little girl," Cortaro said.

"Think they'll get married?" Hale asked.

"I will beat him within an inch of his life if he pulls that 'I'm not ready for family' crap. Yarrow's the responsible type, good kid. He'll do the right thing."

"Or else."

"Or else," Cortaro grunted.

Hale's gauntlet dinged with a priority message. The captain looked at his arm but made no effort to answer the call.

"Maybe it's nothing," Hale said.

"I don't hear anything." Cortaro rubbed a finger against an ear. "Chinese grenade hit awful close a couple years back. Kept me from hearing my old lady's honey-do's for years."

"Balls," Hale said and looked at his screen. He rolled his eyes. "I just want to take a god damn shower."

"What is it?" Cortaro held up a hand and stopped Orozco from walking down the ramp.

"Valdar wants me on the *Breit*. Something about an anomaly on Jupiter. He only wants me and Steuben. Get our Marines quartered and fed. Keep them close. I don't know what the next move will be."

"Yes, Captain."

"Oh, and put Yarrow on a twenty-four-hour local pass after he gets his foot treated."

"Yes, sir."

Hale turned around and saw Steuben still in his seat, staring at the mechanical hand. He went to his XO and said, "You up for the next bit?"

"I am always ready." Steuben looked up, the skin

around his cyborg eye twitching.

CHAPTER 19

Hale looked out from the *Breitenfeld*'s hangar deck over the surface of Jupiter. The last time he'd seen the giant of the solar system was when he'd stood on the surface of Europa, dodging Toth fighters.

Steuben shifted from side to side. "I don't like this."

"What, the view?"

"No, waiting with the gate wide open for whatever brought us out here. Valdar brought a significant portion of the fleet here to investigate the anomaly, leaving the Ruhaald practically unguarded," Steuben said. "Also, the great red eye of this planet bothers me. There was a similar world in my home system. Its atmospheric patterns changed quickly. Whenever *Ulundialli* formed an eye, the *gethaar* took it as an ill omen."

"I heard some of the crew say the jump gate signature formed right over the Great Red Spot," Hale said.

Steuben growled. "I will not share this with the *gethaar*."

Captain Valdar and Captain Gor'al stepped onto the flight deck.

Hale tapped Steuben on the arm. "Here we go." Hale was about to turn around when he saw a glint of light just beyond Jupiter's edge. The glint became a crystalline ship within seconds, heading straight for the *Breitenfeld*. Hale reached for a rifle that should have been on his back, but it was locked away in the armory to prevent another unfortunate incident like Standish and the others had gone through with the Ruhaald.

The crystal ship slipped through the force field separating the flight deck from the void, causing an uproar from the crew. Hale felt a sense of calm, and a memory of his grandfather came to him. He and Steuben went to the two captains, not taking their eyes off the strange craft.

Sections of the ship opened, spilling glowing tentacles the size of thick ropes toward the deck. The crystal plates glowed faintly.

+Greetings.+

The word stung Hale's mind, but it was a feather's

touch compared to the General's voice.

Two people dropped from the Qa'Resh's tentacles, Stacey and Pa'lon.

Stacey shivered, and her eyes opened wide when she saw Hale.

"Ken!" She ran over and stopped short when she saw Steuben, her gaze on his cyborg eye and hand. She composed herself, her right hand almost saluting Valdar.

"Ms. Ibarra," Valdar said, "I take it you can tell us why the Crucible won't connect to Bastion…and why there's a giant crystal jellyfish on my ship."

"The Xaros are…they're using wormholes. They came to Bastion and…it's all gone, sir. The Alliance is finished. I already sent instructions to the Crucible to stop them from jumping in right on top of Earth, but they'll come for us. In numbers we can't even imagine," she said.

"I take it you're here with more than just bad news," Valdar said.

+We must strike,+ came from the Qa'Resh. +The Crucible must be made whole. The pathway to the Xaros' heart—the Apex—is our only chance at victory. We must strike before the enemy turns their gaze to Earth.+

The words echoed through Hale's mind.

"Our fleets are damaged," Valdar said. "The crews are exhausted. Ibarra says this Apex is a construct unlike any ever seen in the galaxy. How can we win?"

+You had one...once-Torni. She lives?+

"Torni lives," Hale said.

A ball of omnium metal descended from the tentacles and morphed into Malal's faceless form.

"Bring her to me," Malal said. "We have much work to do."

****

Torni looked at a message on her forearm, then to the numbered door in front of her. She raised a hand to knock...then hesitated. She lowered her fist and half turned away.

"You're in the right place." Marc Ibarra popped onto a small screen on the door controls.

"It's not the right place if I'm not welcome," she said.

"I don't understand the Karigole that well, but this rite is for everyone that knew the deceased. It's important for you to participate. Don't want to anger the dead, now do we?" Ibarra asked.

"You don't strike me as the religious type, definitely not the kind that believes in alien religions."

"Darling, in the spiritual sense, I am a ghost. Growing up, I would never have thought such a thing was possible. Then an alien probe drops in the desert and tells me I have to save the whole human race. Who knows what's next? Have you seen the thing on Jupiter?"

"If you're a ghost…then what am I?"

Ibarra closed an eye and winced.

"Tough one, but let's save that for later. Time to force the issue."

The screen blinked off and the door slid open. Inside, a tool chest sat against the wall and a single candle burned on top of it. A mechanical four-fingered hand, a small doll made from twisted grass and a multi-tool sat on the chest.

"Torni," Steuben said as he came to the door. He motioned her inside with the stump of his right arm. "Lafayette would be honored for you to join him."

"I don't…don't understand," she said, staring at her feet.

"He'll explain," Ibarra's voice came from inside the workshop.

Torni entered. Hale and Cortaro sat on a bench across from the small shrine. Ibarra's holographic projection stood behind them. Torni sat down, the wood groaning beneath the compact weight of her omnium body.

Steuben squatted next to the shrine and stared into the flame.

"A Karigole's soul lingers after death. Lafayette waits just beyond the veil, a courtesy so those who knew him can give him one last message before he leaves to join our brothers. Before he died, he wanted me to know that I am *shol mar cul*. It is a blessing and a curse, for it marks me as the last of our centurion to arrive for judgement. If I die well, then it bodes well for the rest. The god of death will look favorably on us all if my death is…worthy. If not, then our souls will be cast into nothing…perhaps returned to the mortal plane if we show promise.

"Lafayette's death saved three peoples from the Xaros. Mine, the Dotok, and yours. That set a high bar."

"The next battle will be something special, Steuben," Ibarra said.

"Indeed." Steuben reached his stump to his face. He clicked his jaw in annoyance and scratched the skin touching the plate over his eye and head with the other hand.

Hale leaned toward Torni and whispered, "Look into the flame and send your message to Lafayette. That's how you get a message to the other side. He'll stay until it goes out."

Torni nodded quickly. How would Mother Superior Wynn react if she knew Torni was taking part in a religious ritual so far removed from the catechism that "heathen" couldn't describe it?

I'm the mind of a dead woman stuck in an alien lump of metal. Maybe it's time to stop trying to make sense of everything.

Torni shifted uneasily, then stared into the flame.

Lafayette. I knew I would die on Takeni. I made my choice to save Hale and all those other Dotok women and children. I made the choice freely, without remorse, without regrets. I hope that you faced your final decision with as much peace and certainty as I did. I hope your end came faster than mine did.

Steuben is a good soldier, a true friend to many of us. I will watch over him, protect him, but I will not let him throw his life away.

The flame flickered.

Steuben turned his head to Torni and gave her a nod.

****

A red wind blew over Mars. Sand bounced over armor lying half-buried beneath the rust-colored accretion as the planet worked to slowly subsume the fallen.

Elias and Bodel approached Kallen's resting place.

Elias went to her head and took a knee. He brushed sand away from her helm. Bodel knelt at her feet.

Colonel Carius stepped through the sandstorm, a black Crusader's cross emblazoned across his chest. The armor touched two fingers to his helm just above the optics, to his sternum, to his left shoulder and then to his right.

"Kallen has fallen," the colonel said. "I see her wounds. I see the scars of battle around us. Who will testify that she died in battle?"

"Witnessed," Elias said.

"Who will testify to her skill in combat?"

"Witnessed," Bodel intoned.

"Kallen came to us with no strength in her body, but with a spirit and a mind stronger than any I have ever seen. No one has ever shown more determination to earn their plugs and their spurs. Her heart was…iron. She will be interred with the fallen below Mount Olympus. May she serve at the right hand of God. May we earn the right to fight beside her again."

Elias grabbed Kallen's hands and bent her arms over her chest. He slipped his hands beneath her shoulders. Bodel gave him a slight nod and the three rose as one. The sound of frozen blood cracking broke over the howl of the wind.

They followed Carius into the red. Armor from surviving platoons formed a cordon through the storm, and each slammed a fist against their breast in salute as Kallen's body passed.

****

Shannon woke up with a deep breath. She stretched her arms out and felt silk sheets against her bare legs. Images of her last dream faded from her mind. She didn't try to catch them; it was a common dream, one she knew by heart: her last day with her husband and son in a Washington, DC, park, just across the Potomac River from the Pentagon. She lost them both on a Tuesday. The moments in her dream were the last time she'd felt joy.

She ran fingernails over her scalp and popped out of bed. Morning sunlight flooded her studio apartment, furnished sparsely and plainly. She looked around for a clock, but there was none to be found.

"What day is it?" Her brow knit in confusion. "Where am I? This isn't my apartment."

Two knocks came from the door, then two more higher up on the wood.

Shannon jammed an arm behind her headboard, looking for the pistol that should have been there, and found nothing.

The knock combination repeated…and a sudden wave of calm spread over her.

Shannon threw a pair of sweatpants over her bare legs and opened the door. A man and woman stood in the hallway, their eyes glazed over. A trickle of drool spread from the woman's mouth.

"Good morning, Shannon," the man said. She heard the words, but with the tilt of the man's head and a slight facial tic, in her mind the words became "Safety. Entrance."

Shannon stepped aside and let them in.

The man looked over the room dispassionately. He spoke again. Shannon ignored the words and took in subtle hand gestures, slight variations in tone, the direction of his eyes when he spoke certain words. His true speech came as a code within his plain speech.

"Do you serve the Naroosha?" he asked.

Shannon answered effortlessly in the sub-lingua.

"I do. What is our task?" she asked.

"The masters are absent, but their mission is ours. Bring the procedural technology to the spawn world and destroy the Crucible. We are few in number, but your position is useful," he said.

Shannon's mind went to Ibarra, the ghost within

the probe. Yes, she'd served him for many decades. He trusted her implicitly, molded the mind implanted in the body to do his bidding without question or compulsion. Perfect.

"Difficult, but not impossible. It will take time to execute," she said.

"This other one is defective," the man said. "Her cortex does not process the sub-lingua properly, but she responds to commands."

"Prompt," Shannon said to the drooler, "jump off the top of this building immediately." She scratched her pinky finger against a temple.

The woman perked up and smiled.

"See you guys later!" She left the room with a happy wave.

"I need a list of our brethren," Shannon said as she went to her window and looked up to the roof. "The Naroosha gave us a task. We will not fail."

TO BE CONCLUDED

ABOUT THE AUTHOR

Richard Fox is the author of The Ember War Saga, and several other military history, thriller and space opera novels.

He lives in fabulous Las Vegas with his incredible wife and two boys, amazing children bent on anarchy.

He graduated from the United States Military Academy (West Point) much to his surprise and spent ten years on active duty in the United States Army. He deployed on two combat tours to Iraq and received the Combat Action Badge, Bronze Star and Presidential Unit Citation.

Sign up for his mailing list over at www.richardfoxauthor.com to stay up to date on new releases and get exclusive Ember War short stories.

The Ember War Saga:

1.) The Ember War
2.) The Ruins of Anthalas
3.) Blood of Heroes
4.) Earth Defiant
5.) The Gardens of Nibiru
6.) Battle of the Void
7.) The Siege of Earth
8.) The Crucible
9.) The Xaros Reckoning (Coming November 2016)

Printed in Great Britain
by Amazon